Blood thieves of Bells Ferry

By

Natasha Sapienza

This book is dedicated to all my sisters in Christ seeking breakthrough. God is more than able. And to my editor and true-blue Southern bestie, Lauren. This book is now all that it's meant to be. - Natasha

Hunter

1. TIME FOR BACKUP

The fading sun peeked in on my dash, and the radio crackled. I cranked it, my heart doing the same.

"Stay inside." Static. "There's—bombing the—fire department on—"

I looked up, my heart jolting. Someone in all black crossed feet away from my truck. I swerved to the left. The truck roared. I looked to the right where the fool had crossed. The open field stretching before the woods lay bare.

"What in the heavens…?"

The radio went dead as I straightened the truck on the road and sucked my teeth. Was I starting to see things now? For sure the radio lit up, but whoever crossed couldn't have gotten to the woods that fast.

I pulled up to the sheriff's office, located right next to Town Hall, with my windows down to spare the quarter tank of gas I'd been maintaining since my last fill three weeks back. Sweat dripped into my eyeballs in the dusky summer sun, but I had to do what I had to do. The world was the Wild West now, and every little bit of everything mattered more than ever.

I jumped out and tramped toward the little brick building's barred entry where a swinging door had been newly added, apparently. Must've landed it from Fred the welder down on Big Shanty Road. Nowadays, extra security was everything; and hopefully, this time, the big boss would agree.

The usual waft of soiled garbs hit me like the bricks that adorned this building. I kept a straight face as I peeked into the Town Hall on the right. The three middle-aged nurses in worn scrubs tended to the elderly on their cots. No one could get to the hospital an hour out in a car because of the gas situation, and even if they did, would it be in operation? We couldn't be sure with the blackout still cutting off most of the country, especially those who weren't prepped for it.

I veered left into Sheriff Hanks' office. He sat at his desk, papers scattered and scribbled on, with head in his hands. His hat lay beside one elbow, revealing his sweaty, bald head. The landline phone sat at the other.

I knocked on the door frame. "Sleeping on the job?"

Hank flinched, then slowly put on his hat and tipped it. "A man's gotta get some shut-eye sometime, don't he?"

"Indeed we do, Sheriff." I stepped inside. "Time to hire some back up— and don't worry, I don't need any extra rations or anything. I'm just here to help carry the load."

The chair squeaked as Hank stretched back. "I told you son, me and Tripp got it all under control."

"Oh, is that right?" I took another step. "Why don't you tell me the real reason you ain't been wanting to bring me on all this time?"

Hank eyed me cool behind that 'stache of his like a man in a poker game anticipating his opponent's next move. I held them right back. Two years I've been in this town, and I know a side-stepper when I see one.

Hank folded his hands, slow and calculated. "Have a seat, son."

"Nah. I think I'll stand for this one."

Hank gave a nod—and a frown. "I checked your file."

I held my own poker face, though my heart skipped.

"Would you hire you if you was me?"

Poker face intact, I kept my shoulders straight as I replied, "If I was in the mess our nation is in now, I think I might."

"Our country may be a mess, son, but I told you, me and Tripp—" The landline rang. He snatched it, eyes glancing up like a kid caught stealing a cookie from behind his momma's back. "Sheriff's office." His brow wrinkled and knuckles whitened. "Hello? Belinda? Belinda!" He shot up from his desk and over to the radio by his window where milky moonlight spilled in. He snatched the headset. "Tripp, do you copy?"

As he waited, I glimpsed out the window. There was only one Belinda I knew of, but perhaps there was another.

"Come on. Tripp. Do you copy?"

"Roger, Sheriff."

"Can you head over to Belinda Cole's place STAT?"

"Negative. Handlin' a situation over at Buck's Grocer."

I turned and rushed out of the office. So it was Belinda Cole, Remington's daughter. As I reached my truck, Hank ran after me with his hat clutched in his hand. I jumped in, and Hank threw open my passenger door.

"Where's your cruiser?" I asked as he clambered in.

"Tripp's broke down yesterday so he took mine."

I gave a nod as I gunned it to the Coles'. "Thought you didn't need me."

"I don't." He unholstered his gun and cocked it. "You're gonna drop me off and keep your butt in the truck, ya hear me?"

I glimpsed at him as I rounded the corner a few blocks away from Belinda's. He gave me his sternest look like some kind of angry principal ready to expel a rowdy student. "What'd Belinda say?"

The sternness melted like wax beneath a flame. "She wasn't sayin'. She was screamin'."

I hit the gas harder and cut a hard right through the woods. The truck bounced through the terrain and roared, but this beaten road would get us there in half the time. Less than a minute, and we pulled up to the gray two story ranch house.

"Remember what I said." Hank hustled out and stalked near the house. He checked out the front door. Locked. He shot by the handle, kicked it open, and disappeared inside.

I clasped my own gun strapped at my waist and spoke. "Praise be to the Lord my Rock, who trains my hands for war, my fingers for battle. He is my loving God and my fortress, my stronghold and my deliverer, my shield, in whom I take refuge, who subdues people under me."

I checked the time on my dash: a quarter past eight. To think I almost didn't come to check on the Sheriff tonight, but I got this itch that I had to get out of the house. I didn't know why I had this hope he'd take me on even though he'd turned me down three times since moving here, but now I knew.

I cocked my gun, slipped out of the truck, and followed Hank's path to the entry. Nightfall muddied the inside. Belinda didn't have time to light a single candle. I scanned the living area. Then the dining and kitchen. All sat clear. The back door stood open. I checked it. Nothing seemed tampered with. The glass was still intact. Did she leave it unlocked by accident? Or did she open it to get in the backyard and someone sprang in?

I turned back into the living room, then crept up the stairs. The steps creaked beneath my weight. If someone was here, they'd be anticipating me the moment I got into the hall.

Gun raised, I kept my eyes and ears as peeled as I could in the dark. The crickets fell silent. The sound aided in masking my movement.

I crept into the hallway and looked into an empty bathroom. Then I entered a bedroom with a twin-sized bed. The moonlight let me borrow a sense that the room sat vacant. I moved on to the next: a door slightly ajar. I kicked it open.

The moon's pale light edged in from sheer curtains by the bed, revealing Belinda lying on her side. I rushed over and set a hand on her. "Belinda! Belinda can you hear me?" I shook her. She rolled over, body limp. I did a quick scan. An LED lantern sat at her bedside. I flicked it on. The dim light revealed Belinda's twenty-year-old face, eyes and mouth open, as pale as the moonlight.

My gut tangled as I checked her cold neck for a pulse. Nothing. I grabbed the lantern and passed it over her. No apparent wounds or sign of struggling. I did another scan around the floor of the bed. No empty pill bottles. One more scan with the LED of her body. I held the light over her abdomen and arms, then drew it closer. Her inner forearm... had two holes like snake bites that covered her median cubital vein.

"What in the…"

Shuffling sounded downstairs. I lifted my gun and stalked to the side of the bedroom door, pressing my back against the wall. Footsteps rattled the stairs with no concern of being heard. I tightened my hold. Someone panted as they drew near, and I steadied my firearm.

A hatless Hank entered the room. I lowered my gun as he sucked in a breath and said, "I told you to stay in the truck."

"I think your exact words were to 'keep my butt in the truck.'" I followed him to the bedside. "Belinda's dead."

"I know." Hank wiped his brow with his arm. "I found 'er here before I heard movement downstairs. Somethin' was down there... All black. It dashed out the back door before I even reached the bottom of the stairs. I followed after it, but it was movin' so fast it looked like a shadow." He rubbed his face with both hands. "Then it disappeared."

"Disappeared?"

"You heard me, boy!" Hank sucked his teeth as he turned away. "At least that's what it looked like, all right?" He unclipped his radio and spoke. "Tripp, you copy?"

"Roger."

"I need you back at the station – pronto."

"Copy that, Sheriff."

My heart cranked up like it had on my way over to the Sherrif's office. That person in black who crossed my truck... Maybe I had seen him. "I think I saw the same thing on my way over to the office."

Hank lowered his radio. "Say what now?"

"Someone walked right in front of my truck before I got to the office. I swerved out of his path, but when I looked back at the open field leading to the woods, he was gone."

Hank closed the distance between us like a K-9 ready to strike. "Now you listen to me, Hunter. If you wanna help us out, you better stay in line. Not a single outburst or I'll make you give up every gun you own, you hear me?"

Though a sting of shame poked my heart, it jumped nonetheless. After everything that happened, I knew I needed a break from the field for a while. But things change in two years. People change. Although I hadn't been active since, I hoped to God now more than ever I was ready for it again because the people of Bells Ferry needed all the help they could get.

My stare found poor Belinda taken before her time. That sleeping giant in me rumbled, and I clenched a fist.

Lord have mercy on whoever—or whatever—took her life, because come hell or high water, we were going to find this thing and put an end to it.

Coryn

2. BILL'S BAD NEWS

I'd do this until my fingers bleed—even though I hate blood.

I moved back from an all-fours position on the living room's wood floors, grasping a polishing cloth, and sat on my calves. The large flatscreen TV still shone black with a connection error message in its center. The screen reflected a murky, but somehow visible mirror of my frizzed-out curls and sweaty face. Goosebumps crawled along my arms. Six weeks of no internet and no phones. How much longer would our connection to the rest of the world be lost? Did I even wanna see what was going on out there…? And once the generator dried up…

I shifted my eyes and grazed the space. Family portraits of the Barnes displayed black and white portraits of parents and great grandparents, while colored ones showcased children and grandchildren. I'd memorized half of Dixie and Gunner's six grandbabies' names since she'd shared so many stories about them. Last she heard, her son and his family were hunkered down safe in a cabin they owned in Idaho, but she hadn't spoken with her daughter and her family in LA since the fall.

Fake daisies adorned every end table, even the Amish dining room table. A giant wooden cross hung above the fireplace, while framed bible verses and smaller crosses decorated every wall. You'd think all the religious stuff would annoy me, given the way my parents were, but here in the Barnes' home, everything… invited. With the hot summer, the fireplace hadn't been lit once, but the whole place just swelled with welcoming warmth…I sighed. Not like my abandoned house next door aka the in-law suite Gunner and Dixie let me rent for pennies.

Holding her broom, Hope sashayed and twirled toward me, her full-length skirt and silky blonde hair swaying as she danced with the broom she'd named Prince Philip. Stopping at my side, she peered down at the shining floor. "Ooh, I can see your pretty face in the floor, Princess Mommy."

I chuckled. "And, my little princess, do you—"

"Actually, today I'm a queen."

"I apologize, dear queen. Do you know why I scrubbed these floors so hard they're shining like marble?"

She tapped her little seven-year-old chin. "Because you're Cinderella?"

I pointed at my dark curls. "Unless there's a Cuban version, no, sweetie. I do this because I want to show Mr. and Mrs. Barnes how thankful I am for all they've done for us."

She smiled, showing off her recently pulled front tooth. "I want to show them how thankful I am, too!" She scurried off, sweeping rapidly. "I can't dance anymore until the ball tonight, Philip, so no more distracting me!"

Smiling, I used the vinegary, lemon scented cloth to wipe the sweat from my face and stretched my legs out in front of me. My knees shone red with specks of blood. But who cared. Raw knees were a small sacrifice in comparison to what Gunner and Dixie had done, taking me and Hope in after those thugs from the Los Daggers gang broke into our house and nearly killed us.

I cringed at the memory. I'd screamed at the top of my lungs, using a skillet to fight off the goons with all my might. Until one of them snatched it from my grasp and held me down while another bear-hugged Hope, telling her to enjoy the show. I kicked as much as I could before the bastard could finally pull my pants all the way off. Gunner showed up with a rifle, and all three of the mobsters were gunned down.

I winced. All that blood… I'd thrown up four times within ten minutes. Thank God Gunner shouted at Hope to keep her eyes closed right before he ended the gangsters' lives. Then he calmly escorted us both out. She was such a good girl and listened. I don't think she'd be dancing with Prince Philip if she'd seen what I did...

"Oh my sweet heaven, Coryn, it smells like lemon pound cake in here!" Dixie descended the staircase, her silvery-blonde hair in rollers and her pudgy body in a pink nightgown fringed with 'fur.' How she managed to still "pretty herself up" for Gunner was a miracle given the current state of affairs. I don't even remember the last time I cared about how I looked, even before the recent downfall of America the Great. Oh wait. An image of that guy I'd refused to let myself fantasize about after that last exchange flashed through my mind. I did care about my appearance that day—though I vowed never to visit that church again, and Mr. Handsome Goodie Good was probably thankful for that.

I stood and slung the cloth over my shoulder. "Just a few drops of lemon essential oil goes a long way."

Dixie reached the bottom and frowned as she stepped into the living room. "Oh, darlin', you didn't need to use your good stuff. That could be worth a lot more now, I'm sure."

I shrugged. "Who better to spend it on?"

"Oh, you stop it. Hold onto that stuff in case your little princess here—"

"Que-ee-ee-een," Hope sang as she swiped her broom near the giant dining table.

"'Scuze me." Dixie continued. "Save your oil in case one of y'all ever gets sick."

"Or," I said, "if you or Gunner do."

"Ha! Nuthin' will kill that man except his own courage."

I shuddered. Gunner's bravery in killing gang members to defend Hope and I surely could've landed him an early grave. He'd even buried all three of the mobsters in my front yard with a handwritten sign that read: *No gang members allowed unless you repent and receive Jesus.*

Dixie turned her attention to the TV. "Still nuthin,' huh?"

I shook my head. "Quiet as always."

"Good Lord, when will all this end…" She said it more to herself than to me. "Time to shut off the generator and have us some breakfast." She swiped the cloth from my shoulder. "Everyone's gettin' too skinny in this house." As she put her arm around Hope and led her into the kitchen, I trailed close, stomach gnawing on my backbone. So far, gun-slinging men like Gunner kept a lot of bad guys at bay from Bells Ferry, though every now and then, a few fearless ones sprang up like weeds to test their fate.

I entered the kitchen, beginning to swell with the bittersweet aroma of brewing coffee. I breathed it in nice and slow like I had every day for the past week of living here. No generator and having lost my job as a wedding video editor immediately after the Law Abiders lost the war in Washington to the Freedom

Fighters two months ago, hot coffee became room temperature brews until I ran out of my last few bags then had to resort to tepid tea.

Me and Hope took our seats at the wooden island as usual, while Dixie finished whipping up breakfast. After setting a mug of beautiful, steaming coffee and a plate of four boiled eggs with a few strawberries in front of me and Hope, Dixie sat across from us. "I'm sorry we're short on strawberries 'cause the season is endin', but Big Mama Nugget and her crew ain't slowin' down their egg makin' anytime soon! You gals could use some extra protein, anyhow." Her rollers jiggled slightly as she shook her head. "And you're supposed to be *Latinas*."

I laughed at her *Gringa*, Southern accent. "Only half Cuban. My mom was a white girl like you."

"Was she now? Then you must've taken after your daddy, huh?"

"Yes ma'am. My mom used to say, 'Now I'll never need to wonder what your father would look like as a woman because I'm lookin' at her.'"

Now Dixie laughed. "Hey, you did that Southern twang like a pro. Keep it up, and maybe, people will start believing little Hope here is yours."

I reached over and stroked Hope's blonde tresses as she devoured the strawberries. "Sometimes I just let them believe she's my little sister. Easier than explaining, you know?"

Dixie nodded, her blue eyes sympathetic as she clasped her mug and sipped.

I looked at the gold wedding band on her ring finger. "Or maybe you don't."

Setting the mug down, Dixie looked at Hope, already with clean plate, cooing at the Yorkshire picture on her cup. "Little miss queen, can you please head up to your room and help the princess find her glass slipper?"

Hope gasped. "A barefooted princess! Oh no, she won't be ready for the ball tonight!" She hopped off her stool and bustled out of the kitchen. As her swift patters up the stairs faded, Dixie focused on me. "That wild bear out there may have managed to keep his parts to himself til our wedding night, but that doesn't mean I'm a perfect li'l angel. My sins may be different than yours, but they're still sins."

I took a long sip of coffee. Not according to my parents. When they found out their daughter got knocked up by a boy from the Christian private school they'd spent so much money to have her attend, they pulled me out and homeschooled me until graduation. Then they stopped taking me to church when I started showing. They said they'd suffered enough shame to have to hear it from the congregation, too. Though I still believe at least the youth pastor and his wife, Cindi, wouldn't have been judgmental, especially since it wasn't like I was proud of what I'd done. But mistakes are still embarrassing, especially to Christians. The worst kind being the ones you can't hide or make disappear… Maybe God did deem some sins as worse than others.

I huffed. "Wish my parents were as forgiving."

Dixie sighed. "Sometimes, it's harder to forgive those we love the most."

I rubbed my mug's handle, fighting back tears. I didn't know how to forgive my parents, but what did it matter now, anyway? They'd been dead since the year after Hope was born.

"Darn Satan babies!" Gunner marched into the kitchen, shirtless in dirt stained overalls and cowboy boots, a holstered gun on his hip. "I found 'nother snake near our 'maters!"

Dixie leaned back. "Did you get 'em?"

"Ya darn right I did! Knocked his ol' head off with my ax. Sucker had to've been, I dunno, for or five feet long, I reckon."

I looked up at him. "Can you get any braver?"

"Sure can." He stood behind Dixie and clasped her shoulders with soiled hands. "Ask my girl here 'bout the time her sister called from the bar sayin' a couple of fools were givin' her a hard time with payin' their bill."

Dixie laid one of her hands atop his. "Don't start boastin'. You lost a tooth in that fight."

"Yeah, well, they all paid up, didn't they?"

"Yes, hon', they sure did."

He released her shoulders and slapped his belly. "Now what'cha got for breakfast, darlin'?"

"Eggs."

"Again?"

"Now don't you go givin' me a hard time or it'll be the same thing tomorrow."

"All right, all right." Gunner walked to the stove where the pot of boiled eggs sat and began scooping some out with his dirty hands, making them muddy. "Where's the strawberries?"

She winked at me. "I gave sweet little Hope the last of the picked ones and I don't think there's any more out there."

"I can go check." I guzzled the remaining delectable sips of my coffee.

Dixie waved me back down. "Don't think I didn't notice these floors. You've earned your break, little lady, so just—"

Rapid knocks at the front door interrupted her.

"Stay here." Gunner unholstered his handgun and treaded out of the kitchen. Dixie and I followed—keeping a ten foot distance. He peered out the front window to check, then quickly opened the door. Bill, their celery-stick neighbor, rushed inside, his sunburned face somehow pale and sweating profusely.

"What's goin' on?" Gunner asked as he shut and locked the door.

Bill sank onto one of the leather couches like a withering stalk. Staring ahead with unblinking eyes, he said in a trembling voice, "It's all gone. It took it all."

"Took what?" Dixie sat beside him.

Like dragging something heavy, his distant, slow-moving eyes landed on me. "Her blood."

3. PRICKED

I could feel the blood fleeing my face as if scared off by Bill's bloody—or lack thereof—announcement.

"Now what on God's green earth are you talkin' about, Bill?" Gunner dropped into the armchair across from his wife and Bill while I trembled down onto the loveseat.

Celery stick Bill kept his petrified gaze on me. "She was young… like you."

My stomach churned. With all of this creepy news and attention, at any moment, I'd vomit red eggs on the guy.

"Who are you talkin' about, Bill?" Dixie snapped her fingers in front of his face. "Snap out of it so we can figure this out."

Finally, he took his death-grip stare off of me. "Belinda Cole, 'bout a mile down by the farmer's market."

Dixie covered her mouth as Gunner clasped his forehead. "Remington's oldest?"

Bill gave a nod. "Me and Jesse were goin' down there 'cause we heard they got more gas, when 'bout a block from the Coles' place, we saw a big ol' crowd. People were cryin' and all shook up. They said Sheriff Hank and Deacon Hunter found her in bed last night, white as snow, with two small holes in her forearm. Dr. Johnson went in and said the cause of death was extreme blood loss. Based on the holes, Dr. Johnson said it looked like someone used needles to draw out all her blood."

A wave of dizziness crashed over me as my heart hammered in my chest. What kind of depraved human being would do such a thing? And to a young woman while she slept? A young woman like me…

As Dixie began to cry, Gunner's tone softened, but still maintained a certain hardness. "Do we have any idea who could've done this?"

"Not a clue so far. But the town is holdin' a mandatory meetin' tonight at First Baptist Bells Ferry."

My heart jumped at the name. The place with that Hunky Goody Good who I stormed away from in the church parking lot. The place I vowed never to go again.

"We'll be there." Gunner clasped his gun's hilt. "We'll find that murderer and make sure this doesn't happen again." He rose from his seat. "C'mon, Bill. Let's check around town, make sure everyone's got their windows boarded up good and the dogs got enough food. We'll need 'em."

Dixie stood and gave him a kiss.

"You wearin' your gun, sweetheart?" he asked.

"Sure am." She lifted her nightgown, exposing her upper thigh where a small gun sat in a holster.

"Good." Gunner turned to me. "Give Coryn one, too." He and Bill marched out, and Dixie wiped away her tears.

I swallowed, my throat extra dry. Whoever this poor Belinda was, the Barnes clearly had a relationship with her. And not to sound like a horrible person, but I wasn't as sad for her passing as I was scared. I didn't know her like the Barnes did, or many people living here for that matter, since I kept to myself as much as I could. People here always said hi and engaged in small talk, but I rarely ever picked up names—or offered mine. Running away from a small town to an even smaller one sounded like a good idea at the time.

I rose. "Did you know her well?"

Dixie nodded. "Used to babysit her when the Coles were goin' through a rough time financially, and both of 'em were workin' two jobs."

"I'm so sorry…"

She fanned her face. "This world's gotten crazier, Coryn. I just can't wait for Jesus to come back." She walked toward the stairs and beckoned me. "Let's get you set up."

I bustled forward, bumping into the armchair on my way. "I've never shot a gun before—or even held one."

"First time for everything, darlin'."

She reached the top of the stairs and led me through the narrow hall, passing the bathroom, then mine and Hope's bedroom, where she danced again. This time, she had a bed-sheet draped around her chest like an oversized gown. My stomach knotted as we reached the last door on the right and traversed into Dixie's bedroom.

"I don't think I'd be able to… kill someone," I said.

Dixie strode to her closed walk-in closet and opened the door, revealing half a side with clothes and another half with a wardrobe. "When y'all were almost killed, you and your daughter, did you defend yourself then?"

As she removed a key from her bust and unlocked the wardrobe, I looked over my shoulder toward the hallway. When that gangster had his tatted arms bear-hugging my helpless Hope, rage swelled through me from my head to my toes. I swung my skillet like a sword and would've done whatever it took in order to save my baby girl's life… but that pan only stalled the monsters at best. Then Gunner came and did what I might never could.

Dixie opened the wardrobe. Four rifles hung in the middle, three handguns on the left, and two shotguns on the right. A shelf beneath them carried various holsters and smoke grenades.

"Whoa," I breathed. "You guys sure you're Christians?"

She snickered. "The Bible says God put authorities in the government to bear the sword, to act as avengers who carry out God's wrath on the wrongdoer. Now that the authorities have been overthrown, who's gonna defend the innocent and helpless?" She grabbed a pistol and handed it to me. "We are, that's who."

I swallowed and gave what I was sure had to be a pathetic, unconvincing nod. She was right, I guess…

"That's a semi-automatic," Dixie said. "Easy to shoot, easier to hide than some of the others. Already locked and loaded. Just take off the safety right here, cock it, and you're good to go."

I held the weapon in both palms like it were a baby bird fallen from its nest. "But what if Hope gets to it?"

She snatched a thick, black waist belt. "This is a belly band. Tuck that in here, and make sure to wear it all times."

"What if she hugs me and finds out I'm wearing it?"

"You tell her it's not a toy. Guns are not safe to mess with, and only Mommy can touch it." Dixie closed the wardrobe and locked it. "She's a good girl, isn't she?"

"Yes, but—"

She pointed at the boarded up window above her giant, leopard-print bed. "Aren't there worse things to worry about out there? You heard Bill."

I shivered, his words haunting: *"She was young…like you."*

Dixie continued. "Between gang-bangers, violent drunks, desperate folks, and now these blood thieves, it's find a way to defend yourself or die at their ruthless hands."

I bit my lip and lifted my shirt. While Dixie strapped the belly band around my abdomen, I said, "I just wish there was, I don't know, a different way to defend myself."

She finished stuffing my new pistol away. "Pray about it."

"Pardon?"

She shrugged. "Jesus said ask in my name and you shall receive. So, ask him if there's another way you can defend yourself. Who knows, maybe you'll become a swordsman or somethin' else instead." Without any more bizarre advice, she walked out of the room as if… leaving me to do just that. Pray. Right now…

I laid my hands against my still-knotting stomach. It tightened more. I hadn't spoken to God since after I told my parents I was pregnant at sixteen. I didn't even know if he was really there or not. He let me fall for that douchebag who managed to convince me I was his dream girl that he planned on marrying someday, blah, blah, blah, then had the jerk's kid!

Hope.

My heart stung. Though her father was an absentee pig, she wasn't. She was an angel… How something so sweet, beautiful, and precious could form from the sperm of that con-artist was nothing less than a miracle. I glanced up at the crown molding ceiling and sighed. Even though I'd messed up massively, maybe Hope was proof that there was a God who was benevolent sometimes, at least…

Stomach twisting and heart racing again, I inched toward Dixie and Gunner's bed. Slowly, I sank to my knees and propped my elbows on the soft mattress. I closed my eyes and took a deep breath in. "Hi…if you're there. I know it's been a while, but I guess desperate times call for desperate measures, right?" I forced a laugh. If God was real, he'd totally know how fake that was. Maybe he wouldn't care. Or maybe he'd roll his eyes at the friend who hadn't called in years. "I'm sorry. You know—if you're real—that I was never good at this. I guess I'm just so visual it's kind of hard to pray to someone who's invisible. But whatever, I get it. Faith is trusting in what I can't see so… Here I am."

Tears began to swell in my eyes. "I feel so lost. And scared. I never imagined this country—my home— would become this ridiculously dangerous wasteland. And the things people are doing to each other… What they almost did to me and Hope." Now the tears flowed from my eyes like a leaky faucet. "How am I supposed to raise my daughter in this world? It's bad enough she's had to grow up without a father and grandparents. It's always been just me, and I feel like I can't protect her anymore. It's out of my control, and I'm just so scared of losing her…" I crossed my forearms and nestled my face against them. After a minute, I remembered the whole point of this was to ask that bizarre question Dixie suggested I take up with Jesus, but desperation and confusion don't leave much room for pragmatism.

"If there's some other way I can defend myself and Hope and anyone else who may need it, some way that doesn't involve guns—or swords—can you please show me? I want to be able to help, but just… I don't know… differently." With a final sigh, I wiped the tears from my face and finished my terribly ineloquent prayer. "In Jesus' name, amen."

A knock sounded by the doorway. Dixie stood in the hall, smirking. "Gunner's gettin' on my nerves about the strawberries. Still wanna go check that patch so you don't have to see him get his butt whooped?"

"Sure." I hustled to my feet, the snug belly band a super uncomfortable reminder that I was locked and loaded, and strode from the bedroom. I stopped outside of mine and Hope's room. Now she swayed slowly with her princely broom. I opened my mouth, but quickly closed it. With what happened to Belinda and all of this increasing madness, I didn't want Hope outside—at least until the murderer was caught.

I hurried downstairs, snagged a bucket, and stepped out into the vast backyard. The mid-afternoon sun shone bright and high on the green farmland below. I think Dixie had said she and Gunner owned ten acres of land. Enclosed by a barbed wire fence, the barn stretched to the left, the "small" crop field to the right, and the garden straight ahead.

I walked through the pathway of blueberry bushes and eventually reached the rows of barren strawberry plants. As I scoured through the leaves for juicy red goodness, I glanced over my shoulder at the forest. With long, snaking roads enshrouded by dense woodland and only smatters of clarity along the rolling hills—and being home to one of the darkest cities in the state—the beautiful countryside of Bells Ferry was the perfect place for predators to stalk.

I breathed in a trembling breath. I hated this… fear. But in the country's current state, it was inevitable, like a chronic cancer. It could fade for a time, or even seem to disappear, but then after believing you were okay, it'd spring up again worse than ever. Because the truth was things just weren't getting any better.

President Moore's tight face and hardened eyes etched themselves in my mind. He'd barely gotten into office. The country was a near-perfect split on the vote I chose to sit out on. Leading up to the election, both sides spoke of the other as Enemy Number One. Riots continued to breakout everywhere from college campuses to grocery stores.

Bells Ferry kept it peaceful because most everyone here was on his side. They believed he would fight the 'moral decay' and kick out the career politicians – and he did. That's really when all hell broke loose. You'd see politicians getting dragged out of their homes, videos coming out of trafficking rings backed by big namers in our government. The horror stories of children…

I shuddered. It was like a giant boiling cauldron that had been pushed over. The White House was stormed by the Freedom Fighters who wanted Moore gone, and the Law Abiders came swarming after them. Thousands and thousands of them. The military did their best to fend them off, but in the end, they evacuated the president while the White House got trashed.

Simultaneously, shootouts and street fights ignited all over the states, and sleeper cells came crawling out of hiding.

I trembled more as visions infiltrated my mind of TVs displaying the massacre and live streams of people dropping like flies at whizzing bullets or getting blasted to bits by grenades. It felt like watching a gruesome war movie directed by Mel Gibson, but it wasn't a movie. It was real.

Then the blackout hit.

To this day, we don't know if rebels caused it or if the government itself put everyone in darkness to help abate the madness.

I shook my head. You'd hear of people in other countries who have dictators as leaders, like in Dad's country, Cuba; or terrorists running the government, and how they're able to just raid people's homes and businesses, hacking at them with machetes. Even kids participating in the brutality, and it just seemed so… impossible. But America proved that you didn't need to be a third-world-country to partake in such tribal-like violence. You just needed enough hate.

Something pricked my hand. I recoiled, a thick bubble of blood on my index finger. A smudge of purple bordered the cut. I peered into the plant. In the midst of it, a thin, violet stalk with a thorny tip stood. I frowned as I carefully clasped the stem and plucked it from the ground. I rubbed the rough exterior gently between my fingers. A spark ignited at the thorny tip. I gasped as the flame rapidly spread to the stem. Not because it burned, but because… it didn't.

I poked the fiery plant. Nothing; just flickering brightness, like an illusion. Or maybe a hallucination? Did Dixie spike my coffee with some crazy whiskey concoction or something? I did take her advice to pray, which was something I hadn't done since before I was pregnant with Hope, but I did it because I'd been desperate for something, anything, besides my current reality. Desperate for a spark of hope, for change… Or maybe I'd snapped and become schizophrenic; all the fear finally got to me and, like, broke my brain or something.

Coryn. A thought penetrated, dousing my own frantic ones.

I froze, eyes still on the unreal, heatless flaming stem in my grasp.

You are not alone. You will see greater things than this.

The purple stalk stopped burning. It wriggled and curved as a snake would, then coiled around my wrist like a triple-banded bracelet. I gawked at my new piece of super weird jewelry. Then, somehow, despite how much wilder this day kept getting, something odd and foreign happened within, calming my pounding heart. Something that felt as impossible to have as a heatless fire. Peace…

I looked up as clouds rolled over the sun, and without another thought, I spoke words to the sky, something that I hadn't done since I was a kid. "What do you want me to do?"

Hunter

4. HI AGAIN

Murmurs of worried women and pissed off men mingled in the old Baptist Church as they swelled up to its high ceiling. Colored light flooded in through the stained glass on the throng below, mostly white fifty-somethings and older, and only two black families, including Dr. Johnson's. Every pew sat full with folks lining the walls and crowding aisles; but, at this point, there were much greater threats than breaking the fire code.

"I can't believe some folk!" a short lady with thick glasses and puffy hair like a Collie's screeched as I nudged through toward the stage. "Sucking peoples' blood like a darn vampire! Must be on drugs of some sort to pull that one off, I tell ya."

I forged onward past the woman who hadn't got all her facts straight. Dr. Johnson confirmed someone used needles to draw out Belinda's blood, but that still didn't answer the question of how the suspect was able to move the way Hank described or the way we'd both seen him disappear. We'd get to the bottom of it, but for now, we needed to get a move on with this meeting before more rumors spread like gangrene.

Pastor Mitchel Sligh stood behind the podium on the risen platform. Pink-faced, but fully present as always; and Mrs. Sligh, as I called her, even though she'd been my mother-in-law, flanked his left, proper and pronounced as usual in a silk top and red heels. I couldn't blame her. If looking good made her feel better about the situation, then let it be. The more normalcy we could maintain in this jacked up world, the better. Behind them stood Sheriff Hank in what appeared to be a backup cowboy hat.

As I mounted the stage, my old dad-in-law turned his pink face to me, then gave me a bear hug. "Thankful you're back in action, son." He let me go, then Mrs. Sligh followed suit and chimed in, "We need you in this fight now more than ever." As she released, I posted on Mitchel's right. This was my home, and I'd do everything I could to keep it safe. I scanned the crowd. Rex Ellington and his wife Lauren and their sons, Ryan and Miles; Bill Bailey, Gunner and Dixie Barnes; and next to them, a familiar face jumped out at me and my heart did what it did the last time I saw her: race like a horse turned loose.

Her pretty browns looked around with her curls a mess as she held the hand of another familiar face, that sweet little blondie of hers with a pair of headphones on. Then the brunette raised her eyes up — to me.

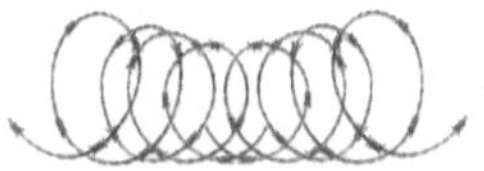

Coryn

I squeezed Hope's hand as my stare landed on that undeniably hot, dark-haired, green-eyed church boy whose face I never wanted to see again. I ignored how my heart quickened and focused on Hope. She hummed softly in her own little world, rocking the headphones of my old CD player. I used two of my last five AA batteries, but protecting her innocent mind from the nightmarish words surrounding us was worth it. Gunner and Dixie stood to my left, conversing with Bill and a few others.

"You heard somebody got the blood sucked out of 'er?" a woman with glasses and a silvery afro said. Another lady with similarly styled-hair replied, "Some people got demons in 'em, Maryann. How else can you explain such depravity? Don't make a lick of sense otherwise."

Demons. A phrase I'd started hearing more often after the whole pregnancy scandal. Mom would enter my room and pray against the demons who had "enticed me into fornication." She just couldn't accept that no one but Eric himself had lured me into his twin-sized bed with his good looks and bad boy charm, that I chose to sleep with him because he alone influenced me to… and I was dumb enough to think he'd only love me more after I gave him my virginity. Alas, guys love sex, but they don't always love the girl giving it to them.

I inched to my left, using the fluffball hair of one of the gossipy friends as cover. I'd noticed the probably late-twenty-something-year-old hunk both times I'd visited this building; and, thanks to Hope, he also noticed me…

"All right! Settle down, folks!" Pink, piglet-faced Pastor Mitchel clapped his hands. His Martha Stewart- like wife clapped along with him, though she didn't seem half as composed.

Slowly, the anxious chattering calmed, and once again, he spoke. "Now I know we are all very upset about what happened to the poor Coles', but we've got to focus on amping up the security around here. And it's got to start with our bravery, not with our fear."

The room quieted all the more. Despite his exasperated appearance, he carried a strong cadence that demanded attention. And the guy had been raised a preacher's kid so that passionate voice was built in— or engrained. His eyes spotted the Barnes. "Gunner Barnes and Bill Bailey already got a team of men to put up more barbed wire on all the fences, and they're done boarding up most of the windows. We got our nightly watchdogs, Rick Riley and Ned Flack, posted up in the water tower, but that's only on the South end of town so we're going to need to set up more posts on every side. Do we have any volunteers?"

A number of men raised their voices and offered their services, all with military backgrounds. A few even claimed they had night vision binoculars, resulting in six more watchdogs. I pulled Hope in closer. Already, Bells Ferry felt a tiny bit safer. Dixie smiled at me and rested her hand on my back, tenderly, like a mother would.

Pastor Mitchel squinted over the mob before him. "Where's Jace Myers?"

"Here, sir." A lanky old man with a shiny bald spot standing along the right wall raised his arm.

"How we doin' on ammunition?"

"Fine," the old man replied. "Most everyone's been bringing me their used cartridges, and my apprentice is really starting to get the hang of it so we've been able to pump out more in less time."

"Good." Pastor Mitchel pointed at him. "Let's get this man another apprentice. Who can help make ammo?"

A saggy-shouldered teenage boy wearing a Star Wars t-shirt raised his hand.

"Great," Mitchel said. "Now Sherrif Hank, Officer Tripp, and one of our deacons, Hunter,"—he gestured to the annoying holy hunk—"are still gathering information from the Coles, but we have to assume for now that all of the younger women in our town are prime targets."

I gulped and glanced around. In the crammed room of maybe 600, probably about the entire town, there stood only…a dozen visibly young women—including me.

I wanted to facepalm—or face punch—myself. Moving into an even more obscure, quiet little town where I could just work from home and not be surrounded by similar-aged people who'd want to befriend me seemed like a smart, safe idea. And it was. People were still kind and greeted you in the store, smiled and waved as they drove by, but I was younger. The only places people felt comfortable inviting me to was one of the two churches in Bells Ferry; here, the ancient First Baptist Bells Ferry, or the barely two-years-old nondenominational Seed Planters Fellowship. I'd chosen to visit this church twice, but only because Hope's best friend invited her to their Christmas service every year, and I couldn't say no to my sweet little girl's pleading.

I glimpsed at Hunter, the apparent deacon. And sure, maybe I came to get a snap shot of Mr. Hot Baptist Boy who'd acted as an usher during both years' services. The second time, he came running out to me and Hope in the parking lot because she'd left her favorite babydoll. His sweet, deep voice and gorgeous smile was way too memorable. Even his polished politeness, whether it be from picking up women on Saturday nights or practice greeting church folk on Sunday mornings. "Ma'am, I apologize for running after you like this, but I believe this doll belongs to your little girl."

I stammered out a pathetic I-haven't-dated-in-over-seven-years, "Thank you."

"My pleasure. You young ladies be safe now." As he turned and began walking away, Hope called after him.

"Wait!"

He gracefully obliged. "Yes ma'am?"

"Aren't you going to kiss my mommy goodbye?"

I died inside. I really think my heart stopped for a few seconds as I stood there, totally shocked, trying to figure out what to say; but Hunter beat me to it.

An unsettlingly attractive smirk lifted his lips. "Pardon me?"

"You're clearly a prince." Hope lifted her doll. "You brought me baby Ariel just like Cinderella's Prince tried to bring her her lost slipper, but she was gone already, so he couldn't kiss her."

I grabbed Hope's hand and again tried to say something, but Hunter, like he had previously, responded before I could spit out a correction or reprimand of some sort.

"Now, I don't think he was trying to kiss her just yet, ma'am. Remember, he waited until the end of the movie – after they were married."

Even though I knew he was just teaching Hope a moral lesson, I couldn't help but get all hot in the face. But I turned cold real quick. "Yes, because good old Christian boys like yourself wait until the girl they're chasing is their wife." I spun around, marched to my sun-baked, raggedy Civic with Hope jogging to keep up, and I didn't look back.

I averted my gaze from Hunter in the here and now. I always dreamed and even prayed a few times for Hope to have a good father figure in her life or an actual step-dad who would love her like his own… But I'd been down this road before. A guy like Hunter was probably in a serious relationship where he likely slept with the girl behind his pastor's back or he had a bunch of secret flings with church fangirls. And the only thing distracting him from his conquests was the fact that the world was falling apart.

"So for the unmarried women," Pastor Mitchel said, "We are going to set up trusted watchdogs that will keep guard inside the home with another single or widowed sister here from the church." He raised both palms as if conducting a service where he'd just asked his congregation to stand. "Will the unmarried women aged thirty and under please raise your hands?"

Me and the twelve other women held up our arms. Hope peered up at me and lowered her headphones. "Why are you raising your hand, Mommy?"

"Just answering an adult question for the minister, that's all. Keep listening to your music, angel. I like hearing you hum."

She slipped them back on as Hunter looked our way. Hope waved at him. He flashed his beautiful smile, and my chest burned. I lowered my hand. Him smiling during the apocalypse should be forbidden.

"We're gonna clear out before dark, but I ask all the young women to please stay behind so we can pair you up with your watchdog." Pastor Mitchel addressed a few other concerns, including an accusation that someone was stealing grain, and dismissed the gathering with a final word of encouragement. "Whatever darkness comes, remember: No matter how strong, it can never overpower the light."

Dixie and Gunner told me they'd wait for me and Hope outside. As everyone departed, their shoulders and sweaty arms brushing past, I stared at the purple stem around my wrist. Its fire had shone bright, but didn't scorch me. The light was beautiful and bizarre, like a melting sun. Then the stalk curved around my wrist and hadn't budged since—even though I'd poked at it a lot and tried a few silly mantras to see if it'd do something magical again.

What was its purpose? To remind me I wasn't alone? That there was a God who could do crazy things that defied nature and had power to burn or not to burn? I couldn't figure it out. But I would. Soon.

"It's quite creepy, isn't it?" A pretty twenty-something woman with wavy, chestnut hair stood beside me as the other girls were chatting around us. Pastor Mitchel and a group of men and women — Hunter included — spoke with two of the girls, apparently pairing them up with twin brothers who rocked long, gray beards tied in a double ponytail and another Martha Stewart-type lady. I nodded at Miss Pretty Squirrel Hair.

"I'm Krista." She held out a hand.

"Coryn." I shook it briefly then played with Hope's straight tresses.

"She's beautiful," Krista said.

"Thanks." I really wanted to say, "Clearly, she doesn't look like me," but thought if I kept my mouth shut Krista would do the same.

"How old is she?"

I could've slapped this woman, then guilt poked me. "Seven."

Krista smiled, so warm, so country-kind. "God's perfect number."

I actually returned a real smile. Maybe Pretty Squirrel Girl wasn't too bad; and admittedly, it felt kinda nice to bond with a fellow near-aged woman, especially one who wasn't married. Maybe she could relate to a plethora of poor prospects, though I never had many men knocking at my door and that was one of the precious perks of moving to the boonies.

Hope removed her headphones and gasped. "Mommy! Are these all princesses that the prince is going to meet and try to fit the lost slipper on so he can marry the right lady?"

I stiffened and whispered sharply, "Listen to me, Hope. Mr. Hunter is not a prince, so when he comes over here, you better treat him like a normal human be—"

Pastor Mitchel, a middle-aged woman using a cane, and Hunter walked toward us. I pursed my lips and rested my hand on Hope's shoulder as they stopped across from Krista.

"Hello there." Pastor Mitchel eyed me. "I've seen you before haven't I, dear?"

I offered a small voice. "I visited your last two Christmas services."

"We've visited." Hope gave a dancing finger-wave to Hunter. "Hi, Prince Hunter. Remember me and my princess mommy?"

I squeezed her shoulder. Why she had to not only look nothing like me — but also act nothing like me — had to be some kind of God-inflicted entertainment that he threw together just so he could get laughs out of my reactions.

Hunter smiled. "I do remember you ladies. How's baby Ariel doing?"

I blinked at him. Did he seriously remember the name of Hope's babydoll?

Hope beamed, but then swiftly frowned. "She's still at our old house by Mr. Gunner's. We left her there 'cause the bad men came in and tried to hurt me and Mommy."

Hunter's smile melted.

Pastor Mitchel looked at me, his pink forehead creased. "Where are you ladies staying now?"

"With the Barnes," I answered.

Pastor Mitchel's mouth twisted a tad like he'd gotten to the sour part of a sweet candy. "Oh, so you have Gunner to look after you then."

I nodded, wishing I could read minds and know why he acted funny at the mention of Gunner.

"Well then, as long as he and Dixie will have you, you should be fine." He faced Krista, though Hunter's stare lingered on me like… a concerned big brother.

"Now, how about you, young lady?" Mitchel asked Krista.

"I've been living down on Trickum Road by myself for the past month-and-a-half." Tears welled in her hazel eyes. "My brothers got into the military and my parents had gone up to Texas to visit my grandmother in hospice while I stayed back for school. Then the whole"—she glanced at Hope—"ordeal happened a week later, and I haven't heard from any of them since."

The woman with the cane and Pastor Mitchel nodded empathetically and slapped Hunter's back. "Hunter and Miss Mildred, the church secretary, will be good company for you then. They'll stay with you until this all gets figured out."

Pastor Mitchel's Martha Stewart wife scurried over. "We've gotta get these folks home. It's almost dark out."

"Right. Y'all are in good hands," Pastor Mitchel said. "We'll be praying for you."

Hunter concentrated those sparkling green eyes on me. "Y'all be careful now." He spoke with sobriety, no trace of his previous lightheartedness.

"Thanks," I replied.

"Thank you, Prince Hunter," Hope said before I could stop her.

I sighed inwardly as he raised his palm, and she gave him a high-five.

As he walked ahead with Krista and Mildred down the wide center aisle, the other eight girls and their watchdogs trailing, I forced myself to look away then followed along toward the double doors. I kept my arm around Hope. It's almost nightfall. Now the term brought with it a certain doom, like it had somehow become evil in itself.

Six weeks into this shambled state of the Americas, and the bad guys who'd tried to pillage Bells Ferry were amping up in darkness. They wouldn't relent. They'd be back, but we'd be ready for them. Wouldn't we?

Hunter

5. BUMP IN THE NIGHT

finished hammering in the final plank on Krista's bedroom window and brushed the sweat from my brow. Night danced in like Jezebel at a bar ready to bring any man she could to his knees.

I did one final perimeter scan, then headed back toward the front. Wind pushed against the porch setting off a wind chime by Krista's bright-red-bullseye of a door. I tramped up the steps and removed the chime from its hook. The quieter things were outside, the better.

The door opened. Krista stood in the entry, her pretty hazels glancing around. "Everything lookin' good out there?"

"Yes ma'am." I carried my tone like a man playing poker. "You're all set."

"Oh, thank you, Hunter." She stepped aside. "I don't know what I'd have done without your help."

I gave a cautious nod, walking in as she locked up behind me and rubbed her arms. "Would you like some water? I wish I could offer you some tea, but heaven knows when I'll ever be able to do that again."

"Water's good." I scanned the living room. The lit fireplace cast its light on the empty couches. "Where's Miss Mildred?"

"Oh, she hit the hay already," Krista said as she bustled to the kitchen. "Poor thing kept nodding off on the couch so I offered her my bed instead."

Turning away from the couches, I set the hammer down on the dining table, then took a seat. Krista returned with two glasses and handed one over before sitting across from me. Those hazels batting, she looked distant, yet near at the same time. The white sweater she wore dangled off one shoulder.

Coryn's face sprung in my mind like a bear-trap. That face I could never forget… How were she and her babygirl right now?

"I never imagined I'd be afraid in my own home," Krista said. "I always had my brothers or my momma and daddy with me, but now…" She shook her head, eyes shining. "I'm sorry, I'm such a mess."

"Hey, you don't have to be sorry." I set my glass down. "I'm sorry you have to go through all this alone."

She smiled through tears. "Well, not anymore, right?"

I shifted in my seat, but donned as natural a smile as I could. "You know Jesus?"

She coughed over some water. "Pardon me." She cleared her throat and wiped her mouth. "I mean, yeah, I think we all grew up in church around here."

I knew that much. She'd visit First Baptist Bells Ferry regularly and always made it a point to say hello. "I mean do you read His book, talk to Him, and hear back from Him?"

Krista clasped her glass with both hands. "I read sometimes and I say my prayers, but I wouldn't say He responds much."

"Would you like Him to?"

"I think that'd be nice… especially with all that's going on these days."

"Well, why don't you ask Him?"

"Now?"

"I don't see why not."

She shrugged, the sweater sliding down further. "I'd rather do it when I'm alone." She set her cup down. "All this talk about being alone, how about you? Before the war, I'd seen you at church all by your lonesome."

I took a sip as that knot way down tightened. I held onto the cup rigidly as I answered, "My wife died four years ago."

Krista's mouth fell open. "Oh. I'm so sorry, Hunter." She leaned forward, the other side of her sweater slipping down, bearing both shoulders. "May I ask what happened?"

I kept my hands on the cup. "Cancer."

Krista sighed. "How old was she?"

"She was twenty-four when she passed."

"And how long were you married for?"

"A year." I took another sip, a long one. Even though I had made peace with it, it wasn't something I'd shared with another woman before, one right around her age—and Coryn's. "And how old are you?"

Krista smiled, something lurking behind that pretty Southern charm. "How old do you think I am?"

I leaned back in my chair to clear the space between us some, regretting the question I'd used to change the subject. "I'd say twenty-three, twenty-four, somewhere in there."

"Wow, you're good at this." She stayed in her leaned-over-the-table position, setting her elbows on it. "My turn. I'd guess you're about… twenty-seven?"

"Twenty-eight."

"Ah, close enough." Her tone changed, the fireplace's flames burning in her eyes. "Like we are..."

I gripped the glass tightly. I hadn't been with a woman for over four years. After Allison, I kept away from them as best I could. Not that there were many eligible ladies in Bells Ferry, anyway. Except the one across the table, inching closer and closer… and the one at the Barnes' with her precious babygirl.

I set my cup on the table. "Listen, I'm not—"

Suddenly, darkness swallowed the room as the fireplace's flames extinguished. Krista shrieked. I rose to my feet and snatched the gun at my hip.

I felt around the table and got in front of Krista. She clung to my arm. Something creaked in the corner across the living room. I pointed my gun through the darkness. A clank rang in the kitchen. I adjusted my aim. A vibration rumbled against my skin: slow at first. Then faster and harder.

"What is that?" Krista whispered.

I held firmly to my gun. Whatever it was, it wasn't natural. Something fell near the fireplace. Iron clattered onto the floor. The fireplace pokers.

Something whipped past, a cool draft in its wake— and the vibrating got worse. Much worse.

"Oh God help us," Krista breathed.

A chair moved, right behind her. She shrieked as I grabbed her and pulled her in, circling as I did so and entering the hall. I backtracked with Krista close at my side, not letting her go for a second.

I reached her bedroom and stepped in, leaving the door open. The clamor of dining room chairs falling over and kitchen drawers opening spread through the house.

A single candle on the nightstand revealed Mildred as she stirred. "What's goin' on?" she mumbled as she sat up. I directed Krista to the mattress and sat her down beside the old woman.

The candle flickered wildly as I pointed my gun at the door. "Jesus, don't let me miss."

Another cool draft whipped past, dousing the flame.

Darkness hung thicker in the bedroom, no light seeping in from the boarded up window. Another shriek, this time from Mildred.

A dark figure stood in the doorway. I shot, but the figure darted to the left. I fired again, and it moved to the right. The candle reignited. The figure darted past like a dragonfly. He swiftly made his way around the room with a chuckle leaving his throat.

Another shot. Another miss. Another shriek.

I spun around. Mildred sat screaming while a second man in a black cloak sat atop Krista. A white hand held a device with a large needle at her arm. I fired. His head snapped in my direction. Black covered his eyes entirely, like I was gazing into a deep, endless hole. Blood dripped onto the hand holding the needle.

He hissed at me like a cougar, and I pulled the trigger. The first man appeared at his side and snatched his arm. The candlelight dimmed and relit. When the light strengthened, the two of them were gone.

Hunter stood in the doorway of Dixie's guest bedroom. A smile covered his lips with his green eyes on me. He stepped closer toward the bed. My heart hammered, and somehow, now I was out of it standing beside him. He kept walking, though, not even realizing I stood right beside him. He kept his gaze rapt on Dixie's bed. I followed his wholly devoted attention.

Krista lay on the mattress in a red nightgown, her legs exposed and a smile just as wide as his. A rock entered my stomach as he climbed onto the bed. A laugh left Krista's pretty lips, her mouth open, ready for him. I covered my eyes, the stone in my gut now simmering like soup left on the stove. Of course as Miss Mildred limped off to the couch for a snooze, Hunter would throw off his good church boy facade and have his secret fun. Why did I care, anyway? In times like this, meaningless sex could exist, but no one would be looking for true love. Fear didn't allow for that.

A gunshot pierced the night. I shot up in bed, ripped away from my nightmare. The LED lantern on the nightstand in Dixie's room shone Hope still asleep beside me. Three more shots fired. Gunner's frantic steps raced through the hallway, followed by Dixie's scuttling. She scurried into our room as Hope began to shift. Another two shots fired.

"Mommy?" Hope groaned as she slowly sat upright. "What's that sound?"

I held her tight as Dixie's arms wrapped around us, my heart pounding and skin crawling all over.

"It's okay, angel," I said as yet more gunshots rattled. "It's going to be okay."

Dixie began to sing an old familiar hymn, her voice loud in my ears, but welcomed. Anything to help distract from the gunshots. "Be Thou my vision, O Lord of my heart. Naught be all else to me, save that Thou art. Thou my best thought, by day or by night. Waking or sleeping, Thy presence my light." As she continued, Hope hummed along.

I closed my eyes, shutting out the darkness though the black of my closed lids mirrored it. Something deep within my pounding heart urged me to open my mouth and sing along with Dixie and Hope. So I did.

"High King of Heaven, my victory won. May I reach Heaven's joys, O bright Heav'n's Sun. Heart of my own heart, whate'er befall, still be my Vision, O Ruler of all."

The stem bracelet around my wrist emanated warmth. Or at least I thought it did. Maybe I was just heating up from my rushing blood. But either way, that strange, still rare sensation washed over me; that quelling…peace. My heart rate normalized and the skin crawling ended.

After maybe half an hour, Hope fell back asleep. Another half an hour after that, the front door downstairs opened. Dixie and I crept out of the guest room into the hallway. Gunner turned on a lantern by the couches, and we quickly descended the stairs to join him. Sweat dotted his face.

"What happened, Gunner?" Dixie asked.

He panted, eyes glancing at me before fixing on his wife. "They got another girl."

Dixie gasped as my heart hammered again. Another girl. Meaning another young woman like me. So Pastor Mitchel was right – they were targeting us.

"But they didn't kill her," he added quickly. "Hunter caught two of 'em while in the process of drainin' the girl's blood."

Krista. Now my heart skipped. "Are they okay?"

Gunner gave a nod. "He shot at the goons, but…" He shifted his gaze beyond us, as if trying to discern something far off, then slowly shook his head.

Dixie waved her hands. "Come on, spit it out already! Before I have a heart attack!"

Gunner's brow wrinkled. "They disappeared."

"Disappeared like, they ran off and disappeared into the woods?" Dixie asked.

Gunner stared at her, and for the first time since I'd met him, fear lived in his eyes. Maybe it was the first time Dixie had seen it, too. As the same look consumed hers, I spoke gradually. "They literally… vanished?"

Gunner lifted his hands. "Into thin air."

I sank onto the couch.

"There's more, ladies," he continued. He paused to address his wife. "You might wanna sit down."

Dixie rubbed her arms as she sat next to me.

Gunner plunked in the armchair and rubbed his hands together as if he were cold, too. "When Hunter fired on 'em, one of the men was… dodgin' the bullets."

Trembling overtook me. Fear shoved its way into my heart and forced all the peace out of it.

"Hunter was able to shoot the one trying to draw out the girl's blood, and when he did, he said the other one grabbed the man on Krista and the candlelight went out for a few seconds. When it turned back on, the men were gone."

"How can that be, Gunner?" Dixie held herself as if trying to keep warm. "How can these blood thieves dodge bullets and disappear like ghosts?"

"Not sure. The only thing I can come up with is somehow, they're gettin' these unreal powers from supernatural forces."

I instinctively touched the stem around my wrist. Warmth emanated from it again. As if confirming Gunner's assumption, it felt stronger that time.

Dixie clasped her forehead. "Oh sweet heaven. As if gang bangers aren't demonic enough, now we got enemies usin' weapons greater than knives and guns?"

Gunner rose from his seat and sat beside her. Taking her hands, he peered into her eyes. "We've got supernatural weapons, too, darlin'." He managed a smirk. "Ha! The fact that Hunter was able to intervene and we didn't lose another girl is proof that the prayers of this town are workin'. He even landed a shot on one of 'em. Now they know Bells Ferry is its own force to be reckoned with." As he wrapped his arms around his wife, my stare riveted to the purple stem wrapped around my wrist. Since I didn't dig guns, Dixie suggested I pray for another way to protect myself and Hope. I did, and no more than fifteen minutes later, I'm out by the strawberry patch, get pricked by this strange stalk that ends up igniting into heatless fire, then it latched onto me.

Already, it proved to have some supernatural elements to it. It emanated warmth after I sang that old hymn, and it did it again after Gunner's observation about the blood thieves. Could it also guide me by confirming truths, like a sixth sense?

I looked up at the front door and imagined all of the swaying shadows of the forest and nightfall. All the obscurity and confusion they caused to those without bright lights to guide them. Then I imagined the purple stem igniting in my hand: its brilliant, beautiful light that shined even beneath the rays of the sun. Yeah, this thing could do some nature-defying feats; and for whatever reason, it chose to reveal that fact and cling to me.

Why it—why he—chose me, and what more the stem could do, I was still figuring out. Somehow, I just knew that tomorrow night more answers would come.

6. ROOMMATES

$\mathcal{N}$ow the anxious murmurs had become louder, faster, more desperate, and confused in the old church. Late afternoon sunlight seeped through the stained glass windows on either side of the auditorium, where once again, the whole town crammed together to discuss last night's events.

I stroked Hope's hair as she bopped to the music playing through the headphones over her ears. Already, only a quarter of battery life remained. I knew I couldn't keep up this whole protection thing for long. Eventually, fear would find her, too; but hopefully, I'd be prepared to help her navigate through its dark, cold waters without drowning in it myself.

"You don't need to fear, y'all." Gunner stood to my left with Dixie, preaching to Bill and those nearest to them. "Krista is fine, and Hunter chased the goons off."

"Chased?" Maryann, the white Collie-haired woman said. "I thought the blood thieves disappeared out of sight!"

"Well, yes, but—"

"That sounds pretty terrifyin' to me."

Gunner opened his mouth, but before he could respond, Pastor Mitchel shouted from behind his podium. "Quiet down, folks!"

Once again, his Martha Stewart wife, in royal blue heels today, stood on his left while Sheriff Hank, Officer Tripp, and Hunter flanked his right. Despite slight darkness beneath his eyes, no doubt from staying up all night keeping watch over Krista, he still looked super hot in a short-sleeve shirt and jeans.

I bit my lip. Lust was a sin, and I was in God's house. I really needed to stop. Unfortunately, it seemed the only way to do that was to not look at the guy—or to remind myself that he was probably a wolf in sheep's clothing.

Krista stood close to the risen platform with her long, squirrel-colored waves laying against a flowered dress. After what she went through the night before, looking pretty seemed like a superpower in itself though she didn't need to try very hard. The people around her, mostly elderly or in their fifties, stared and whispered, making even me uncomfortable. Poor thing. She must be traumatized, and now, she had to deal with extra attention and lots of bombarding inquiries about her face off with death, too.

As the gathering quieted, much quicker than yesterday, Pastor Mitchel continued. "What's been happening in our town – in our country – is horrific, yes. But we've gotta choose to focus on the good." He held his palm out toward Krista. "This precious young lady is still alive thanks to the quick actions of our brave young deacon Hunter and our prayers." He pointed at the crowd before him. "Your prayers."

Somehow, the room quieted all the more.

"Now, what we're facing shouldn't be too alarming. Remember the man in the tombs in Jesus' days? He was so strong he broke the shackles his town had used to bind him. He had supernatural strength, because he had a legion of demons in him."

I grasped Hope's shoulder. Before yesterday, I didn't believe in demon possession. I knew we all were made with free will, and people could choose to do terrible things to others… But after what Hunter said those men did, even though it was unbelievable, the wood on the windows hadn't been broken. And he would've heard them if they tried to break in through another window or door, right? So somehow, they got into Krista's room undetected and left without leaving a trace of their visit – minus the two marks in Krista's arm and the bullet holes in her walls. What they did was indeed supernatural.

I looked at the purple stem on my wrist. And so was what I experienced two days ago…

"Since we now know beyond a doubt that what we're facin' is the forces of hell itself, we can't just fight with physical weapons."

"Yeah, but they're still human!" a man hollered. "And a gun did chase 'em off!"

A few others loudly agreed.

"Right," Hunter spoke now, "With my last bullet, too. What if I'd missed?"

The throng silenced like death itself.

"I'd have nothing but my fists. And with the way one of them was moving…" His gaze landed on Krista. "We both would've been dead long before morning… Unless God intervened." He paused, every eye on him. "The fact that I was even able to land a shot on one of them was a miracle in itself. And you better believe we are still standing here because of God, not because of me or my gun."

A number of people applauded at his mini sermon, but he wasn't done. "Yes, we can prepare ourselves as best we can, but if we won't include prayer in this fight, we've already lost."

More applauds broke out as Hunter stood there with his bulging chest and arms like a Southern Superhero. Although he could probably kick some regular human butt, he didn't have superpowers like the guys who tried to kill Krista last night…

Pastor Mitchel gave Hunter a nod, then addressed the townspeople. "For extra measures, we're going to be doubling up the security for each young lady. Do we have any volunteers to help watch Krista?"

"They can stay at our place," Gunner called.

My heart rate spiked, and my palms moistened. For fear of Krista staying with us who was just targeted last night, yes; but also… I glanced at Hunter. That meant Prince Baptist Boy would be an ever-present, indefinite guest in our new home—if we survived through the night since death stalked Bells Ferry like a hungry lion.

Pastor Mitchel continued. "If you still have generator juice, leave your lights on or keep your lanterns burnin'. Light seems to be something they don't like."

Warmth emanated from my stem-bracelet, just like it had after I sang that hymn and when Gunner guessed the Blood Thieves were getting their powers from supernatural forces. I touched the stem. Did that mean Pastor Mitchel was right about the blood thieves disliking light? Was it only because criminals preferred to go undetected and unseen… or because demons feared it?

After addressing a few more concerns, like a shortage on grain, which a few people volunteered to temporarily solve by sharing more of their food, Pastor Mitchel dismissed us. So far, the people cooperated amazingly well, sharing with one another as if whatever they had didn't belong to them. Though that kind of generosity and brother's keeper-like sacrifice was inspiring, food was growing sparse. I held Hope's hand, remembering our own shortage on strawberries. Eventually, the rest of the Barnes' garden and crops would get low, too. Maybe we would only go hungry and not starved.

I fought back tears. Hope and I had gone hungry before, but there were food stamps and pantries then. Who knows when – or if – the government would return, and it would probably be years until such programs came back… if ever. And everyone could keep farming, but sooner or later, more raiders would come. How long could Bells Ferry keep this up?

Hunter and Krista approached Gunner and Dixie. As Hunter shook Gunner's hand and embraced him, Krista's dark-circled eyes passed over Hope, then onto me. Like a groundhog popping out of its hole, Krista threw her arms around me and squeezed. A little jarred, I released Hope's hand and gently rubbed Krista's back. Though her broken embrace felt kind of awkward at first, my discomfort quickly melted away. This poor woman – like me – might have lost her parents and brothers forever, and probably didn't have any friends, either. And here we were, two young, single women without family in the midst of the hardest times in American history. Like that wasn't enough weight for us to bear, now we were the prime targets for deranged, demonic men who – for some odd reason – wanted our blood.

She released me and wiped away tears from her eyes. I had so many questions I wanted to ask: What the men used to try to draw her blood, how they appeared, if they'd said anything… But I knew if I were her, I probably wouldn't want to relive that nightmare over and over again so soon.

"Thank you again for havin' us, Mr. Barnes," Hunter said with his perfectly polished politeness.

"Gunner's fine," he replied.

Dixie put her arm in his. "We don't do formal at our home. Ask Coryn here."

Hunter looked at me.

I smiled, palms moist. "They're very hospitable, but yeah, guns are allowed at the dinner table."

As Hunter chuckled, butterflies fluttered in my stomach. Then the memory of my ex's country charm stomped them out.

Hope removed her headphones. "Are Prince Hunter and Princess Krista staying with us, Mommy?"

I nodded, singed at Hope's pairing of the two.

She jumped. "Yay!"

"We have an extra mattress we can lay out in the guest room for you, Krista," Dixie said.

"And we can bring our old futon in there for you, Hunter," Gunner said. "It'll be a tight squeeze, but should work well enough."

"Sounds good," Hunter replied. "I appreciate it."

"Me, too." Krista pursed her lips as if trying to stop herself from crying.

Hunter made this cute, sympathetic face at her before speaking again. "We just have to get some things and we'll be over soon."

Gunner slapped Hunter's buff bicep. "Bring every bullet and Bible you got."

"Yessir." Hunter smiled at Hope, then at me, making my stomach flutter again. "See you ladies in a li'l while."

"See you," I replied.

Krista gave me another hug. This time, I hugged her back. We both could use more hugs, more love…

As we walked outside and parted ways, I couldn't help but watch Hunter and Krista walk off side-by-side down the road. Prince Hunter and Princess Krista. They did look good together.

I clasped Hope's hand and forced my attention on the hilly road leading to the Barnes'. I needed to stop fantasizing about romance.

The sun danced off Hope's golden strands as she skipped. My babygirl needed all the love I could give. In this new life, she'd never get to experience walking down an aisle in white. She might never even have a first kiss…

I shivered despite the summer heat. What if something happened to me? What if the Blood Thieves got me? What would that do to my daughter, losing the person closest to her? She barely knew Gunner and Dixie. She'd be devastated and scared, and the security and joy of her childhood bubble would burst. She'd be thrown into the dark, confusing maze of this dangerous world. Death was banging on all of our doors, especially mine and Krista's, and who knew when it'd break through to seize its loot. It could happen tonight…

You are not alone. That intrusive but calm, gentle voice intercepted my anxious thoughts. *Neither is Hope. Do not be afraid.*

I looked up at the skies and let out an unsteady sigh. Maybe I really had become schizophrenic. Hearing these voices in my head that weren't my own, saying things I'd never say to myself. Like sure, you could die a slow, agonizing death tonight, leave your precious girl behind, but don't be afraid, Coryn. That's just silly.

"We've got supernatural weapons, too, darlin.'" Now Gunner's words echoed in my mind. I released another breath, this time more steady. Why not keep praying? What did I have to lose from doing so? I could still have my mental health and someone really was up there listening, who actually did show me something supernatural, something I could hold onto—literally.

Listening wasn't the same as protecting, though. Mom and Dad weren't protected from that car accident. Death wasn't something anyone was protected from. Sooner or later, we'd all face it; and sooner or later, I'd have to face it in the form of the ruthless and very powerful Blood Thieves. Hopefully, I'd live until morning.

Hunter

7. RUN AND WAIT

"You're really something, Hunter." Krista walked beside me up her porch steps, the afternoon sun burning at our backs.

I held my peace as she unlocked the front door, brushing her hair to the front. Her bare back flaunted in a flowery, strapless dress. It suddenly felt hotter out.

She opened the door and stepped inside, but I stayed put. She paused. "Taking in the breeze?"

"Just givin' you some privacy while you gather your things. I'll get mine after."

She gave a nod. "So professional of you. The Sheriff paying you to watch over me?" Then she smiled. "Or is this something you wanted?"

Ignoring her innuendo as darn best I could, I replied, "I want everybody safe, ma'am." Coryn's beautiful face entered in like a sweet song, then that precious girl of hers, along with her words when I asked about her babydoll. *"She's still at our old house by Mr. Gunner's. We left her there because the bad men came in and tried to hurt me and Mommy."*

I balled a fist. Krysta's eyes lowered to it, and she slowly stepped back outside. She stood right in front of me and looked up at my face. "Like I said, you're really something, Hunter. You're doing a great job, and it's because of you I'm still standing here right now…"

Her hand clasped my fisted one. Her touch sent me flinching, but I kept my tone professional. "Krista, I'm thankful to God He kept you safe last night, but —"

"You should take a little credit for that, too. He did use you, didn't He?"

"Yes, but—"

"All I want, Hunter"—she set both hands on either of mine now—"is to thank you."

I exhaled a shaky breath. It'd been so long, so long since I'd been this close to a woman. I knew about Krista for some time, always making herself known at the church. She never failed to put on her Sunday best and flash a smile. I always found her pretty, sure, but I just couldn't pursue another woman at the time. To be honest, I didn't even want to. I just wanted to help people. Serving at the church as a deacon was good, but I longed to serve in the field again; and now, I finally had that. The only thing missing was a woman by my side…

Krista tugged on my hands, leading me to the door. I planted my feet at the doorstep.

She turned, head peering over her exposed shoulder. "You really gonna make me beg, Hunter?"

My heart pounded. Sweat compounded between the searing summer humidity and her words.

She glimpsed around at the woods, then took another step toward me. "I mean, I could—"

I tore my hands away from hers and hightailed it to the forest. I ran and ran, leaping over branches and logs, dodging trunks. Brush thrashed, birds chirped from every angle. The sun broke through the canopy in flashes. My heart burned in my chest, part of me screaming to go back, to enjoy a woman while I had a shot. I'd waited long enough, hadn't I? Just one time and never again. God would forgive me.

A root caught my foot. I lunged forward and turned to the side. My shoulder smashed into the ground. As pain ripped through it, I flung over on my back, gritting my teeth. Through the trees, bits of blue peered down on me like God's eyes… as if they were filled with tears.

The burning in my chest was vanquished as fast as it started. "Forgive me, Lord," I said through gritted teeth. "Forgive me." I sat up, holding my busted shoulder. "I love You more than a passing moment." I sighed. "You know what I want, and you'll give it to me in the right time." I grunted. "Help me wait for as long as it takes."

Taking in a slow, steady breath, I rose to my feet and walked on toward the Barnes.'

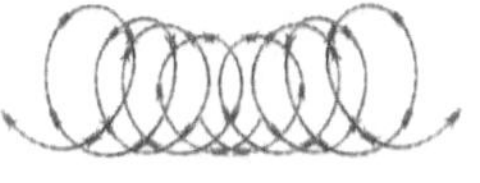

Coryn

The high sun reigned down on the empty strawberry patch like a king over his impoverished subjects. I breathed in the hot air, thankful for the brief break Dixie offered as she did puzzles with Hope inside. I was still processing the meeting from earlier. A second woman almost died last night, confirming all of our suspicions that ladies like us were being targeted… for our blood.

A shiver defied the heat as I looked down at the place I'd been pricked. Why? What were they doing with it? Selling it? Using it for an underground hospital or something? But then why were they acting like… real vampires? The way Hunter described it, it sounded like something out of a horror movie. Yes, I knew there was a high likelihood that God existed, but vampires? That was something entirely different. Creatures that looked like humans, but could only live —and live long—off of blood. But if they really were these supernatural beings, why didn't they just use their teeth? Why use a device to get it?

Something cracked behind me, and I spun around. Emerging from the woods, grasping his shoulder and looking like a hot mess—literally—Hunter approached. His jeans were smudged with dirt, a few leaves lay in his brown hair, and sweat lined his collar and abs like he'd been doing yard work for hours.

I froze as he drew near, limping a bit. "Picking berries?" he asked.

I glanced at the bare bushes. "Not exactly. Just catching some air. And… you?"

"Just took a run in the woods – agh." He winced. "And maybe a fall."

My eyebrows scrunched together as I sized him up. "Where's Krista?"

"Just wanted to give her some alone time."

"Why didn't you bring your things?"

"I can get them later."

Eyebrows still dipping, I took a cautious step toward him. "May I?" I asked, looking at his shoulder.

He gave a nod as I slowly lifted my hand. I lifted his sleeve gradually, but even so, he still grimaced. Red and blue the size of my palm marred his sunkissed skin.

I gasped. "How fast were you running?"

He managed to flash half of his killer smile. "Pretty fast."

I shook my head. "You sure you weren't being chased by a bear or something?"

He chuckled. "That honestly would've been better." His smile dissipated.

I eyed him. He held my stare for a moment. Something in me moved. I stepped back. "We don't have any ice, but you can get some cold water on that at least." I turned and walked ahead of him.

He lumbered behind, grunting here and there. I slowed my pace, face smoldering. Thankfully, the sun was as hot as it was because, although a *Cubana*, I was also half *Gringa* like Mom so olive skin didn't exactly mask blushing. I fought the urge to walk faster, to get away from this limping man, but guilt kept me in step with him.

"Where's Hope?" Hunter asked.

"Doing puzzles inside with Dixie."

"Hope said you lived close to the Barnes' before this?"

"Yeah, they let us live in their in-law suite." I looked to the left where our old house lay vacant, my heart suddenly heavy. I pursed my lips as tears welled. Would we ever step foot in it again?

Hunter followed my gaze, then said, "I miss my place, too. But—" He looked up at the Barnes' as we neared their back door. "—It's nice being hosted by a great couple for a little while."

I swallowed back the rest of my tears. Though I enjoyed being alone with just me and my babygirl, Dixie had often brought comfort, and Gunner, his laughs. I'd have missed much of that if they didn't take us in. I glimpsed at Hunter. Quiet, eyes fixed and watchful. Every bead of sweat glistened on his striking face. His encompassing form larger and… imposing.

"I'm going to check in on Hope," I said quickly.

"Tell her I said hi."

"You're not coming in yet?"

"I'll enjoy the heat a little longer, and Krista should be here soon, so I'll be heading back to get my things." He smirked in a smug way that suddenly made me want to flick him; but instead, I cranked an eyebrow and marched inside, leaving him and his antics behind me.

8. NIGHT TERRORS

This is the nicest awkward I've ever felt. The Barnes,
Hope, Hunter, Krista, and I all sat at the huge dining room table, almost done with our tomato, potato, and carrots dinner. Gunner, at the head of the table, shared a number of battle tales: gun fights, bar fights, and Dixie fights. "B.C., before Christ," he'd quickly add. And Dixie, of course, who never seemed to run out of stories about their six grandbabies: Lexi, Audrey, Lawson, Trevor, Randy, and Bart. She and Gunner both got emotional more than once, but they always collected themselves quick, thankfully. Hope seemed to pick up on their sadness sooner than I'd expected, and I didn't like it. She still had six months until she turned eight. Her innocent, safe little bubble… It was cracking.

"So, what were you studyin', Krista?" Dixie asked, twining her fingers together and resting her elbows on the table.

Krista rubbed her glass mason jar of water. "Education. I love kids." She smiled at Hope, who was eating her carrots by hand.

"Do you have any siblings?" I finally included myself in the conversation. Up until now, I'd been the silent spectator, but I was starting to make myself feel awkward. Hunter, chewing his boiled potatoes, looked over at me, probably startled by my sudden self-inclusion.

"I do," Krista replied. "Three brothers."

Hunter chuckled. "I didn't know it was three of 'em. I'm sure they drove you crazy, huh?"

"They sure did. I always wanted a sister, but I was the baby, the girl they kept trying for... So they stopped with me." She let her eyes linger on him, then her smile faded for some reason.

"Aww." Hope licked her fingers. "I always wanted a sister, too. But I wouldn't mind a li'l brother."

I dropped my fork. It clanked against the plate and I quickly picked it up. My face was likely as red as the three tomato slices I had left. I kept my eyes down, which perhaps only added to the awkwardness of the now silent dinners. I didn't want to think of baby-making or having a man, especially when an eligible one sat at the table with a beautiful woman he just saved last night—and who knows what went on beforehand… God, please let someone change the subject.

Gunner burped. "Whew! S'cuse me!"

Hope giggled. "That sounded like a bear growl."

"I'm tellin' you, dear," Dixie pointed her fork at him. "That man was raised in the woods."

"You better believe it." Gunner wiped the remains from his fingers onto his pants. "Poppa always said that playin' sports and wearin' clean, fancy clothes wasn't gonna teach nobody responsibility. Only shows ya that you're better than somebody else 'cause of how they look or talk. That's why havin' plants and animals growin' up is important. Try takin' care of somethin' that matters so much it affects more than just yourself. Not a trophy for the team that'll sit around collectin' dust or some letters on a piece of paper, but actually havin' lives that depend on your showin' up or they go hungry, thirsty, and could even die. That'll teach youngins everything they need to know about life… Well, almost everything, anyway."

Silence followed his granddad mic drop of wisdom. I looked at Hope, my heart warming. Though being a single mom had its many more-than-difficult moments, Hope taught me so much about myself… about life, about patience, gentleness, even timeliness; because even a missed nap or a late breakfast would make her a toddler terror. But most of all, she taught me about, well… hope.

Gunner shifted a bit, then focused on Hunter. His tone toughened just enough to be noticeable. "Now

Hunter, I know you've been a part of First Baptist Bells Ferry for about two years or so now, right?"

"Yessir."

"See, me and Dixie here used to be members there, but when that new Seed Planters church opened, we started going there."

Hunter raised his palms. "Hey, you haven't offended me. As long as they're teaching the truth and living it, they're good in my book."

"Wish Pastor Mitchel could say the same," Dixie spat out a little too fluidly.

Hunter took a sip from his water. I fiddled with my own glass. At least the awkwardness wasn't coming from me now.

Gunner cleared his throat. "You only been here two years, right?"

"That's right." Hunter put his glass down. "I moved from North Carolina."

"You have family here or somethin'?"

"Sort of. Pastor Mitchel was my wife's father."

Gunner and Dixie both paused before swallowing the bites they'd just taken.

I also chewed slowly, trying not to stare too hard.

"After Allison passed away," Hunter continued, "He'd always invite me to come work at the church."

I squeezed my glass, heart sinking. So he was a widower, and so young… His wife had to be in her early or mid-twenties… like me.

Hunter's tale flowed from his lips almost like he'd rehearsed it. "A few years went by, and after a lot of prayer, I believed God wanted me to take Mitchel up on his offer. So, here I am."

I couldn't help but sneak another glance at Dixie after her remark about Hunter's ex-father-in-law. She twisted her fork and her mouth like the two were having a confusing dance. What was the beef apparently she, too, had with the Piglet-faced Pastor? Come to think of it, they had made a few snide remarks about him here and there whenever talk of a town meeting cropped up, but I didn't like to probe. Getting deep meant getting dirty, and I had enough of that on my hands with my own family. Even though they were gone now…

"Well, Coryn," Gunner wiped his mouth with a handkerchief, "I suppose you want to put the little princess to bed soon."

Hope gobbled up her last bite of carrots. "Are Princess Krista and Prince Hunter going to come, too?"

Wishing I was black now that my face was doubtless redder than the frickin' tomatoes, I opened my mouth, but Hunter spoke first. "We can head up with y'all in a few minutes, Princess Hope."

She grinned, a piece of carrot in between her top teeth. "Ooh, I just love sleepovers!"

I caught sight of the holes dotting Krista's forearm, the unpleasant reminder of why this sleepover was happening to begin with, and swallowed hard. "Okay, honey, let's get you ready for bed."

"Before you go on to bed—" Hunter pushed his chair back as he stood. "I got something for you."

I eyeballed Hunter as he smiled almost deviously and exited the living room while Hope bopped up and down with a new boost of energy—just what I needed before bedtime.

He returned in no time, bulky arms behind his back. He stopped and kneeled before Hope, continuing to bounce, and revealed what he'd been hiding: a ginger-haired, puffy pink-dressed babydoll.

"Ariel!" Hope screamed and snatched it from his hands and death-squeezed the babydoll, kissing her over and over. "Oh, I never thought I'd see you again!"

As the Barnes and Krista oohed and awed, my heart jumped, fell, and nearly burst all at once. I couldn't help but clasp it. My tongue had a thank you on it, but I just couldn't get it out.

Hope paused smothering her babydoll and tossed her arms around Hunter's neck. "I knew you were a prince! I just knew it!"

Hunter's warm smile and frame melted at my sweet Hope's embrace, and for a split second, I almost wanted to hug him myself.

As Hope released him and returned to my side cradling Ariel, Hunter stood straight, seeming even taller.

I forced out a choked, "Thank you."

"Anytime," he said with a subtle somberness that made me shift. The first time he'd returned Hope's babydoll was just collecting it from an empty pew. This time, it required going to an abandoned house that could've hid squatters – or even worse, the blood thieves. Why would he even consider doing that?

"What a prince, indeed, huh, Princess Hope?" Krista approached and grasped Hunter's bicep. My dream of him approaching her on the guest bed slammed into my brain like a car collision. Something in me kindled with anger.

"You be sure to find yourself a nice prince like him someday," Krista continued.

I set my arm over my daughter, the kindling worse. "Okay, it's way past your bedtime, young lady, so if you'll excuse us—" I veered my daughter toward the stairs. Every moment closer to putting her to sleep weighed heavier and heavier. Never had I been so terrified of bedtime, even when we were alone in our house, snuggled closely on my full-sized bed, knowing there wasn't a man with a gun in the home to fend off gangbangers and looters. But bad guys with guns weren't the same as bad guys with… superpowers.

I breathed in as we entered the upstairs bathroom and did everything with trembling hands. Guns, guns, guns. I hated them because they killed so many, yet we needed them to kill or be killed ourselves; but now, it seemed they were hardly enough for these Blood Thieves who could appear and vanish seemingly at will. These Blood Thieves, who even buff Hunter had a hard time fending off. Hunter, who barely saved flirty squirrel-haired Krista last night from having every last drop of blood sucked clean out of her.

We stood in front of the mirror as I brushed Hope's hair while she kept hugging the babydoll. Her gaze – so small, innocent, and shining with life – searched mine. "Mommy, why are you scared?"

I tightened my grip on the brush. "I'll be fine, sweetie."

"Are you sure?"

"Yes," I lied. I could die in a few hours, and so could she, but pretending was better than telling her the truth. For now, at least. I'd take that lie to the grave – if I lived long enough to see this whole mess through to its end.

Her eyes drifted to my wrist. "I like your pretty new bracelet. Who gave it to you?"

I stopped brushing. "I don't know."

"It was a secret gift?"

"Sort of."

She yawned. "Can I have one?"

I set the brush down. "Maybe one day. Now let's tuck you in." I slipped my arms beneath her and raised her up like a princess. As she giggled, I held her tight. This could be our very last night together. "I love you, Hope."

"I love you, too, Mommy."

Tears filled my eyes as we walked into the guest bedroom. I laid her and Ariel down on the bed, and she peered up at the night table's lamp. "Are you going to shut the light off?"

I stared at the warm light, mimicking the sun. Fake, like I had been. "Not tonight."

"Is that what you're scared of, Mommy? The dark?"

My heart stumbled in my chest. The tungsten glow blended with her blues, making them falsely appear green, like a lake surrounded by trees. A lake that stretched on and on… She looked older. Wiser.

An ache rose in my chest. "I—"

A knock softly rapped the door.

"Uh, come in," I called, admittedly thankful for the interruption.

The door opened and Hunter ambled into the room, courtly with a polite bow of his head. I breathed with more difficulty, some of that kindle returning, too, as if the air thickened at his broad presence. He paused, his countenance also lightening the area somehow. I disdained it.

"I can wait outside the door 'til Princess Hope is all tucked in if you'd like."

"It's fine, Prince Hunter," Hope said in her little voice, just as quaint as his. As he shut the door behind himself, a heaviness crept up. How I wish she could always believe in fairytales… and how I wish I still did. "But Mommy doesn't want to turn the light off 'cause she's afraid of the dark."

I kept my mouth closed, still at a loss as to how I should respond because that truth couldn't be hidden anymore, not even from her.

"Well…" Hunter eased onto the bed, right next to me, sinking in the mattress. His whole presence was larger than it felt outside. "You know who isn't afraid of the dark?"

"You?" Hope asked.

He smiled that criminally beautiful smile—that I despised more than anything else about him, the one that made him seem so genuine, and yet the same one that made girls like Krista crawl into his lap when he had them all to himself. "I was going to say Jesus."

Not even Hope could remain somber. She smiled back, lightening some of the weight from me. "Maybe he can help Mommy not to be."

As I found a loose thread on the blanket to play with, I held my tongue again. Hope wouldn't understand why Mommy didn't want to talk to the God. She believed was perfect and good all the time. She had enough burst bubbles for now. She'd find out the truth about him later.

Hunter gave a few nods, the warmth from his encroaching frame on the bed now emanating just inches from me. "She can always ask him."

Hope lowered the blanket from her chest and shot up like a dang Jack-in-the-box. "Let's ask him, Mommy!"

I shook my head as I lifted the blanket over her. "Not now, honey. Go to sleep." I swiftly pecked her and Ariel's cheeks, avoiding Hunter's face, and laid down next to Hope. Hunter stood, the mattress rising to its proper height at the relief, and adjusted something at his waist—no doubt a gun—before sitting on the futon, which set right under the only window in the bedroom…

A tremor infiltrated my core, and I looked away. I forced my eyelids shut and feigned sleep. If only I could will myself to disappear for a while – or teleport. I cringed. Like the Blood Thieves…

It took a few minutes before Hope's breathing slowed and quieted. Her gentle breaths defied our reality—the one she still wasn't fully aware of... But how long would that last? Her illusion of safety was going to shatter sooner or later, and what could I do to help her then?

I sat upright and turned away from my baby as if doing so would stop the thoughts. Between the looters, the gang-bangers, the lack of food, and now all this lack of sleep, I was on the verge of breaking; but I couldn't bring myself to dream. Not tonight. Maybe not ever. But who cared anymore? What was I even fighting for? Maintaining an illusion? A glass cup just waiting to be knocked over? Ugh! How much easier death would be than this.

"Coryn?"

I flinched at Hunter's voice. It was soft. Cautious. He surveyed me from his post on the futon, his gun now laying on the cushion beside him—another reminder that at any moment it could all break. The lamp's gentle glow rolled off his shoulders like the setting sun over a hill with his fitted green tee that did more than bring out his eyes. "She's gonna be okay."

I sucked my teeth, acid on my tongue. "How can you say that? Are you also a prophet or something?"

He shook his head, unmovable, like that hill in a valley standing tall and firm. "I've made wrong predictions before."

"That's comforting." I looked away.

"But just because I confessed them out loud doesn't mean I didn't know the truth deep down."

I kept my eyes on the wall across from me, decorated with photos of Dixie and Gunner's adult children. One displayed their daughter, LillyAnn in a puffy wedding dress beside her husband, Denver, in a burgundy tux. They looked to be no older than me and Hunter… I lowered my gaze to my flowery pajama pants that Dixie let me have from 'the good old days' when she could still fit in them. The good old days… like when people could spend countless hours on planning their perfect wedding, finding the best venue and dream dress, and invite those they loved to celebrate before they danced the night away. Would those days ever come back? Or would something even worse happen before they could?

An exhale just loud enough for me to hear left Hunter's lips. "I knew my wife was going to die."

My stomach hollowed. I forced myself to look at the Holy Hunk whose handsomeness bothered me less —only for the moment. For once, his eyes were lowered.

"God showed me, but I kept telling myself – and everyone else – that she was going to make it."

My voice softened like butter left on the counter. "How'd he… show you?"

Hunter lifted his green eyes. They reached across the space between us. Though sadness dimmed his usual light, something stirred beneath that I couldn't quite pinpoint. It both scared… and thrilled me.

He opened his mouth. Another gentle tap rapped the door. It opened, and Krista's pretty face peeked from behind it. It opened more, and in she walked, slowly and gracefully with a tray of steaming mugs like a perfect country hostess. Her silky hair lay restfully down her shoulders, freshly brushed, over a pretty pink gown, making my own flowery second-hand pajama pants look like a mockery. What was it with these Southern gals and their ability to maintain themselves even though the world was going to hell? And better yet, why did Krista care about looking good when we could literally die tonight?

She held out the tray. "Coffee anyone?"

"Have any sleeping pills instead?" I asked.

She smiled a painfully pretty smile. "I wish."

Hunter's sadness seemed to melt at her presence. A smile curved his lips as he grabbed a mug. "Thanks, Krista."

"It ain't the sweet tea I would've liked to offer you back at my place." She gave a generous smile. "But you can thank Mrs. Dixie. She insisted even though that was her last batch."

Sweet tea? What the hell did that mean?

Hunter sipped, then jumped, grunting as a splash of scorching coffee attacked his shirt.

Krista gasped as she handed our mugs to me and rushed to Hunter's aid like a paramedic—with a smirk on her face. "Hunter Freeman," she lulled as she took the mug from him and produced a handkerchief out of nowhere, wiping the side of his mouth and chin. "You saw the coffee was steaming, didn't you?"

He tugged on the wetness by his collar. "Clearly, I wasn't thinking straight." His tone pinched just enough to make Krista roll her eyes, all the while still smirking gladly. For some stupid reason, my own chest sizzled like the mugs I held. For a moment, I wondered how Krista would react if I accidentally spilled coffee on her as she came for her cup, but when she reached for it, the two holes in her forearm reminded me that she had been through plenty last night.

Guilt washed over as I inhaled the bitter sweet fumes and took a sip of Dixie's last brew. My tongue thanked me, though my heart didn't.

Krista sat down on the futon beside Hunter, confidently, like she'd known him for more than just two days. Her pretty smile now faded like the sun at dusk as she spoke somberly. "I wanted to say I'm so sorry for your loss. I'm sure she was amazing."

Another small smile found itself on Hunter's mouth, as if he couldn't be sad around Ms. Country Kind Squirrely-haired Krista. "She was."

"How old were you again when you got married?"

"She was twenty-three, and I was twenty-four."

"Wow." Krista shook her head, her smooth hair moving freely, no moose or hairspray needed – unlike my frizzy curls. "So young."

"God knows why he does what he does," Hunter said. "One day I'll know why, too."

The light flickered, and I peered back at it. The flickering continued at a rapid pace.

Hunter stood and walked over to it. "Could be a bad bulb."

I looked down at the purple stem coiling my wrist, almost expecting it to light up to affirm what Hunter said, but it didn't.

I focused on him, heart hastening. "I don't think so."

The light popped, swathing the room in darkness. A pulse suddenly filled the air. Painful, pounding, and intrusive.

I reached for Hope, but cold fingers grabbed my wrist. I gasped, a scream trapped in my throat. The stem glowed brightly, unmasking who—or what—held onto me.

A pale face emerged from the darkness. Sharp cheekbones rose to a pair of ebony eyes, not a hint of white anywhere in them. The purple from the bracelet hung onto the hollow-looking orbs, and they glinted… Like a thirsty animal. "So you're the one they told us about."

Another pop – Hunter's gun. The man released my wrist and lunged at him as fast as a shadow. With a crash into the dresser, the men collided to the floor and grappled. I snatched Hope and pulled her off the bed. The bedroom door burst open. Gunner stormed into the room with an LED lantern and a shotgun, Dixie right behind him with her mini handgun. Krista grunted.

I searched the room for her. She stood next to the closet—but not alone.

Though snowy-haired, a woman with a beautiful – but lifeless – face, free of any wrinkle, stood behind Krista in a black catsuit. She clung tightly to her with one arm, while the other held a massive, two-pointed needle at Krista's forearm.

Another scream locked itself in my throat.

Tubes connected to the needle by a wristband the woman wore. Krista's eyes began to roll.

Gunner aimed his shotgun, but the attacker pivoted in a jolt with Krista from side-to-side like a sped-up dance. Krista's legs hung limp as the woman dragged her to-and-fro as if she were merely a lifeless puppet being mastered.

"My God," Gunner breathed.

Krista's attacker laughed, a low rumble that stabbed me with shivers. "Tsk, tsk. Using his name in vain."

"What's happening, Mommy?!" Hope cried.

I pulled her head into my chest. My body quaked. God, help us!

The purple stem pulsed warmth, reminding me of its presence. A sudden surge of heat poured up my arm, and a violet glow emanated from my skin. The young man grappling Hunter jerked his head in my direction as he slammed Hunter's into the wooden planks, breaking them in half. The scream I couldn't release suddenly found its escape.

The man disappeared. The violent pulsing worsened. It was all around, coming from every angle, thrumming and pushing against my skin.

He reappeared a foot in front of me and Hope. Still holding her, I freed one hand and shoved him. A flash of hot, purple light burst from my palm. For a few moments, the pounding vibrations dissipated as if blown back somehow. Violet sparks spread across the young man's chest as he convulsed, like being shocked by a defibrillator. He staggered backwards into the closet doors past the white-haired woman who still dragging Krista around like a ragdoll. Gunner fired his shotgun. The bullets slammed into the man's chest, and he crashed backwards, breaking the closet doors as he collapsed within.

The woman growled and threw Krista down. Dixie fired, but the woman vanished. As Dixie and Gunner ran to Krista, I surveyed my arm. The purplish glow and warmth slowly faded.

Hope backed away from me as tears cascaded down her cheeks. Her eyes shined with fear. I reached for her, but she recoiled.

"It's okay, sweetie. It's just Mommy." I tried to keep my voice calm, but desperation drowned it.

More tears and fear welled in her eyes. She ran out of the room.

"Hope!" I rose.

"Get the first aid kit!" Dixie ordered Gunner. As he rushed out, my eyes found Krista. She lay pale on the floor by the mattress, her eyes closed and mouth agape. My heart slammed against my chest. No. Please no.

Hunter also lay on his side on the floor, faced away and not moving.

My heart raced a million miles an hour as I turned and ran out of the room. "Hope!"

Gunner rushed into the hall. "She's in our room."

I took in an unsteady breath, though I couldn't stop the shivering, and quickly closed the distance to Gunner and Dixie's bedroom. Hope lay face down in a pillow sobbing. My heart shattered. Her bubble of innocence had finally been destroyed by the very real monsters who probably killed both Krista and Hunter —right before her eyes.

A new emotion surged in: rage. How could God allow this to happen? He let that wolfish punk take my trust, take all of me and trample it, not even caring that he'd gotten me pregnant because his parents wouldn't shame him the rest of his life like mine had. They'd ignore it like they ignored me that night I came banging on their door, begging them to just hear my side of the story. Then the gangsters, and now the Blood Thieves. Sure, God was real, but he let all of this happen to me and now to my little girl! None of this felt like love. None of it!

I stepped toward my baby, her sobs the worst sound in the world. I sat beside her gently and laid my hand on her back. She shuddered, and the pillow muffled her voice. "Did they kill Krista and Hunter?"

I pursed my lips, head reeling and heart aching worse and worse. I don't think I ever heard her say their names like that… No princess or prince moniker. Her fairytale had ended in the worst way possible. "I don't know. Dixie and Gunner are taking care of them."

She raised her little head and looked at me. "And that bad man. You hurt him. Your arm…"

I examined my right arm. The stem remained, but no light emanated. *"So you're the one they told us about."* The now-dead man's words invaded. Who told them about me? Was I being watched? Did someone see me when I got pricked and the stem crawled onto my wrist? Or was it… some*thing*.

Demons.

"Coryn."

I shrank back. Gunner stood in the doorway, sweaty and red-faced, blood stained his hands. I shivered again. That couldn't have been Krista's blood… Gunner beckoned me over.

I turned to Hope. "I'll be right in the hallway, okay?"

She nodded. I hesitantly walked away from her and into the hall with Gunner. Nausea eased up my throat.

"Krista's alive," Gunner said.

I let out a sigh and spoke quickly. "And Hunter?"

"He is, too. Barely."

As another sigh freed itself from my mouth, Gunner peered over his shoulder. "But that young man is dead. Looked to be nineteen or so." He shook his head, then his eyes gleamed. He spoke quietly, but stern. "You gonna explain how they knew about you and why your arm lit up like a darn firework?"

I breathed in and looked up at the ceiling before divulged into the situation to catch him up to speed.

He clasped his moist forehead, smearing blood on it. "I done lost my ever loving mind... I need a beer and some serious prayer to figure this one out." He paused before he whispered, "Me and Dixie are gonna get things in order in there as best we can so keep your daughter preoccupied."

I winced. All that blood in our room. Getting rid of the… My throat burned, and bile swelled up, but I forced it back down so I wouldn't vomit all over Gunner.

He started to leave before he paused to say one more thing. "I don't know how you did that back there, but I do know this: they're not gonna be just after you now. They're gonna be after all of us."

Hunter

9. OWL EYES

Thunder rumbled in the distance as I danced in the kitchen by the stove and stuffed a bowl with popcorn. "Oh it's coming, ma'am!" Popcorn in tote with a box of chocolate raisins, I slid into the living room where Allison waited on the couch with the remote in her hand like a gun. The dim light from the TV screen couldn't hide the light in her beautiful smile as I dropped beside her.

Blonde hair piled onto one shoulder, wearing one of my tees, she looked snug as a bug. "You took long enough." She snagged the chocolate raisins first, like always. "What were you doing in there, putting on a dance recital?"

I set the popcorn in our laps and wrapped my arm around her. "Gotta warm up a beautiful gal like you somehow."

She laughed as she unpaused her movie of choice —a rom-com, again, as usual. I'd have gone for a thriller, just because I like it when she jumps on me, but the storm might help with that tonight.

A bright flash mocked our sheer curtains, followed by another clash of thunder. Allison recoiled closer.

I held her tight. "Just focus on the movie—or me." I winked.

She elbowed my side as she fed me a chocolate raisin. "Now Hunter Freeman, you know I've been wanting to see this movie since I saw the trailer three months ago. You ain't gonna go robbing me from it for another minute." She set her gaze on the screen while I swallowed the treat—and my hopes of skipping the movie for something better.

Lightning flashed and thunder bellowed a moment after, this time rattling the windows—and zapping the TV. I set the popcorn aside as darkness covered the living room. As swift as the lightning, Allison crawled into my lap with her head on my chest. "Darn it, Hunter."

"What you mean, 'Darn it Hunter?' I only prayed God would intervene so I wouldn't get nightmares about Hallmark couples."

"I can't believe you did that."

"God knew I was only half-serious."

"Well you got what you wanted—halfway."

I sucked my teeth. "Come on now, don't punish your man like that."

She yawned. "I'm sorry, love. I'm just feeling really tired, actually." She yawned again. "Really tired…"

Lightning struck and thunder smashed. My eyes opened.

A blurry pink glow filled a room. I lay on something. I turned my head, and sharp pangs sliced my skull. The room blurred more. Someone lay on a mattress on the floor. A woman. A woman I'd… never seen before. More pangs attacked my head. The pink light darkened until it turned black.

Coryn

"You telling me she's some sorta superhero?" Pastor Mitchel sat at his desk in the office behind the church, pale faced for once. He tugged at the collar of his long sleeve button-up, damp with sweat. Perched beside him, Pastor Rhett from Seed Planters, in a causal tee, retained his tan hue and observed like an owl—a handsome one.

Gunner sat on my left and Hope on my right across from the ministers. She kept her eyes down the entire time. Headphones were useless now. Dixie had stayed home to tend to to Krista and Hunter… who could both be dead before we got back.

"I saw what I saw, Mitchel," Gunner said.

"You sure you're not drinkin' again?"

Gunner rubbed his chin. "Oh okay, so you wanna bring up the past now, huh?"

"No, I was just askin'—"

"—'Cause I can bring up the past, Mr. Judgey Judge."

Rhett raised a calm hand. "Our enemy isn't flesh and blood, but a very crafty spirit." He finally broke his silence. His brown eyes stared as if he analyzed my very soul. "Can you show us?"

I shifted in my chair. "I don't know."

Mitchel leaned in, his fingers twined. I locked onto the stem on my wrist and willed it to light up. I rubbed it, poked it, wiggled my wrist; all that and it still clung dormant. Two or three very long, awkward minutes passed by until the sound of chair legs scratching wood broke the silence.

Mitchel rose. "I'm gonna see if anyone's willin' to volunteer to be an extra guard at your house."

"I'll be the first," Pastor Rhett said as his soul-stare bore into me. I felt like some kind of weird artwork at a museum that both perplexed and amused him—that he stubbornly needed to figure out.

"Thank you, Pastor Rhett." Gunner stood. "You're a good man."

Mitchel's mouth tightened, and he walked out first.

Pastor Rhett rose. "Anything for you and your precious family." He looked at me and Hope. "And for you and yours."

I offered a fake half-smile. The man was maybe an early thirty-something and kinda handsome. Attracted to holy-roller pastors, too, now? What the freak was wrong with me?

"Thanks." I grabbed Hope's hand. She flinched. My chest stung like a million needles. I don't know what was worse, my daughter knowing about and fearing the demented Blood Thieves – or fearing me.

"Can I have a moment with you two?" Rhett asked me.

My grip on Hope tightened. Gunner's shining blue eyes asked if it was okay. I turned to Rhett. "I guess."

"I'll be waitin' for you girls right outside, 'kay?" Gunner said.

I gave him a real half-smile. Gunner. Our gun-slinging protector who'd die for us in a heartbeat as if we belonged to him…

Rhett set his serious soul stare on me again. "I can't imagine what you're going through. The fear, the confusion, the doubt. But I… had a dream about you."

My hold on Hope tightened even more. She looked up at me and finally broke her nearly two day silence. "You're hurting me." She even spoke differently.

"I'm sorry, sweetie." I loosened up as Pastor Rhett continued.

"That stem on your wrist, did it… prick you?"

I blinked at him. How would he know that? "Were you watching me?"

"So it did?"

"Well, yeah. Accidentally, I guess. I don't know."

"And it was glowing purple, like how Gunner described your arm?"

"Yes…"

"Amazing…" A small smile etched his lips, but it quickly vanished. "Hope?"

She peered up at him.

He slowly kneeled, bringing his face eye-level with hers. "You see this pretty bracelet your mom is wearing?"

She looked at my wrist then nodded.

"God gave it to her for a reason. Do you trust him?"

Hope lowered her eyes again. "Prince Hunter does."

Rage flickered inside of me, and I unleashed some. "Yeah, and look at where that got him." I squeezed my lips shut, instantly regretting my words. Thick tears flowed from Hope's eyes, silent, haunting, like the weight of them crushed her ability to let out a sob for the friend she could very likely lose before the day's end.

I addressed Rhett as he straightened. His soulful stare was now softer, wounded. "I know you're a pastor and all, but I'd really appreciate it if you'd stop bringing up God to me and my daughter."

He failed to hide his hard swallow. My stomach fluttered some at my own harshness, and I quickly exited, taking Hope with me.

Gunner cleared his throat as he stood waiting for us in the small hallway.

My face warmed. I suppose I was louder than I meant to be.

"Let's see if we have any more takers." Gunner led us into the sanctuary where the pews sat crowded with bantering Southerners. Pastor Mitchel stood atop his risen post with his wear-on-your-hip bride, more humble this morning in a taupe skirt and wedges rather than heels. Even her blonde hair looked less touched.

As we walked down an aisle to find seats, many heads—and whispers—followed. I shivered. Another reminder why I never bothered to go back to church after Mom and Dad died. Not everyone was like Gunner and Dixie, and my old youth pastor and his wife Cindi; And maybe weird Pastor Rhett, and Hunter…

My heart trembled. As much as I didn't like being around him, I didn't want him to die, especially not like this… at the talons of merciless animals who stole the blood of women in the dead of night.

Gunner pointed to two empty seats in a middle row for Hope and I. As we squeezed past, Maryann, the Collie-haired woman, flinched.

Pastor Mitchel tracked me with his stare. "You know what, let's just have Miss Coryn come up here and tell you herself what she saw and did."

My palms instantly moistened. Stand up there in front of all these judgemental Christians and tell them about my bizarre supernatural encounter? Um. No pass go. Not gonna happen.

Mitchel beckoned. "Come on up here, dear. People wanna figure this out, and see who else wants to volunteer."

I narrowed my eyes, rage returning. You know what, yeah. I'll play his little game. We'll see how humiliated he feels when his cozy little members prove they're all a bunch of religious hypocrites. I kissed Hope's temple before rising.

Gunner spoke low. "I can tell them, Coryn. No worr—"

"No, it's fine." I shimmied my way through, then marched down the aisle toward the altar. Pastor Mitchel took his wife's hand, who nervously glanced at me and offered a weak—and plastic—smile as they stepped aside.

I positioned myself in front of the podium, queasy and lightheaded before this eager audience. Hope sat among them, and though her bubble had been decimated, I considered my little girl's listening ears. "Not even a week ago, I was in Gunner and Dixie's field picking strawberries. I got pricked by something, and turns out, it was some strange plant I'd never seen before. It was glowing, or on fire or something, but it didn't burn—"

"Like Moses and the burning bush!" an old man in a cowboy hat hollered.

Several folks shushed him.

I went on. "The plant wrapped around my wrist, and last night, when the Blood Thieves showed up, my arm emanated this purplish light and I just... pushed one of them, the light sparked on him, and he fell back."

Gasps then quiet filled the room.

"Then Gunner shot him. The other one disappeared."

As more silence stuffed the place, I kept my focus on Hope. Her golden hair now nappy, face leaner, and clothing wrinkled and stained... My chest thrummed slow. Even though we'd always struggled, this was next level. Despite the odds stacked against her, my little girl still had a hope and a future in this land of the once-free. Maybe she'd never get married or have kids of her own, but at least she could pursue a dream. Now, she only had merely surviving to look forward to. Something I'd done my whole life. I could handle it for myself, but for my angel?

"I'll volunteer." A man with a beer belly and a cap, wielding a shotgun declared. "Me and good ol' Denny here don't like mosquitos."

"Thank you, George." Pastor Mitchel gave him a clap. "Any other takers?"

Surprisingly, a handful of other gun-toting men offered their services, though the only fierce thing about the majority of them was their weapon. Another pang stung my heart. How many of these guys would die this week?

Hunter's beautiful and bloody face smacked my mind. I hurried off the platform as Pastor Mitchel dismissed the gatherers. A gang with Gunner met me at the foot of the altar with my sweet babygirl in front of them. Those beautiful blues peered up at me, glistening like bluejays in summer, but brownish circles darkened them. She'd tossed and turned all night for days. Awake or asleep, she couldn't escape the terrors of the night—and neither could I.

"Let's hurry back." I gripped Hope's hand and strode to the exit, and though I hated to do so because of how permissive of it all God had been, I prayed Krista and Hunter were still alive.

10. HUNTER WHO?

"It's a nightmare." Standing with her back to the TV in her candlelit living room, Dixie wiped fat beads of sweat from her pale forehead. Streaks of blood stained her white nightgown, what she donned last night before the attack. I sat on the couch with Hope, Gunner, and the country guardians all crowded around on their feet. Everyone's face shown just as pallid. "They're both hardly breathing. It's a miracle they still are at all."

Hope squeezed my hand. I flinched at her sudden touch. Tears fell from her eyes. I squeezed back, heat rushing to my toes. These beasts needed to be stopped. But how?

"Are you going to fight them again, Mommy?" Hope's voice sounded alarmingly older and… angry.

Everyone's attention shifted from Dixie and rested on me. The choking silence brought on a wave of nausea. Whatever I did last night, I clearly couldn't do on command. I miraculously escaped death, but who knew when the teleporting, hyper-fast murderers would return for round two? How many would they bring next time? Yes, we had five more guns; but against these Blood Thieves, the weapons were more like sticks, and the guardians like sitting ducks. Then I focused on Hope. "I'll do everything I can to stop them." Part of me trembled inside. It was a half-true promise. I wanted to rid the earth of these vermin, but wouldn't leaving this place be better? They seemed to be after me, and any other woman around my age. If we all disappeared, lived underground or something, wouldn't everyone be safer? Well, as safe as you could be in a land without law.

I focused on Dixie now. "I wanna see Krista and Hunter."

Face still drained of color, Dixie gave a nod and took my place beside Hope. She stood. "I wanna see them, too."

"Not now, Hope, maybe—"

"I want a chance to say goodbye if…"

"They're gonna be okay, Hope. Just stay with Dixie."

Head bowed, she sank back onto the couch. My own head low, I ascended the stairs. My heart drummed slowly like my steps. What if Hope was right, and once again, me trying to protect her would only hurt her more? If they did die… My knees weakened when I reached the door, slightly ajar. Crackling candles shed weary light in the bedroom. I inhaled a deep breath and stepped inside.

Vanilla cupcake iced with the coppery stench of blood wafted in the air. My neck cooled, though sweat dampened it. Krista lay in her twin-sized mattress, and Hunter on the futon. A bloodied bandage wrapped his head, his skin so light, and purple encircled his puffy eyes. I tiptoed toward Krista, my gut tangled. Her chest barely lifted. I knelt beside her, tears falling. This sweet woman didn't deserve this. She didn't deserve to die this way – or to live this way. Why'd I even pray for her to survive? Perhaps it was better for her to die. For all of us to just die.

"She's… alive." Hunter moaned. I hurried over to the couch. Eyes closed, his head swayed back and forth as he mumbled.

"Hunter?" I asked. My hand found his, cold and clammy against mine.

"She's… here…"

"Who's here?"

Hunter groaned. I clasped his hand tighter. His green eyes gradually opened. They shimmered in the candlelight, glassy and reddish. Hunter's gaze met mine. "Allison?" His fingers flinched beneath mine. "You're here."

My stupid heart fell at his confused words, and I spoke the truth. "No. It's me, Coryn."

"Coryn…" He blinked tiredly. "Who's Coryn?"

My heart sank even deeper, goosebumps rising on my skin. His eyes struggled to focus on me, at times grazing, then trailing off somewhere beyond me. "I need to… see my…" His eyelids fought to stay open, and his hand lay limply in mine.

I tightened my hold. "Hunter. Hunter, please. You're okay. You're gonna be okay. Just rest."

His eyelids gradually closed. I quickly pressed my head to his heart. A slow, steady beat pulsed against my cheek. I exhaled, my goosebumps still in place. His head wound… What did that beast do to him? He didn't even know who I was. And Allison… He brought up his ex-wife. Was he just delirious from the concussion?

I left my head on his chest though the smell of blood began to smother me. Tears hazed the sight of the man who ran after me and Hope to give her back her babydoll. He didn't have to do that, just like he didn't have to volunteer to protect Krista and me.

The tears left my eyes and fell onto his blood-marred shirt. He didn't deserve this either. Wasn't he a believer in God? But then he lost his wife, and now his own life was hanging on by a thread. He hadn't forsaken his God even after all that, but where was his God now?

"Where are you, huh? Where are you?!" I couldn't fight back the sobs though I stuffed them inside as best I could so I wouldn't disturb him. A soft knock rapped the door. I swiftly sat up and released Hunter's hand. The door creaked open.

Dixie stepped in with a fresh bandage and a bowl in her hands. "How's he doing?"

I wiped away tears. "He woke up briefly, but seemed confused."

"Yeah…" She sat beside me and set the bowl down. Whiteish water filled it. "His wound was bad. Real bad."

My dry throat found a small voice. "Was?"

"I was able to stitch it up, but…" She raised the bandage. "Can you lift his head? Be real careful."

I swallowed nothing, absolutely nothing. My already tangled stomach began to churn. I took in a breath and forced my hands to obey. Trembling, I gently slipped them beneath Hunter's head. It felt so heavy, so… frail. I bit my lip as Dixie undid the bandage. The breath gushed from my lungs. A swirl wracked my brain. A bulging, dark gash on the side of his head raised from beneath his hair. Hope had gotten a few bumps in her young life, but I'd never seen anything like it.

Dixie sighed as she tied on the new one. "I know, dear. All we can do is our best and pray God does the rest. That's all we can do now." Though she purposed to sound strong, I'm sure I could hear a shiver in her beneath. Was Dixie breaking, too? How couldn't she when everything kept bleeding all around her? The Cole's daughter, now Krista and Hunter. Dixie finished with a wide yawn, and I slowly set his head back on the pillow.

"Did you get any sleep?" I asked.

"Barely a wink."

"Maybe Hope can join you for a nap, and I'll take over watching Hunter and Krista for a few hours."

Dixie's tired eyes widened some. "You sure?"

"I think Hope really needs it. Last night was…"

"Don't have to tell me twice. I'll fetch 'er." She gave me a kiss on the temple before leaving. I adjusted myself on the floor so I could see both Hunter and Krista, though it tore me to shreds. The moments of labored breath, the silence... My heart kept skipping beats, and I had to do some breathing exercises to fend off panic attacks.

As time dragged on, I busied myself with thoughts of the past. Before the fall of life as we knew it, I had many nights of tears. Many nights of tossing and turning, worrying about how I'd feed Hope. Then I'd go to get gas, and the cashier would randomly hand me a card for a food pantry. Once, I opened our front door to groceries – which had to be the Barnes, though they never took credit for the act of kindness; And as painful as it had been, I still had so many days full of Hope's laughter, her silly princess antics and barefooted adventures in the woods, though I never let her go too far in.

Times where she'd creep into the living room while I was editing late and ask for water, only to take the tiniest sip and ask if she could watch me edit for just a little while. I'd always say yes, and she'd crawl into my lap to ooh and ahh at the bride's dress. Then she'd ask me what each person in the bridal party was called, and why they did certain things like toss flower petals or carry the rings on a pillow.

I pushed my lips together. Now those hard times seemed like the good old days. I'd trade them for the here and now so fast if I could... but I couldn't. I'd never be able to undo everything. Would anyone, really?

Hunter stirred. I grasped his shoulder, flinching a bit at my own desire to touch him, to hold onto him…

His eyes slowly opened and settled on me. The tiniest glimmer shined in them, and my heart leapt. "Coryn?"

Another leap as I responded. "Yes, Hunter. It's me."

A smile crawled on his lips. "I'm not dreaming still, am I?"

My mouth dropped open, but I quickly shut it. He wasn't… flirting? Was he tired? Delirious, even? Maybe he didn't mean it in that way since he'd literally been sleeping a lot and he knew it.

"You're—" He winced.

"Just relax. Don't overdue it, please." I tried not to sound as desperate as I felt seeing him like this, but I still held onto his strong arm; though admittedly, it didn't feel that way at the moment…

He closed his eyes with another wince. "What… day is it?"

"It's a Thursday, I think. It's only been a day since we were—"

"My head." He let out a low groan, and my gut groaned with him as he asked, "What happened to me?"

"The Blood Thieves came last night and attacked us. Your head got slammed against the floor." I winced myself at the memory.

"Blood Thieves?" He seemed more and more confused with each answered question.

"Yes, but we can talk about it later. Just go back to sleep—"

"So I'm not dreaming." He slowly turned his head toward the left, his gaze landing on my hand still stubbornly clenching his bicep.

A flash of heat rushed into my face, and for once, I felt thankful for the darkness. He turned his head back toward me, sucking in a breath. Now my stupid hand clasped his cheek. I ached so bad for him in this battered state. I didn't know the last time I hated something more, and... it scared me.

"How long have you...been watching...over me?"

Face still warm, I replied quietly, "Just a few hours. Dixie was looking after you and Krista before, but she's napping now."

His brow creased. "Where's... Hope?"

I shook my head at him in disbelief. Asking about my little girl when he was lying limply on a couch with a giant cut in his head? "She's napping with Dixie."

He winced, brow creasing again. Another groan that made me cringe. I caressed his clammy forehead, barely letting my fingers brush his cool skin. I was afraid of agitating his agony further. He shut his eyes and set his hand over mine. He breathed in slowly as his cheek pressed deeper into my palm. My shoulders tensed at his sudden return of affection.

His eyes opened again. They focused on me with a new keenness—and something else. My brain tripped over itself as I just focused back on him. How could he look this good even with half the color drained from his face and thick gauze wrapped around his head?

Just like that, his eyelids closed. My heart stopped. I pressed a hand to his temple. A gentle pulse met my skin. I released my thousandth shaky breath. Every part of me felt suddenly very heavy. My own eyelids began to close. My upper body sagged. I couldn't fight it anymore. I stretched myself out beside Hunter and gave in to sleep.

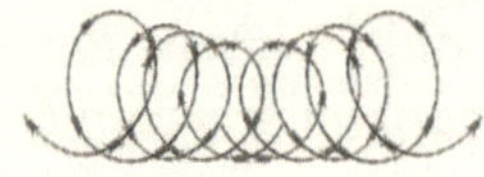

My eyes opened. My head lay on something firm. How long had I been out? Rays of light crept in through the window by the guest bed. They rested on my legs—and someone else's. My heart hurried. I peered up, my cheek still resting atop Hunter's chest…

My body tingled at the reality. So close. He felt so good. Too good. Stubble dotted his chin and neck. His firm jaw relaxed, and his lips slightly parted. He breathed deeply, heavily, stronger than he had when I last tended to him. He couldn't have healed that quickly. Did I sleep for hours… or for days?

Hunter's green eyes opened much brighter, and certainly more alert. They peered down on me, and for some reason, I couldn't move like a fence post in the ground. I left my head right where it was, suddenly not caring at all that I was this close to Hunter—or that he knew it. Fear filled me and somehow fled me all at the same time. Something I thought I'd never let myself feel again came creeping in like the sun over the horizon. Hope…hope that maybe…maybe I could let him see me.

Hunter's eyelids narrowed suddenly. His eyes grew wider as he slowly sat up, forcing me out of my paralyzed state.

I raised myself beside him, his face turning dark. "Allison… Where's my wife?" He looked around the room, then stopped on Krista. "Who's that? What's going on?"

My heart cranked a few notches. "Hunter, that's Krista. We're still at Dixie and Gunner's pla—"

"Ma'am, I don't know who you are, but I need to know where my wife is." He spoke clearer, though he appeared more and more confused with every passing second. He rose to his feet and touched his head, wincing. As he staggered, my hand found his back. "It's okay, please, just keep resting—"

He recoiled from my touch as if he'd sinned, then strode to the door. "Allison? Allison!"

Heart racing, I followed behind. Dixie and Gunner hustled up the stairs, but they halted in the doorway. Both in different clothes than the ones they wore last time I saw them, and with guns strapped, the whole scene appeared extremely sketchy.

Hunter froze, his muscular shoulders tight and… very intimidating. "What's going on here? And where's Allison?"

Gunner and Dixie swapped glances before Gunner raised both hands. "Hunter, son, listen to me—"

"The TV's workin'!" one of the men hollered from downstairs.

With hands still lifted, Gunner spoke as tensely as Hunter's body. "Please join us, and we'll explain what's happened."

Hunter looked back at me. His shimmering eyes sent a chill through my bones. He really had no idea who any of us were—who I was. He reluctantly obeyed his apparent captors and trailed them to the living room. Hope, bright-eyed and seemingly better rested herself, shot up from the couch and dashed over. She threw her arms around his hips. "Oh, Prince Hunter! I thought you were gonna die!"

The tenseness in his frame visibly eased, though his taut face appeared more confused. He allowed her to hug him and offered a weak smile before focusing on the TV against the back wall.

A lean woman in a black hoodie stood trembling in front of the White House's graffitied and crumpled entrance. The sun beamed on her terror-stricken eyes.

"The body was first seen this morning at approximately 6:02AM."

The camera panned up. Gasps filled the room. I rushed toward Hope, still holding Hunter, and buried her head in my chest.

Roped to the flagpole on the White House's roof was a bloodied President Moore.

I scooped Hope into my arms and strode through the kitchen out the back door. The sun hardly warded the cold seeping into my soul. I kept walking. On and on through the barren rows of strawberry bushes until I reached the edge of the forest that hedged the farmland. The trees huddled on the hills, all high and mighty, but where was God? Wasn't he always supposed to be in control? Yet everything was a mess. The entire world was falling apart, and it seemed like all God was doing was falling asleep at the wheel. Hope's head pressed hard against my chest, like she sought to climb inside and never come out again.

I weaved my fingers into her matted blonde waves and shut my eyes on it all. I fought for her my whole life, but this? This is a battle I just couldn't win.

"Coryn?" Pastor Rhett's voice jarred.

I turned toward him with Hope's head still above my heart.

His deep brown eyes did their soul searching thing; and yet again, I couldn't deny how handsome the holy-roller was. He peered at the swelling forest behind me. "You're not planning on taking a hike, right?"

"No, I just didn't want—" I lowered my gaze to Hope.

"Of course." He put his hands on his hips and peered at the empty patches around us. "Hope, did you gobble up all the strawberries?"

Her head halfway peeled from my chest, and a tiny smile lifting her mouth. "No."

"Did you pick them all for your momma and she's the gobbler?"

Hope giggled. "Maybe…"

Miraculously, a smile sneaked onto my own lips, and I seized on the opportunity to distract my baby—and myself. "Hope! How could you throw me under the bus like that? You promised you'd never tell anyone about my secret strawberry addiction."

She giggled some more, letting her head move away from my chest completely now. "Don't make me tell him about your super top secret coffee addiction, too."

I mock gasped. "You wouldn't dare!"

Rhett lifted a fist to his chin. "Oh now Hope, you've gotta listen to your strawberry gorgin', coffee hordin' momma, you hear?"

Hope burst into loud giggling, and my entire chest burned as I laughed with her. Her gorgeous laugh echoed in my mind like a favorite song. When was the last time I'd heard it?

Pastor Rhett smiled, and it seemed like the sun itself brightened because of it.

"Thank you," I mouthed.

He gave a little nod, and I couldn't stop my stomach from fluttering. Seriously, I was losing it. Absolutely losing my ever-loving mind. I just needed some more alone time. Away from handsome men who—

"Rhett, Coryn, quick!" Dixie hollered, standing by her back door, face white and sweaty. "It's Hunter!"

11. REVENGE

I set Hope on her feet and clasped her hand, trailing Rhett toward the house. As we neared, shouts rang from within. Dixie stood by the open back door, her face pallid—aside from a bluish mark on her cheekbone.

My stomach hollowed as Rhett strode inside. I turned to Hope. "Stay right here with Mrs. Dixie."

Hope nodded, her little face wrinkled with concern.

As Dixie embraced her, I followed after Rhett. Four of the older men, including Gunner, pinned Hunter down on the living room floor. Rhett charged in, adding a fifth man to the mob of restrainers. Two of the men had bloody lips, and one man sat on the couch holding a bloodied handkerchief over his nose.

"Son, if I didn't know what happened to you two nights ago," Gunner grunted, "I'd have done knocked you out." He pressed his elbow on the back of Hunter's neck. Red-faced and fuming, Hunter's eyes found me. I gasped and covered my mouth, chills running all over my skin. His brow creased again like it had before he started losing it in the room. Something shined in them. Fear? Guilt? I don't know what, and I don't know if he did either, but as if shot with a tranquilizer gun, he finally lay still, submitting himself to his struggling captors.

Gunner held fast, still grunting between words. "You gonna let us finish explainin', or we gonna have to tie ya to a chair?"

Hunter, something still stirring behind his gaze, at last lowered it from me and replied, "I'll listen."

Gradually, Gunner, Rhett, and the others eased off Hunter. As he rose, he dusted himself, everything about him bulging—and frightening. The men cautiously encircled, and though it felt almost like a betrayal, I didn't blame them.

"Sit." Gunner gestured to the couch—next to bloody-nose whose eyes were glued on Hunter. Slowly, he complied.

"Coryn," Gunner said, "While we wait for Randy to finish fetchin' Mitchel, why don't you explain to Hunter what's been goin' on here over the last few days."

Fear clawing at my heart, I instinctively rubbed my purple stem. Hunter watched my every move.

Although sweaty and red-knuckled, he appeared unscathed, minus the gauze wrapping his head. My mind threw the image of bruised Dixie at my brain. I flinched as if I'd been the one punched. How could he have hit her…? This is not the same man who'd just put his hand over mine and asked about Hope two days ago… was it?

I swallowed before opening my mouth. "As you may have seen," I said as I glanced at the TV which was black again with the error message floating across it, "America has just gone through a civil war. I was renting the in-law suite next door from the Barnes before everything collapsed. Thugs broke in and tried to—" I winced. "Hurt me and my daughter. Gunner came and shot them all. Then we moved in with him and Dixie." A sudden surge of anger flashed through my limbs. "Whom you gave a nice lick to."

Hunter huffed, his face hard and those broad, intimidating shoulders squared. "Ma'am, I may have lost my cool a few moments ago, but I'd never lay a hand on a woman."

Gunner chuckled. "He got a good lick on Wylie, but you really think he'd still be conscious if he'd laid a finger on my lady? Nah. She got a bit too close and got elbowed." Now he huffed. "Maybe next time, you'll listen when I say get back, darlin'."

My cheeks burned, though some relief eased my trembling. I found Hunter's face, still too hard for my liking. I held my shoulders back, though I softened my tone. "Right. That's not the Hunter I was beginning to know."

He turned his head slightly, his eyes signaling something again, and like me, some of the hardness eased off of his glowering face.

I cleared my throat before continuing. "This is gonna sound crazier than the collapse of our nation, but.." I rubbed my weird bracelet. "While out in their strawberry patch, I got pricked by this and… Well, it can…"

A few of the men gasped—minus Rhett, who just did his signature spirit-searching ogle. Hunter's eyes widened. His stare dropped to the stem on my wrist as it glowed purple.

The burning in my face returned with ferocity. "Yeah, it does things I don't quite understand yet, but it helped us survive these men who've been targeting the younger women in our town." Anger rose in me again as I pictured Krista now lying nearly dead upstairs, but a tenderness I couldn't even hide lay just beneath as I added, "And you've also been helping us stay alive."

Hunter put his hands over his mouth and rubbed around his chin. I despised how even his brooding looked good, but the confusion in his eyes certainly did not. All of this information was like new to him, but it wasn't. When would his memory return? If ever, that is…

Fighting shivers, I recounted what happened when the Blood Thieves last attacked, and also awkwardly admitted how I'd glowed purple and propelled my attacker backward. Hunter sat quietly, studying me as if I'd been the one who'd lost my memory and assaulted everyone.

Without thinking, I finally shared what I hadn't with any of them. "I know this all sounds super bizarre, and it is; but I also know you're a man of faith, as are Gunner and Dixie. She challenged me to pray for a way to defend myself." I patted my waist where the gunless bellyband hid beneath my gray top. "One that didn't involve guns, and right after, this thing… found me."

Hunter's green eyes still scrutinized, but some of their sharpness softened. "So Allison is really…"

I wished I could just lie to him, but I knew that would only make things worse so I nodded instead.

As tears filled his eyes, a knock hammered the front door. All the men jumped to their feet.

Gunner strode to the entry as he removed his pistol. "Who is it?"

"Pastor Mitchel!" came a shout from the other side.

Gunner unlocked the door and revealed Pastor Mitchel, pink-faced beside pudgy Randy, one of the volunteers. As they marched in, Pastor Mitchel embraced his old son-in-law. Hunter seemed to break, and he wept into Mitchel's chest like a boy who'd lost his first dog. Knees now too weak to stand, I sank onto the armchair. I let my face find my hands and let my own tears flow. This sucked. All of it. How long would

Hunter now have to re-grieve everything he'd lost? He seemed to have come so far in his healing journey only to have to start it all over again. And yet we were supposed to believe God is good?

A warm hand rested on my shoulder. I flinched as I looked up. Rhett stood beside me, looking down on me. A few wrinkles lined his tan forehead, and those deep browns peered into me—a little too closely. I shrugged his palm off and hurried outside where Hope waited with Dixie.

Dixie glanced toward the living room as she released my little girl. "Is it safe now?"

I sighed. "Yes."

"Phew." She touched her bruised cheek and grimaced. "I don't need one of those fools accidentally elbowin' my pretty face again."

I laughed as Hope gripped my hips. "Mommy, is Prince Hunter okay?"

I looked back where the open door revealed Hunter wiping away tears as he stood before the large cross over the fireplace. I donned the most convincing tone I could, "He will be, princess. Soon." My voice dipped to a whisper. "I hope…"

Sirens pierced the air. Hope and I trailed Dixie inside where all the men, except Hunter, filed out of the front door. We continued trailing Dixie to the yard. In the distance, Sheriff Hank's police car sped our way.

I clasped Hope's shoulder. As badly as I wanted to wait with her inside, my legs locked me in place. The car parked in the grass, and Hank hurried out, his cowboy hat shading his tense, mustached face as he approached.

"What's goin' on, Sheriff?" Mitchel asked.

"The Los Daggers gang is comin'. Y'all get inside now! And I mean yesterday!"

My heart thrashed as I snatched Hope's hand and wheeled her inside. As the men scrambled behind, guns in hand, Hunter lifted his shirt revealing an empty holster. "Where's my gun?"

Gunner answered, "You'll get it back soon enough, but for now, we've got thugs to deal with."

"I'm gonna need my big girl gun." Dixie tramped up the stairs and I followed with Hope.

"Thugs?" she asked, her voice squeaky. "Like the ones that—"

I led her into our guest bedroom where Krista still lay on her mattress, who was barely breathing. I steered Hope into the closet. "Now listen very closely to me, Hope. You stay in here, and don't make a sound. Do not come out for anything until I come and get you. Do you understand me?"

Hope nodded vigorously, tears already piling. I quickly grabbed my MP3 player from the end table drawer and turned it on. One bar of battery remained. I set it to Hope's favorite playlist, a mix of children's songs and a few Christmas ones she'd heard at church. I raised the volume to full blast and set the headphones over her head with viciously trembling hands. I peered into her blue eyes and kissed her forehead.

Several rumbles of illegally loud exhausts pierced through the air like an army of roused hornets.

I looked at Krista, laying lifeless like an unintentional invitation. I bustled toward her, stubbing my toe on the wooden bed frame along the way. Now limping, I swore under my breath, then carefully scooped her into my arms. Her skin was cold and body limp so I pressed my head to her chest. A faint thrum met my ear.

An orchestra of slamming car doors thudded from outside. I hobbled to the closet and put Krista beside Hope, hugging her knees and humming. I gave her one last kiss on the head before closing the wooden doors.

A few shouts in Spanish rang outside. I dashed out of the room, closing the door behind me. Downstairs, Dixie and the men peered through cracks in the boarded windows. I found a place near Gunner.

"There's at least ten of 'em," he whispered.

"Ten." My knees quaked as Gunner ordered men to upstairs windows and the back door.

The shouts outside ceased. The hush reminded me of the night when the Blood Thieves prowled…

I glanced at the ticking mantel clock mounted atop the fireplace: 7:18. The sun would only last for less than an hour. Who else would show up?

The stem warmed my wrist where it still glowed purple. A faint thump sounded above. Then another, and another. Their steps followed the tick of the clock as each second passed.

"They're on the roof," Mitchel whispered.

"Thanks for the news report, Pastor Obvious," Gunner replied as he gestured for two men to go upstairs. They slipped away, guns ready. Now only Rhett, Dixie, Hunter, Mitchel, bloody-nosed Wylie – who was posted at the back door – Hank, and I remained.

I touched my waist and froze. I'd left my gun in the bedside safe. A bang rattled the front door, then the back. Shards of wood burst in every direction as the door knobs flew off. Dixie, Mitchel, and I ducked behind furniture while Gunner, Rhett, and Hank flanked the front door. Hunter quickly disappeared into the kitchen.

The door bolts at the top of each entry remained intact. More bangs followed. The holes around where the knobs were widened, splinters of wood flying. Oh my sweet Hope. What the freak am I doing in the middle of a gunfight without a freaking gun? Even if I had it, God knows if I'd even be able to hit a target—a fast-moving, violent, ruthless, tried to kill-me-and-my-baby kind of target.

Gunner held up his palm like a guy from those cop shows on TV. After another moment, he stuck his pistol in the hole and fired two shots. A man yelled and rapid shots pierced through the door. AK-47? Everyone dropped low. More shouts roared, leers and cuss words in Spanish, the mantel clock steadily ticking. My heart slammed within. I panted as sweat poured off me in buckets. What do I do? What do I do? What do I do?

"You *gringos* think you're getting away with killing my brother and cousins?" a man hollered from outside. "None of you is walking out alive! You're all mine!"

Something crashed into both doors. A burst of flames rose outside of the holes. Another crash and both doors caved in. Wylie was on his butt against the wall by the back door with his rifle clenched. Another round of rapid fire. Wylie crawled over to the sink. He opened the cabinet and set his rifle down. He spotted the fire extinguisher, grabbed it, and crawled back to the door. As he doused the flames, more gun shots rattled the house. Wylie shouted, and blood seeped from his chest. He collapsed as the flames in the front door grew.

"Get the extinguisher!" Hank commanded as Dixie elbowed her way across the floor to Wylie. Body quaking, I did the same. Bullets continued to spray. Dixie clasped Wylie's arms and dragged him toward the couch. My ears rang as my hand grasped the cold metal of the extinguisher. I chucked it across the floor to Rhett. As he fought the flames, the back door crashed down. A tan man with a bald head smothered in tats carrying an AK stepped inside.

Hunter reappeared. He grabbed the AK, rammed the man with its butt, swung him around, and trapped his neck with it. The man gagged as Hunter dragged him across the kitchen. Shots popped. I scrambled behind the island. More shots fired—from upstairs. I rose and raced to the second floor landing.

Dixie's bedroom door stood open. Pudgy Randy sat at the foot of Dixie's bed with the boarded window above it broken in. A handgun appeared and fired. Randy groaned and dropped to the ground. More shots blasted from somewhere else in the room. An AK rattled through the roof from above. More groans in the bedroom. My limbs locked in place. An upside down, tatted face emerged in the window. The man grinned at me before he swooped in. My limbs remained paralyzed in the hall. As he drew near, he licked his pistol. "*Que linda eres.*" His dilated pupils gleamed. White powered his nose.

He hauled me onto his shoulders and carried me into Dixie's bedroom. The door shut behind us and he locked it. Side-stepping dead Randy on the floor, the man tossed me onto the bed. A grin stretched beneath a skinny finger as he shushed. My parted mouth refused to scream. I closed my eyes. A headache battered. Shots raged downstairs. I still couldn't move, completely frozen.

A cold hand squeezed my wrist. "Cool bracelet, *linda.*"

I forced my eyes open. His ugly face, so cruel, so thirsty, chilled every inch of me. I wanted to shut him out, but now my eyes were locked on the beast before me. He rubbed his hands together and grinned all the wider.

Jesus. Please. Help me. Violet light poured into my hand.

"What the—" His grip loosened.

My body instantly unlocked. I slapped his cheek. Purple light dotted his face and swelled into his eye. It faded, leaving his pupil pale white as if bleached. He clutched it as he scrambled off the bed. He stumbled over Randy's corpse and toppled to his rear. "My eye, my eye!"

Yells rang from everywhere. I rushed off the bed, hands trembling. As I inched closer to the thug, he scooted back, terror in his exposed eye.

"What are you, a witch?" he spat.

"No." I raised my glowing hand. "I'm just a single mother."

A funnel of light streamed from my palm and crashed into his face. He toppled backwards with his entire head engulfed in pulsating purple.

"No, no! You can't—you—" He peered up and spoke at someone—but it wasn't me. "You're not real —you're not..." He rocked his head back and forth several times before laying very still.

Goosebumps traveled down my arms. Who—or what—did he just see?

Gut in a ball, I treaded to the top of the staircase. Hank lay against the wall by the front door, bleeding from his side. Dead. So much death everywhere. My empty stomach rolled.

Hunter, Gunner, Rhett, Dixie, Mitchel, and Wylie were out of sight. Were they dead, too?

I peered back at the guest bedroom where my baby hid with Krista. Time was ticking, and night was falling. It seemed all of the extra watchmen were dead. The gangsters needed to leave—or be killed, too.

I crept down the steps. Gun shots rang from somewhere further outside. I reached the bottom, glancing at Hank. His lifeless eyes had lost their and looked beyond me. I quickly averted my stare, bile stinging my throat. *Tick, tock,* the mantel clock taunted.

A track of blood led to behind the kitchen island. My head spun as I followed the trail. The stench was overwhelming, just like before in my house next door. All the blood. I can't do this… My head reeled. I tried to focus on something. Anything. Someone coughed— a woman. I inched around the corner.

Dixie sat with a large pistol against her chest, holding her nose with her free hand. Wylie was dead on the floor beside her.

"Get your butt down, girl!" she hissed.

I quickly sat. The coppery odor worsened my nausea. I forced my eyes on her. "Where's Gunner and the others?"

"They drew the men toward the barn."

"They're outside?"

"That's what I said, ain't it?" Her shimmering gaze dropped to my purple hand. She blinked, all sass removed. "You turn superhero on me again?"

"I…guess?"

She chuckled. "Sometimes I dunno if I'm actually awake or if I'm dreamin'."

I nodded, but this wasn't a dream. It was a living nightmare.

AK shots clattered outside.

"Lord help 'em." Dixie cocked her gun. "Watch your baby." She rose to a hunch and headed to the back doorway, stepping onto the broken-down door.

I rose. "Dixie, no—"

"I'm not leavin' my husband to die out there." She looked at Wylie, then at Hank. "Enough of us have gone to be with the Lord already."

Before I could say another word, she stalked outside. I covered my mouth and walked to the doorway. Two shot up, lime green convertibles sat parked with doors ajar. Dixie looked both ways as she stalked across the open. Only a faint line of orange colored the sky, quickly being overpowered by a graying purple.

Please, please don't let her—

More shots fired. Dixie ducked and raced toward the barn entrance. I cringed as I clasped the doorframe. Could I bear to watch her die, too? She'd become almost like a mother to me, and the grandmother Hope never had. Another shot. Dixie closed in. A hole pierced the wall by the entrance as she disappeared inside.

I pressed my back against the wall by the doorframe. How long could I keep Hope up there? Nowhere was safe. Bad guys with guns lurked, the Blood Thieves could come tonight, and downstairs, many dead men lay. If Dixie and the others died, how could I fend them all off alone? One bullet in the right place, one surprise attack from the Blood Thieves, and I'd join Hank and the rest of them. And even if I managed to survive... How long could I hold onto my sanity?

The light faded from my palm. A deafening silence plagued the air. Except the ticking mantel clock. I peered out again toward the barn just as the last of dusk's orange glow dimmed to nothing. Minutes went by. I checked the clock on the stove. 8:28. Four long minutes passed. No gunfire.

The clock on the stove went black as everything was was suddenly shrouded by darkness. Oh no, the generator must have died... I glanced upstairs, and my heart dropped.

Hope.

12. NEW BLOOD

I raced upstairs past Hank, all the blood, and stench suffocating everything. I barged into the guest bedroom and slammed the light switch. Nothing. I squinted in the darkness. The closet remained closed. I shoved open the wooden door. Hope lay on the floor with her arm over Krista's waist. My heart stopped. I dropped to my knees and shook Hope. She turned, eyes wide, but the headphones still over her ears. I sighed as I clasped her. "Oh, thank God. Thank God. Thank God."

I kissed her cheek, wet with tears. I pulled back. She slowly removed the headphones and looked down at Krista. "Mommy… I think Krista is gone."

My heart bounded to life again. The pounding quaked in my throat. I reached a trembling hand to

Krista's neck. Her cold skin shocked my fingers. I waited for a pulse, but it never came.

I pulled Hope into my embrace again, clenching my mouth shut so a sob couldn't confirm Hope's words. I kissed her cheek once more. If nothing, I have her still. But for how long?

"It's dead, Mommy." Hope placed the MP3 player in my palm. I swallowed another sob. Carrying her, I stepped out of the closet. I dropped the MP3 to the ground and kicked it under the bed. What do I do now?

I stood in the darkness with Hope. Why were we still alive while so many others around us were not? Why did we deserve to live? We weren't even God's children like these folks thought they were. Why am I still standing when I don't even want to fight? Dying would be so easy, so much easier than all of this.

Why am I here, God? Why did you put me here? The only good thing I have left to hold onto is Hope. The Blood Thieves... My knees quaked, and I sank onto the bed still clinging to my daughter. They'll come. They'll come back for me – for us.

Fear no evil, for I am with you.

Warmth hugged my wrist. I glimpsed down. A faint lavender glowed around it. Or was it my imagination? How could I still be sane? A miracle? Or was it delusional to believe in those now?

Shuffling and whispers filtered in from downstairs. I squeezed Hope.

"Mommy," she breathed.

"It's okay, honey. Just be quiet." I carefully set her down and took her hand. I crept to the doorway and eased my head through. Low voices. I couldn't make out who they belonged to. I slipped back into the room and gradually closed and locked the door. I led Hope to the closet and sealed us inside. I shut my eyes against the darkness. Oh, God, help me to fear no evil. Help me, please.

I held my breath. The stairs creaked. I squeezed Hope's hand. Her soft breaths reminded me of when she slept. Remarkably, she managed to sleep peacefully most every night since we left our home and moved in with the Barnes except after what happened with Hunter and Krista... Her bubble had popped, but some peace remained, at least in the unconscious.

The door knob rustled. Hope's breathing hastened and she squeezed my hand that pulsed from the pressure. The rustling strengthened.

"Coryn?" Pastor Rhett?

Was it really him or was it my imagination again? Silence ensued.

I leaned closer to the closet door. A gentle knock tapped the bedroom door. "Coryn? Hope? Are you there?" Yes, that was Rhett.

I jumped to my feet, still holding onto Hope and rushed to the door. I opened it. In the darkness, I could make out more than just Rhett's figure.

"Oh, thank Jesus!" Dixie embraced me and kissed both cheeks before doing the same to Hope.

"You can say that again." Gunner. My heart nearly burst with gratitude as he hugged me. "We lost a lot of good people, but I'm thankful you and Hope are still around."

I squinted through the darkness toward the other three figures that were standing behind in the hallway.

I could barely bring myself to ask the question, but somehow, I did. "Who else made it?"

"I'm still here," Hunter replied.

I let out a sigh I barely cared to hide, more gratitude filling my now racing heart.

"Prince Hunter!" Hope released my hand and charged through toward his voice. He grunted as she slammed straight into him. A soft chuckle left his lips. "I've never been called that before."

The glow in my heart dimmed. No... He still didn't remember.

"Yes you have," Hope said. "I call you that all the time, silly."

"Right…" He cleared his throat. "I'm sure you do, sweetheart. I'm sorry, I forgot."

My eyes adjusted to the darkness, and I could find his sad eyes on my babygirl who loved him so darn much, then me. He knew we knew him, but he didn't know us.

"I forgive you." She returned to my side and took my hand. "Now what?"

"We... Well," Gunner paused and peered back at one of the men that stood beside Hunter. "We got a new member of the family."

I blinked in the darkness. "A family member?"

"Rhett," Gunner said, "You can go ahead and turn that thing on."

A white light clicked on from an LED lantern in Rhett's hand, revealing everyone's ragged, sweaty faces, including Pastor Mitchel—and a tatted up man in a bloody white sleeveless shirt beside Hunter—whose gauze looked bloodier.

"Coryn," Gunner said, "This is Rico, our new brother in Christ."

I choked Hope's hand. "Pardon me?"

"I'll explain after we get this place cleaned up if you know what I mean." Gunner glanced at Hope. "Ladies, y'all take a rest in here, and we'll come and bring you somethin' to eat soon." He looked at the closet, then at me. I shook my head.

Gunner sucked his teeth and gestured for Rhett to get Krista. I turned Hope away as the solemn pastor who'd probably done a number of funerals, but not forensics, lifted the only woman I could relate to, the sweet and beautiful young woman who had comforted me even in the midst of her own trauma, and walked out.

Dixie closed the door behind them and walked to the closet. She rummaged around and returned with a small lantern. The dim light shined off her tired eyes, and her silvery blond hair never looked so disheveled. Wrinkles and blood sullied her clothes—and mine. We looked war-torn, all except for Hope. Though her hair was matted and in desperate need of a deep conditioning, her clothes remained relatively spotless. She looked like a child who'd just been playing all day while her mother got lost in chores and work... If only that were our reality.

Apparently out of tears and words, I walked her to the bed as Dixie set the lantern on the futon against the wall. As Hope lay on the mattress, she yawned, and her eyes toward the closet. "I didn't get to say goodbye."

I pressed my lips together, my heart aching too much to respond. What could I say anyway? My seven-year-old daughter had just witnessed someone die, someone she deemed a princess. The pain threatened to cut through all my shock and pour out, then Dixie quietly slipped onto the bed. She set a weary hand on Hope's head and brushed wild tresses aside. "Sometimes that happens in this life, dear." She spoke slow, so quiet. "But ya know, Princess Krista knew the king... So you could say she's just sleeping—"

"Like Sleeping Beauty."

Dixie smiled. "Exactly, but instead of a prince like Hunter kissing her awake, her spirit's already up there walkin' around in Heaven with Jesus."

Tears fell from my eyes.

"If we trust in Him, we'll be saying hi again soon enough." She bent down and kissed Hope's forehead. "You get some beauty sleep of your own, too, now." She peered at me as she patted the space beside Hope. "You too, Momma."

I nodded, too exhausted to fight, though the image of Hunter's bloodied gauze gnawed at me. Would anyone tend to it? "And you rest, Auntie."

She chuckled. "I believe Auntie Dixie will." As she made her way back to the sofa bed, I lay beside Hope, whose eyes already closed and breathing softly. Swiftly, the shuffling downstairs died out, and sleep overcame.

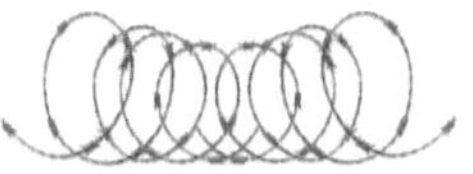

"What are you doing here, Coryn?" Mom sat at her white kitchen table. Her mostly-dyed blonde waves lay on either shoulder. Her face looked younger and blue eyes brighter. She looked as beautiful as always. The Marilyn Monroe of her time. But something seemed… different.

"You tell me." I stood in the entryway between the kitchen and the dining room, squaring my jaw—and my shoulders.

Mom maintained all composure, her eyes agleam and happy despite the shade I just threw at her. "I'd rather not speak my hopes aloud."

"Well that's a first. Mrs. Always Right Christian finally out of words?"

A small smile wrinkled the edge of her mouth. "Well, out of some, yes."

I tossed out more acid. "I'm thankful for that."

Her smile vanished, finally moved. "Are you?"

I leaned against the wooden frame. "I didn't like the stuff I heard, but…" My heart thumped, heavy and slow. "I wish none of it happened, because then maybe I'd miss you more, but then I wouldn't have Hope… And she's better than a do-over."

Mom rubbed her painted nails. "I wish I got to see her grow up."

"You do?"

"Of course, Coryn. I may not have liked how it went down, but that's still my grandbaby."

"Why didn't you ever say that when you were here?"

"I did."

A pile of letters bound by a rubber band appeared by her hands.

I opened my eyes, panting. Murky light crept in through the boarded window above the bed in the Barnes' guest room. Dixie snored on the futon, a pile of gauze and a bowl of whitish water by her leg that was hanging over the side close to where Hunter lay on his stomach on the mattress Krista had been on. His elbows were propped on the floor and eyes closed, whispering. The bloody gauze from last night still marred his head.

Hope turned toward me and nestled her face into my arm. She muttered and continued breathing slow. Hunter's green eyes spotted me. Face hot, I adjusted my gaze to the ceiling, though I couldn't unsee the gauze.

He whispered something more and slowly sat up. "How'd you sleep?"

I managed to turn my head in his direction, looking at that gauze again. "Miraculously well. You?"

He stretched his formidable arms. "I did more praying than sleeping, but I'm glad one of the prayers was answered."

My face burned more, and I temporarily focused all my attention on carefully reclaiming my arm from being Hope's pillow. "Did you guys finish…" But I couldn't finish my question.

"We did."

I exhaled. I don't think I've ever been more grateful for men in my entire life. Hauling and disposing of dead bodies? Cleaning up the mess? My stomach gurgled, and my throat stung. How many more times would they have to do this…?

I finished slipping my arm away from Hope and got up. I stepped toward Hunter with my eyes still on his gross head dressing. "May I…?"

He touched the gauze. "Ouch."

"Yeah…" I grabbed the bowl of liquid and some clean gauze by Dixie's leg that she probably intended to put on Hunter herself eventually, careful not to disturb her beauty sleep, then sat on my knees before Hunter.

Though I tried desperately to keep them still, his sharp green eyes sent shivers to my hands. I touched the back of his head, and he exhaled. Painful still, but strong.

"I'm sorry," I breathed. "You were unconscious when I did this last time."

A small wrinkle occupied his brow. "I… remember."

I stiffened at the confession. "You do?"

"Bits and pieces."

As I softly unwrapped his gauze, he whispered, "I don't mean to make you afraid."

I stopped, my fingers fumbling. I tried to play it off. "Well, you were pretty angry at Gunner and his men. Ans it took several of them to hold you down."

He didn't lower his gaze though I wished he did. "Well, how would you react if you woke up in a place surrounded by armed men and didn't know how you ended up there?"

I pushed my lips together before answering. "I don't know if I'd start throwing hands with women and children around."

His gaze broke from me, looking back at Hope on the bed. He frowned. "I'm sorry, ma'am. You're right. I wish I didn't lose it like that in front of you and your babygirl."

And I wish you wouldn't apologize like that… I dipped my hand into the sudsy water and found a cloth. I wrung out the cold water before gently setting it onto Hunter's head wound. He closed his eyes and exhaled again. I prayed he wouldn't see my stupid shaking.

He opened those mesmerizing eyes. "Thank you, Coryn."

I forced my own on his wound though it made me cringe to do so. "Of course… You got this for us, you know."

His voice turned harder. "There was more than one of them, right?"

"That's right."

"And one of them got real close to you. Grabbed you by the wrist…" His nostrils flared.

I dropped the cloth into the water, splattering some of it onto us both. "I'm so sorry." I rubbed the spots from his abdomen and recoiled. "Sorry." I snatched the gauze like I was swatting a mosquito and lifted it to his head. I froze.

A big grin stretched his mouth. "You don't have to apologize for trying to be respectful, ma'am."

I smirked. "Ah, unlike how you didn't apologize when you tried to preach a purity sermon to my seven-year-old, right?"

His grin wiped right off. He looked genuinely confused, and my heart fell. He didn't remember when we first met… but maybe that was a good thing. I was awfully rude.

"Wait…" He slowly nodded. "In the parking lot at First Baptist Bells Ferry."

I shakily unraveled the stupid gauze. As I brought it up to his forehead, he said, "I meant what I said, ma'am. And maybe one day, you'll believe me."

I gave a nod as I carefully wrapped his wound and decided changing the subject might help my nerves. "Do you really trust Rico?"

"After what he witnessed, yes."

"A bunch of crazy Southerners taking down his whole crew?"

Hunter winced as I continued wrapping, but a gleam highlighted his stunning eyes. "There were six of them in there, guns blazing. It didn't take long 'til our side was out of ammo. First Gunner, then the rest of us. They were closing in, and I shouted for everyone to pray. We all just started asking Jesus to help us, and all of a sudden, several of them started to yell. More gun shots followed along with a ton of groans. Apparently, they started misfiring and shooting each other. That's when Rico came forward, trembling, and his AK suddenly jammed."

I blinked at him. Maybe I was dreaming this whole time.

But Hunter proceeded. "He dropped to his knees, put his hands up, and surrendered—to Jesus."

I finished putting on the new gauze and studied Hunter's expression as he sat back with his elbows resting on his knees. His light skin, brushed with warmth from the fair share of work he'd done outside, remained set and smooth. Not a wrinkle of jesting curled his beautiful lips, and his vivid greens stared right back at me, serious and intense; yet somehow, gentle and... curious almost.

Once again, I couldn't bring myself to look away.

"You're really pretty, you know that?" Hunter spoke.

A breath trapped itself within. Maybe I was dreaming or in a coma or something. Reality seemed to be getting harder and harder to discern; but he seemed so real, so close… like he had been when I woke up with my head on his chest.

His elbows still rested on his knees, and he kept… staring.

I managed to part my lips. "I'm sorry, did you say something?" That stare… was too much. I hated how it made my heart pound.

"You're truly beautiful, Coryn. Inside and out, I mean."

Heat filled my face. When was the last time a guy ever complimented me? Albeit I only ever left home when absolutely necessary, and I stopped caring about how I looked a while ago. Especially after the fall. And right now, after just waking up? There weren't many young women around… Maybe he was just trying to be nice?

"Your daughter is blessed to have you as a momma." He spoke softly, but strongly.

I glanced back at her where she was still cozy under the blanket. "And I'm blessed to have her…"

His mouth lifted. "Whoever her future poppa is, he's gonna be doubly blessed."

My stare dropped to my hands. I rubbed my knuckles, empty of a ring. My hopes for a man at my side had already been dim before the fall. No one would be getting hitched in this economy, and who knew when things would change for the better. That could be years from now…

Hunter's elbow left his knee. His large hand now hovered closer… to mine. I looked up at him. He had a serious face now. I couldn't quite read it. Pity? Concern? The edge of his warm pinky touched the side of mine. More heat spilled into my cheeks. My finger twitched at his touch, and now… I wanted him even closer.

"Mommy?" Hope sat up in bed. "Prince Hunter?" Her eyeballs enlarged like she'd just seen a princess at Disneyland. "Were you two about to kiss each other?"

"No," I answered quickly.

"Well, not exactly," Hunter replied.

I shot him a look, but it was too late. Hope began clapping and bouncing. "Ooh, you're so in love."

"No!" I grabbed the soapy water bowl, jumped to my feet, and clasped Hope's hand. "Let's go freshen up in the bathroom, sweetie."

"So you can get pretty for your prince?"

My grip tightened on her little hand as I whisked her to the door and whispered, "Hope Diaz, you will stop teasing your mother immediately."

"Okay, okay. But may I tell Auntie Dixie?"

"You may certainly not!" I made it into the bathroom and locked the door behind us. My hands shook as I dumped out the water I'd used to clean Hunter's wound, then splashed water on my face. That's just what I needed was for Hope's hopes up that her mommy could find a dream prince in this hellish world we were living in, to make her think maybe someday she'd, too, find a Prince Charming and live happily ever after. Or worse yet, that she could have a daddy of her own some day... All for it to crash and burn. That simply wasn't the reality—far from it. The sooner she figured that out, the better.

I shut the water off and faced her. A twinge of brown shaded her blue eyes, still wide with excitement. Her messy hair betrayed the truth that she'd yet again had a good night's rest even though it was a very late night.

A dull pang poked my heart. I brushed a blonde strand behind her ear and kissed her forehead before pulling her in for a squeeze. I still had my babygirl. We survived another night, another wave of murderers…

Warm tears trickled down my cheeks. This world would crush her dreams eventually, but until then, I'd let her imagine happy endings and a love that conquers all. Even if it was just for one more day.

13. NEXT IN LINE

I love the Barnes, but I didn't think their dining table could get more awkward than it had after that first night with Hunter. That first night when Krista was still with us... My heart bled for my friend. Someone else took her place now.

Gunner sat at the head, eyes mostly down with Dixie on the other end doing the same. Hunter sat on Gunner's right, the only one lifting his sights here and there. Then there were Pastor Rhett and the newbie, Rico, with me and Hope across from them. Everyone ate their corn on the cob, taters, and fresh cow milk with reverential focus. Even Hope somehow caught on, because for the first time that morning, she'd hushed up about princes, balls, princesses, and wedding gowns for a solid, miraculous five minutes and counting.

Rico's tan, toned, and tatted arms flexed as he drank his milk. A tear drop tat decorated the bottom of his left eye, along with an upside down cross, and scant women and skulls adorned his arms. A chill slid down my spine. Images of his cousin's rape attempt slammed across my mind, and how my daughter was almost forced to watch.

I dropped my fork with a cold tater still on its end.

Hunter zeroed in on me. The gauze I'd adorned him with earlier looked better than the previous one. No new stains at least, and those eyes were certainly ever sharper as the days went by. He wore that concerned frown like I were his problem that needed careful tending so as to not worsen. How could he really expect me to just embrace the criminal everyone else seemed to have assumed the best of even though they'd only known him for all of three days?

As my stomach churned, I concentrated on my daughter. She'd seen Rico's cousins and brother and watched them tear at my pants as she screamed and clawed helplessly beneath their wicked grip. All because of Gunner, we sat at this table; and now, also because of him, Rico the thug sat with us.

I rose to my feet, snatching Hope's hand. "Excuse us."

Hunter rose as if to follow us, but I gave him the most threatening look I could throw and whisked my daughter through the kitchen out the back door. At this point, I could use a break from him, too. He was confusing and made the air harder to breathe.

I opened the rickety door, patched and beaten from its gunfight with the man we wasted precious food on. Thick fog and gray clouds hazed the morning sun from somewhere above. The damp air brought with it a gentle breeze that nipped at my arms.

"Where are we going, Mommy?" Hope asked, scuttling at my side to keep up.

"To the strawberry patch." I hurried my pace, breathing in the dampness. The scent of soil invaded, but who cared? It was better than sharing a table with a murderer and holy rollers who'd taken their religion a bit too far this time.

The strawberry patch emerged from the white haze, and I stopped before it. Completely barren of berries, the bush whispered of its plentiful past. It had housed the strange purple stem that still rode my wrist, so out of sorts in its hiding place. It didn't belong here. Maybe we didn't, either.

I moved aside the leaves and peered deep into it.

Hope bent her knees. "What are you looking for, Mommy?"

I answered, almost to myself more than to her, "A reminder of the truth."

Hope watched as I sought for the stem that had pricked me what seemed like ages ago. It still felt like a dream and – had the thing literally not been wrapped around my wrist – I might have believed it was all in my head; but deep in the middle of the strawberry bush, a broken-off shoot hung crooked. Its top half was purple, and the rest of it was brown. I turned to Hope. "Do you see this?"

Bending further to get a closer look, she nodded.

"What color is it?"

"Purple and brown."

My hand shook. That settled it. She could see it, too, so this wasn't some long, comatose dream. America sat in shambles, vanishing vampires existed, and a strange, supernatural power had been given to me—a single, lost, terrified, young woman with a child. Krista and so many others really did die at ruthless hands—like those of the man who sat at table in the place we called home for the last few weeks. I grabbed Hope's hand again, and I marched back toward the house, but when we got to the backyard, I veered left. Beyond the barn, about a hundred yards away, stood our old home…

The fog hung so dense the house didn't appear until we stepped into the front yard. The small, white structure sat beneath the canopy of that massive oak I hated because of all the leaves and acorns that fell from it in the fall. The gutters housed the residue of that season stuffed with browned leaves and gray twigs.

Another chill spilled down my spine as I stopped with Hope at the front porch's bottom step. It wasn't the fog or its biting breeze though…

I took a step forward, and Hope's cold hand gripped mine. It was horrible to bring her back here, but what was worse: here or over there with that living reminder of what we almost went through?

I kept my eyes ahead on the old, wooden front door. We reached the top. Every step still creaked, but I never noticed before how loud the creaking was. I grasped the moist knob and trembled. The door opened. I hadn't seen a point in locking it since I didn't have anything of value in there… At least not in the sight of pillagers. Since it was still his property, Gunner had cleaned up the mess from my first terrifying encounter with the gangs.

I shoved the memory aside as more creaking echoed into the living room filled only with a couch, a pink shag rug, and an end table with lamp—all thrifted finds from Margot's Keep three miles into town. I never cared for a TV. That's probably one of the biggest reasons Hope had such a vivid imagination. She'd occupy herself in this space on the shaggy rug for hours talking to her imaginary friends who always consisted of fairies and royalty. My eyes watered as, still clutching Hope's hand, I journeyed ahead into the kitchen.

Cobwebs dangled in every corner of the tiny space. The country wooden cabinets appeared grayish with dust, as did the old, white laminate countertops. Though the place had been super clean when I first moved in, the Barnes hadn't updated anything but the stove and microwave. The mint wallpaper had been a horror to me at first, but somehow, the vintage hue grew on me. Perhaps because Hope kept calling it our "mermaid kitchen." She always had a knack for seeing the best in everything…

Minus a desk with my dead computer on it, the teeny dining room area just beyond the kitchen sat empty since I couldn't afford – nor did I need – a bigger table. Instead, Hope and I ate right here at the two-seater high top in the corner. I smiled at the third fold-up chair squeezed alongside the two bar stools. Hope usually had a "guest" join us, either her favorite baby doll or an invisible princess. I looked away before a tear could free itself.

Quiet as a mouse and hand still in mine, Hope and I approached the cabinet above the sink. With my shaky free hand, I opened it. A pile of letters bound by a rubber-band sat in the corner of the bottom shelf. I grabbed them even though part of me didn't want to.

"What are those, Mommy?" Hope whispered, glimpsing around the room as if we'd illegally entered someone else's home.

My chest hurt as I squeezed the stack. "I'll tell you later."

A creak sounded by the front door, and my heart lurched. I put my finger to my lips and crept out of the other side of the kitchen that led past the dining room and into the hallway. As quickly as possible, trying to avoid the creakiest parts of the floor, I navigated Hope to the main bedroom. I rushed in and locked the door behind us. Hope gasped and I followed her stare. Above my full-sized bed, a blood strewn message marred the floral wallpaper: *Your daughter is next.*

I rushed Hope to the bathroom on the right, locked the door, and quickly pulled aside the shower curtain. I dropped the stack of letters and fumbled as I cranked the fragile window handle. Resistance met my attempt. I cranked harder, faster. Then the handle broke off. I swore under my breath. My heart pounded in my ears. I pushed against the cool, fogged window. Greater resistance.

I applied more pressure. Come on, come on! After a few moments, the window cracked open. I slipped my fingers through and pulled the top half as wide as it could go. A faster breeze swept past, tossing my hair back. I beckoned Hope. I raised her to the window. She could fit through—but not me.

She grasped the edge and threw her leg over. I held her hands and eased her down along the wall onto the ground. I pointed at the oak, motioning her to get behind it. Without thinking, I grasped the letters and handed them to Hope. She stared at me for a moment as tears swelled up in her beautiful blue eyes, but she held the mail close and ran.

I quietly closed the shower curtain and peered outside. The fog had worsened. It crawled toward the big oak, threatening to conceal it. But maybe that was a good thing…

My chest tightened. *God, please keep her safe.*

The bedroom knob rustled loudly, and the door rattled next, then banged. I peered back out the window. Fog now smothered the tree.

Cold sweat dripped down my forehead. My chest ached from the pounding within. Whiteness seeped into my peripherals—but not from the fog. The throbbing in my temples buzzed in my ears. My bedroom door burst open, and I pressed myself against the side wall.

I could hear the closet doors thrust aside, things being toosed and rummaged through. My bracelet warmed around my wrist as the heavy footsteps came closer and closer. The bathroom knob shook, then stopped. One. Two. Three. Fo—

The door burst open. I pressed my lips together and held my breath as the whiteness clouded my vision. The shower curtain ripped aside.

Hunter.

I staggered forward. Hunter caught me. His hard arms scooped me into his chest, and his heart pounded in my ear as he spoke, "Where's Hope?"

My thrumming temples pummeled so hard my head spun. "Outside... Behind the tree..."

Hunter carried me to the bed and laid me down. He unholstered a gun from under his shirt and disappeared out of the room. I trembled. What was happening? Was Hunter going to hurt Hope? Why was he here? Did he see someone?

The whiteness increased. No. Please. I can't. Hope needs me. I panted. My breaths hastened. Heaving. Every part of me quaked. The pounding inside, everywhere worsened.

Hope screamed.

A gun shot pierced the air.

Heat surrounded my wrist.

The white fog consumed.

And I collapsed inside of it.

14. DIVIDED

$\mathcal{B}$lackness smothered me like death. But its heavy thickness vibrated painfully against my skin like if it were alive… A malignant being that knew exactly who I was and hated me.

I opened my mouth. Nothing. The words clogged in my throat, too weak, too suffocated to speak out. Wherever I was, I couldn't move. I couldn't see. I could only feel the viciousness of whatever watched me. My skin stung beneath the living dark. I willed my arms to lift and get me off the ground. The weight atop me increased. It pressed hard against my chest. What little air I had held onto squeezed out of me. I squeaked, my tongue a rock. "He—he—lp. M—me —"

The darkness shoved me deeper into the floor. A glimmer. Two glimmers. A pair of eyes was right above me, peering down on me; no, into me… They shined so deep yet so hollow…

"Help. Me. Je—"

A growl followed by more pressure. The gleaming ebony irises moved closer.

"Please. Help. Me. Je—Je" —something inside me stirred…slowly…steadily…

My heart pushed against the beast pinning me down. "Help me. Jesus."

The creature flew backwards with a bright burst of light, and I shot upright.

The sun shined down in splinters through the oak tree's canopy in my front yard. Fragments of emerald and spots of blue dotted my vision. Then a swath of sand. Hunter knelt over me. Green eyes alert, edged with anger and... something else. Frantic voices filtered through as shouts echoed in the distance. A walkie-talkie hung on Hunter's jeans' pocket.

"Where is she? Where's Hope?" My head pounded as I pushed my palms on the weed-infested grass. Vertical browns and grays from the trunks helped steady my vision more.

Hunter spoke as solidly as the oak's ancient trunk. "We're looking for her."

"What?!" I scrambled to my feet and staggered.

Hunter grasped my waist. I shoved him away and hurried behind the tree, ignoring the aches and weakness still causing me to stagger. Only grass and more trees. Stupid, endless trees. "No. No, no, no—" I dashed to a trunk on my left, then right, and further into the forest, legs faltering, threatening to collapse. But I had to find her. I had to. The shouting grew distant as a ringing took over. I kept moving faster, slapping bark and brushing aside all the wretched foliage. "Hope!"

I could barely hear my own voice over the ringing. "Hope!" My throat and hands stung. I clawed and ripped at the shrubbery. It almost seemed mocking with its ability to conceal. I screamed my daughter's name deeper and deeper until my voice grew hoarse and begged me to stop. How could I, though? Hope was out there somewhere and she needed me — *No, she's not.*

I froze as the ringing stopped, overtaken by the small, yet terrifyingly loud voice. "What?" I whispered.

They took her.

I took a step back then another, the forest beginning to swirl around me. I continued backward – trembling from the adrenaline – as if doing so would take me back in time before this happened... Before any of it. I panted again as the whiteness clawed at me now, but I can't. I must... fight. Fight. Hope, please. Please, baby, don't leave me.

I bumped into something big and firm. Hands encompassed my biceps, and by now, I knew who they belonged to. The whiteness fled from my wrath. I spun around as heat surged from within like a blazing wildfire. "You!" I slapped Hunter's chest. "What did you do? I heard the gun shot!"

Immovable, he answered steadily, though anger still lined his irises. "I went outside to get her, and I saw a young man in black coming from behind. I fired, but—" His voice darkened. "He grabbed her and disappeared."

"No." I peered into his chest, hoping his heart lied, but I knew it didn't. The fog had dissipated and the late morning sun illuminated the unending treetops. I paced while Hunter stood there watching like some kind of patrol officer. I stopped. "But why were you here?" My voice pitched higher. "You broke into my bedroom and bathroom!"

"I went to check on you and Hope, and I saw y'all walking away from the Barnes'. I wanted to give y'all privacy, but I didn't think it was a good idea to go wandering alone with all that's been going on so I followed at a distance." His tone darkened again, and his eyelids narrowed some. "But as I stood out here, I got a bad feeling, and I decided to go inside. When I didn't hear y'all, the feeling worsened. Then I saw that vile message on your wall so I thought someone had you two." Hunter's green eyes shined, and he frowned. "I'm so sorry I couldn't stop that beast, but I will do everything in God's power to get her back."

Tears blurred his sorrowful face, and I dropped to all fours. A wail ripped from my gut. Why? Why God? Why would you let them take her?! She's just a child! A helpless child! I heaved.

The whiteness returned as it edged into my peripherals, then poured into my vision. My head spun. A warm hand touched my shoulder: strong, firm, and commanding.

Hunter overshadowed as he knelt beside me, his presence still barely breaking through somehow. "Heavenly Father, give us strength. We need You, Lord. We always need You, but now more than ever. Give us the strength to carry on this fight and to not lose hope…"

The whiteness slowly, reluctantly receded as Hunter's voice, roughened with lack of rest, persisted like a ship forging forward on misty waters. "Though evil abounds, it can only fight against the light for so long until it prevails. We ask that You keep Hope safe and lead us to her, Lord. You know exactly where she is, and we know You can show us the way. In Jesus' name, amen."

The dizziness subsided. My breathing gradually calmed, though still shaky. I don't know if it was God's presence or Hunter's, but despite this horrific defeat, an inkling of hope returned; and no matter what happened, I would search for my daughter until I found her. Still grasping my shoulder, Hunter's eyes – so close to mine –searched into me with strength subdued by softness. "We're in this together now, you understand?"

I nodded in submission. Something in me was cracking like a glass on the verge of collapse. No, I couldn't let it open up. Not now, not ever.

I pressed against the grass and tried to lift myself up, but the adrenaline, it completely drained me.

"Can you stand?"

I nodded my head. Not yet, at least…

Hunter's palm left my shoulder. In a moment, both hands were beneath my underarms. Delicately, like a flower being plucked from the earth, Hunter scooped me into his arms. Too weak to fight anything at the moment, I sinned against my heart and allowed myself to enjoy his warm chest. His shirt was damp with sweat as my cheek rested on it. I shut out the flickers of light piercing the forest canopy. In the darkness behind my eyelids, even Hunter's breath right above my head brought unwanted comfort. He came for us. I was so stupid. If I had just stayed closer. If I just didn't go back to what I knew, to what I hoped was still there, then maybe this wouldn't have happened and my daughter would still be with us. With me and Hunter…

A tear rolled. "You came for us," I could hardly speak the words. "And now you came for me twice."

"Three times." He spoke in a certain tone. "And Coryn, I'm not letting you out of my sight again."

I braved opening my eyes and looked up at him as my heartbeat tripped over itself. I looked at his chin stubble, then further up at his green irises as they focused ahead so steadily as if he didn't want to brave looking back at me… Just before I could avert my gaze, Hunter gave me his full attention, and I wished he hadn't.

Even though sweat dripped from his brow, he breathed so steadily like if his body was built for the long haul; and perhaps, after all he'd been through, his heart was, too…

"Coryn." The way he said my name was like it somehow weakened this man made of unbreakable rock. "I…" He hesitated.

And I longed. "Yes, Hunter?"

His stare, though steady upon me, contradicted the confidence he always seemed to possess. "I…"

Hunter's radio crackled. "No sign of her." Gunner's voice. "Dixie, where you at?"

"Headed to First Baptist Bells Ferry with Mitchel."

"Why? Most of 'em are out here lookin'."

"Mandatory prayer meetin'! Over."

"Copy that. Hunter?"

He released one hand and held up the radio while he still held onto me. "Coryn's awake. We're heading over now. Over."

"Copy."

As I took a trembling breath, Hunter broke his gaze from me and returned the radio to his pocket. We reached my old front yard again; and Hunter spoke once more, tender, but guarded. "I found a stack of letters behind the tree."

A pang rattled my chest. "You have them with you?" I breathed.

"Yes."

"Thank you." I swallowed. "I want to drop them off at the Barnes' first."

"All right. We can grab you some water, too, while we're at it."

I nodded. Things blended together as he carried me the rest of the way in silence. Hunter served me a glass of water, and I finally managed to walk again. I tucked the letters in the drawer by my bed. Hunter plucked an apple for each of us on our way out of the Barnes' property.

As we walked through the widening path to the road leading down toward the church, thoughts battled in my mind. What would they do to my daughter? Would we ever find her? Would they kill her right away or torture her first? Would the Blood Thieves ever come back or would they move on to another town?

Something warm and encompassing cupped my hand. I looked down. Hunter's hand held mine. I looked at him, but this time, his eyes stayed ahead. My heart lifted just a twinge in the pain. Hunter was kind. He just wanted to offer a sense of comfort after everything I'd lost, that was all...

I held on tighter. No, I didn't lose her... Not yet, and I had a friend who actually cared about us, about all of us. Even after losing his memory, he managed to show up to protect everyone. I knew him failing to protect Hope pained him, too. Just like he couldn't save Krista a second time...

At the end of it all, we weren't God. We'd made mistakes and lost loved ones. We were a mess, scrambling around trying to figure it out. What should we do but hope? If not even God stopped the war, the best we could strive for was to fight on, to not give up. Even in the midst of this hell, God hadn't called it quits on the world yet. Even though sometimes I kinda wished He did, maybe He was waiting for something. I didn't know what, but time would tell. Wouldn't it?

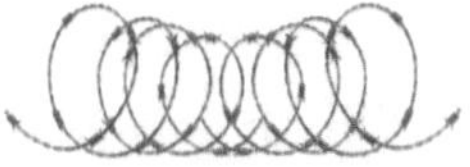

Banter consumed **First Baptist Bells Ferry** as I stepped inside the crowded space with Hunter. Warm sunlight filtered in from the high windows that increased the stuffiness. Underarm stench and sweat smattered. Pastor Mitchel stood on the stage with his wife beside him, pale as a sheet and hair flat. She actually wore jeans and sneakers this time. Mitchel waved his hands, but the crowd ignored him.

"We gotta get these sons of bi—" a man hollered from somewhere in the midst, but his voice drowned out by roars of agreement.

"Hunt 'em all before they take somebody else."

"Our town ain't theirs to run!"

"We're sick of it, Pastor!"

I pressed closer to Hunter. His arm embraced my shoulder like a big brother guarding his introvert sister. Or like a man with his woman… I shoved the thought aside.

"I know everyone's upset. Hell, I am, too!" Mitchel raised his voice. "And I agree, we gotta take these goons down ASAP. But we need a plan! A house divided against itself can't stand. We all gotta be on the same page."

His wife's eyes darted like fireflies, hands clasped together tightly in front of her.

"We know they're after Coryn," another man cried. "Let's surround the Barnes', guns loaded and traps set every night 'til they show up again!"

"Light 'em up!"

Hunter's hand slipped from its post on my shoulder. "Enough!" His voice boomed as it shook me. Every gaze found us – found me. Much of the angry countenances melted into pity.

Women standing nearby rubbed my back and biceps. "I'm so sorry, honey." "We're gonna find your baby." "We're with you."

My heart wrenched, and my tears blurred the onlookers as Hunter peered around. "I know we're all pissed off. Stuff is crazy out here, but us? We don't run wild like the world does. We don't conform to the madness — We overcome it."

Silence. Many reddened men maintained their squared shoulders and taut jaws. Many choking rifles.

Hunter persisted. "The wrath of man doesn't produce the righteousness of God."

Standing across us, one of the flushed men with a USA bandana on his forehead spoke up. "You sayin' we let these demons grab another child?"

"I'm saying we don't let anger rule us. We seek out God and how He wants us to rescue Hope."

I shuddered. Women whispered and rubbed. "It's okay, sweetie. It's gonna be okay." "Come on, let's get you a seat." They cleared a path, and I sat at the end of a pew half-wishing I didn't come, but I needed their help. Didn't I?

"Well, He gave us guns, didn't He?" The man continued, many amening.

"He did, but——"

"We ain't gonna just sit back and get stepped on. America's done been trampled by those snakes, but we're still here! And our town ain't goin' down without a fight!"

Hunter kept his voice firm. "We fight, not allowing hatred to lead us, but letting love compel us."

The man spat on the ground. "I ain't ever gonna love these devils, Hunter. Stop spewin that 'cause you're pissin' me off with all your holy-roller crap." He raised a hand at the surrounding families. "Look around, boy. Jesus hasn't come back yet, and prayin' didn't make 'im come any sooner. So you can sit on your knees all you want. Meanwhile, we're gonna fight!"

Shouts of agreement and more amens resounded in the church, including from the women at my side. The man raised his rifle with both hands while many slapped his biceps and whistled.

Mitchel and Hunter locked stares. Mitchel lifted his pink face a bit, eyes cold. His jittery wife closed the distance between them and clung to his arm as he turned his gaze from Hunter and addressed the USA bandana man. "Come on up here, Kyle."

As the congregants made way, they cheered and continued patting Kyle as he passed through. Hunter's jade eyes sought mine. I gazed back at him as a wrinkle creased his brow.

One of the ladies beside me, maybe in her mid-fifties, clasped my shoulder. "You're in good hands, hon'. Kyle's a veteran, as are many of the men in here. We'll come up with a plan to stop these predators for good."

My chest seared as heat rose from within. The tears turned sour, and I wiped them away. As much as I respected Hunter and Gunner's religion, they sometimes took it too literally. How practical was prayer when these men were able to kidnap my daughter? Prayer didn't prevent that from happening, nor did it prevent Krista and the others from dying, so why would it help in rescuing my babygirl? Everyone in here had guns and the passion to do something to get my Hope back. Every passing minute meant another chance I'd never see her again.

I rose from my seat and nodded at the woman. Hunter's frown deepened, and for once, I wished I could read his mind.

Through the parting made for Kyle, Gunner and Dixie appeared with Rhett and Rico. The gang banger looked at me with shimmering brown eyes before shifting them to the ground.

"Sorry for the madness." Gunner drew close, his white tee drenched in sweat and grayed with dirt.

Dixie brushed back messy tresses. "So much for a prayer meetin'."

"Hunter." Gunner gave an awkward nod.

Rhett also acknowledged him before settling that unsettling see-through-you gaze onto me. "We're with you, Coryn." The way he spoke, it felt like I was the only one in the room.

I couldn't help but shift some. "Thank you, Rhett."

"Of course, anything for you and Hope."

Feeling an uninvited warmth in my abdomen, I stole a glance at Hunter. Something flashed in his eyes.

Gunner and Dixie focused their sights on the podium, and I quickly followed.

"Where's Brock Wilson?" Kyle shouted from in front of it with Mitchel and his clingy wife at the veteran's side.

"Right here!" A bald man with sunglasses called.

"I'm gonna need you and any other snipers and long range shooters. We're gonna stake out at the Barnes' starting tonight. Find all the best vantage points."

"Hell yeah!" Brock and a few other men replied.

"And where's Bill?"

Celery stick Bill, taller than those around him, raised a lanky arm.

"I want you to set up your best traps in the back and by any windows."

"If I might interject—" Gunner crossed his arms. "These Blood Thieves were basically able to teleport."

The amped up congregants quieted and shifted some.

Kyle crossed his arms, too. "You killed one of the bastards, didn't ya?"

"Yessir."

"If they're killable, they're catchable."

Dixie put her hands on her hips. "I thought we were all set on lightin' these sons of guns up, not catching 'em."

"How you s'pose we're gonna find Miss Coryn's daughter if the kidnappers are all dead?"

"Oh, we'll make 'em talk all right!" Brock called.

The more cheers and whistles broke out, the more shivers broke through my facade of calmness. I sat back down. Rhett watched and set a warm palm on my shoulder. Like a reflex, I glimpsed at Hunter. His eyes watched, and even if I tried, I couldn't deny how hard he clenched his jaw as if he held a sucker punch in it. He twined his fingers together, the tips whitening…

I breathed shaky breaths in and out. Right, catch the kidnappers. The kidnappers who had my Hope that may not ever appear again...

"What if they don't come?" Dixie echoed my thoughts.

Kyle spat on the ground, making Mrs. Sligh gawp. "Then we hunt 'em down."

As the gathering clapped and hooted, Rhett whispered, "Let's get you home." He held out his palm, and I hesitated. Something faintly scratched at my gut. A feeling I'd had once before, but ignored. It was the night my ex told me he loved me for the first time… and last time.

Not to make things any more awkward, I resisted the urge to hold myself back. So, keeping my eyes on the floor, I slowly held out my hand.

A familiar, calloused one enveloped mine firmly. Hunter stepped forward. "I got her." Hunter's glare overshadowed Rhett and everyone else. My hand suddenly felt so small in his, so… safe.

I swiftly looked down again as he led me to the door, to what Rhett called home — the Barnes'. And it was true; though a bit crowded now, it had become a dwelling me and Hope grew to feel secure in. But home wasn't home without her, and it wouldn't be until she was back safe and sound.

I tightened my hold on Hunter's hand. Safe and sound? What the hell am I even talking about? America wasn't safe anymore, and God only knew if it ever would be again. Surviving was the new normal. As Hunter led me out into the late afternoon sun, I traced the shadows in the tree-lined path.

I once thought I knew about surviving. To some degree, I did. Food stamps weren't the same as food rationing from your neighbor, though. Fighting to keep the lights on wasn't the same as fighting off gang-banging murderers and blood-stealing Satanists; and warring against my desire to find love and companionship was far easier when I could work from the comfort of my desk, editing weddings with the freedom to merely fantasize I was the one walking down the aisle in white.

Now I had this man I couldn't escape even if I wanted to. Hunter looked down at me as the sun glistened every bead of sweat on his forehead and illuminated that subtle crease in his brow. Even without words, I knew exactly what he was saying: I could try and run, but he wouldn't let me.

15. LOST QUEEN

Night haunted the windows. I couldn't eat dinner, and I barely sipped my water. The answers to my most imminent questions could come tonight. We'd win this fight, lose it, or never even get the chance to wage it. Hope could be lost forever... Gun in hand, I shuddered as I sat in bed. Somewhere outside, Kyle and his men were posted with sniper rifles and other weapons awaiting the prey... or the predators.

I stared at the LED lantern on my end table. Bill did what Gunner called a fine job on traps, but like he said earlier, what good were they really when the Blood Thieves could appear at random—inside my bedroom.

I shifted my stare from the lantern to the foot of my bed where Hunter sat with his back toward me. His attention was on the door where Rhett stood, his wide shoulders tense, with Rico at his right hand. All three toted guns. I trembled slightly. The gang banger had hardly spoken a single word to me since becoming an indefinite guest at the Barnes'. How strange that the murderer feared eye contact with the feeble woman who'd been assaulted by his wicked family.

Rico's hand suddenly relaxed from his gun as he cleared his throat, gaze insecurely on me. "I just wanted to say…" His voice shook, and I braced myself for his next words. "I'm really sorry for what my cousin and them did."

My heart stuttered. Hunter remained unmoved. He'd barely flinched the entire night. Rhett let his eyes wander about the room as Rico continued his confession like I were some priest behind a curtain.

"I kinda wish they met Jesus, too, before they got theirs." He cleared his throat once more. His dark eyes gleamed in the faint light.

My tongue sat heavy in my mouth. Was he being honest or did he feign kindness so he wouldn't 'get his,' too? For a brief moment, our gazes met. Unlike he usually did up to this moment, he held fast to mine. The shimmering… It did seem genuine, but then again, how could someone change so quickly? He'd encountered something terrifying, yes, if Hunter's tale was true.

My heart stung as I studied the back of him, perched faithfully at the foot of my bed. He'd kept his word and hadn't left my side since he carried me out of the woods. He even stood in the hall when I used the restroom, which seemed a bit excessive, but I hated that I liked having him around like a guardian angel or something.

Hunter wouldn't make up a story. I adjusted my focus to the purple stem on my wrist. I'd seen some very bizarre things myself, and it changed me— a little. But I wasn't some cruel mobster who deserved to be locked up in a penitentiary, either. It'd take more than an apology for me to believe he truly 'surrendered his life to Jesus.'

I cleared my throat, and I forced out a "Thank you for apologizing," then copied Rhett's eye wandering. Then our stares crossed paths, too. Even in the dimness, his penetrating irises shone a little too keen. For some reason, though, I couldn't look away.

"You're a very strong woman, Coryn. You know that?"

Ignoring the flurry in my gut, I snorted. "Not really."

"Well you are, and I admire you for it."

Hunter rose to his feet. The flurry in my stomach rapidly turned into a frenzy. He walked over to Rhett. "I need to talk to you outside."

Eye-to-eye, even though he still tried to play it cool, Rhett's relaxed tone dissipated. "Sure."

As they stepped out and closed the door, I squeezed my gun and concentrated on Rico. Back to his avoidance of me. Alone with the gang banger? What was so important that Hunter had to leave me with this man of all people? If he tried something, could I even bring myself to pull the trigger?

Another shudder, smaller thankfully, rattled my upper body. I returned my attention to the lantern. Never have I desired it to flicker and warn of imminent danger, but now I needed it to. I needed the Blood Thieves to come, and the sooner the better.

A radio signal crackled. Rico unhooked a walkie-talkie from his pocket. "Any visitors yet?" Sounded like Kyle.

"Not yet," Rico replied.

"Been nearly three hours since nightfall. Maybe the cowards have other plans tonight."

I shivered. Other plans? I rose from the bed and paced. What good was waiting around for these Satanists when my daughter was out there somewhere? Why wait for them instead of hunting them down right away like some of the others had suggesed?

I stopped by the closet. Right. We had nearly the whole town searching everywhere for Hope. Nobody found anything, not a single clue as to where she could be, so we needed to let them come to us. I stepped closer to the closet. How far could these demonic people teleport from? Did they have some hideout outside of town? Admittedly, the place was small, and the only real spot to hide was in the woods… which there was no shortage of; but despite that fact, we'd searched and searched the forests, and nothing had come up. Just an old shed falling apart. It hadn't held a sign anyone had been in there, at least not for years.

Maybe they could teleport from far out, from the city…

Voices outside of the door raised. Someone slammed against it and grunted. More grunts echoed as Rico, bearing his gun, threw open the door. Hunter held Rhett in a headlock as the two staggered around like MMA fighters wrestling in a ring. Veins protruded beneath Hunter's clutch as Rhett jammed some elbows into Hunter, but they appeared to have no effect.

"'Ey, 'ey, 'ey! Whoa, whoa, whoa," Rico said as he pointed his gun.

Shivering, I aimed mine at him. "Don't you dare."

Rico hesitantly stuffed the gun in its holster, eyes bulging, before continuing to call for the two to stop.

Rhett kicked his leg behind Hunter's, and he briefly staggered, buying Rhett enough time to break away to throw a punch. Hunter dodged the blow, then hooking Rhett's arm in his, his other forearm smashed into Rhett's elbow.

Something snapped, and Rhett sunk to his knee wailing.

I dropped my gun and covered my mouth.

"You broke my arm!" Rhett's face contorted with pain as he panted heavily. Rico's hands flew up like a cop just caught him red-handed.

Hunter marched past him back into the room. As Rico assisted the ailing pastor, my heart rammed in my ribcage. Hunter hardly panted as he towered over me. "You dropped your gun."

I barely whispered, "Where did you learn all this?"

Hunter's face darkened like the sky when a tempest is suddenly upon it. As he opened his mouth, the blue LED on the bedside table flickered.

I snatched my gun and spun around. In an instant, Hunter's arm was around me with his gun raised. The flickering intensified. A shot sounded from outside. Then another, and another. All from different directions. Gunner and Dixie barged into the hall, both wielding shotguns.

"Oh my heavens!" Dixie cried at the sight of Rhett before she entered the room with Gunner.

The flickering and gun shots persisted. Hunter held his hold on me. If it was him or fear that locked me in place, I didn't know, but I knew one thing: they were here.

Brock's exasperated voice tore through the radios.

"We see—" static interrupted, "On the—" more static. "Got Kyle—" He grunted, and another gun shot went off.

"Brock?" Gunner called over his radio, "Brock, do you copy? Over."

My pulse thrummed in my ears. Dixie and Gunner encircled me and Hunter. Everyone's guns raised. I held mine close to my chest. Crackling came through the radio. Then gurgling, and…

"I'm afraid Brock and Kyle won't be responding anytime soon." A voice as smooth and cold as a river in winter leered.

Gunner squeezed his radio, and Hunter squeezed me. I pressed in closer, almost wishing I could meld into him.

"It's only a matter of time before the others are out of commission as well," the icy man chuckled. "Nice formation though, I'll give you that."

"You listen here you son of a—" one of Kyle's men growled through the radio. "Why don't you come on out and fight us like men, huh? Quit hiding behind your witchcraft you pu—" a grunt followed by intense groans.

Hunter's hold tightened, and the others pressed so close their arms brushed mine. The groaning subsided, and the murderer returned. "Now that the pawns are out of the way, let's discuss the queen."

My stomach flopped, the gun limp in my grasp.

"How many more lives are you willing to spare… Coryn?"

Someone coughed through the radio, and my blood chilled. Bill.

"Don't listen to him, Coryn!" Bill cried. "We'll get your daugh—" A wail emerged from the speaker, filling the bedroom.

My head ached. Oh, Bill… I'm so sorry…

"Answer the question, Coryn."

Gunner peered at me as the LED's flickers danced off his wide eyes. Hunter raised his radio to his lips. "Your days are numbered by a God who knows every hair on your head."

"Oh." Another chuckle. "Let me guess... Pastor Rhett? Your cliches betray you."

Hunter's tone lowered, and something churned beneath the surface like lava in a volcano. "Rhett's dealing with the broken arm I gave him, but you're in for something far worse."

"Ah. You must be... Hunter Freeman. The man whose wife was offed by God and whose nasty little temper got him axed from SWAT."

I looked up at Hunter. He kept his gaze on the radio.

"If I recall correctly, aren't deacons not to be quick-tempered or violent? They're supposed to represent the very best of their community, right?"

Hunter's confident countenance waned, something else replacing it... Shame?

"If you're wondering how I know so much about the pathetic pawns and bishops, why, I'd love to indulge you... See, apart from my sources in high places, there's also this beautiful little girl with just as lovely a name who perhaps you're acquainted with?"

My heart punched my ribs. "Hope." I snatched the radio. "I don't know who you are, but I promise you, I'll find you and—"

"So the queen finally speaks. The pleasure is all mine, but I'll be honest, I'm growing tired of all the pleasantries so let's get to the point. If you ever want to see Hope again, you're going to walk out of that house and head into the woods."

I squeezed the radio.

"If you even think of concealing a weapon, I'll hurt your little girl while you watch every single moment. Sound good?"

Dixie whimpered. "Oh, Coryn... No, hun. There's gotta be another way."

Hunter's stare finally found me. He still wore the shame. I almost couldn't recognize him.

I looked down at the gun in my other hand. Then at the bracelet on my wrist. Maybe, just maybe, it'd be a form of protection against these beasts. Though it hadn't lit up in a while... Did that mean God had left me, like he had Hunter when his wife died...?

I tightened my grip around the radio. "See you soon." As I handed it back to Hunter, Dixie grasped my arms. "I can't let you go out there by your lonesome! We'll fight those devils together!"

I gently removed then squeezed the lovely woman's warm hands. "I think we both know how this will end if you come out there with me."

Tears fell from her eyes as she held me tight. "Oh, sweetheart, please... Please don't do this."

Gunner shook his head as he looked at me and gently directed her away from me into his arms. As she wept, Hunter finally spoke with some sternness still beneath the shame. "I told you I'd never let you out of my sight again, and I meant it."

"You have one minute to decide or someone else dies," the man taunted through the radio.

"Hunter, I have to do this."

"No you don't. I'm not giving them what I— What they want. There's gotta be another way, Coryn."

"One way ends with more people dying."

"I won't let you." Hunter's voice cracked. "I can't."

Something else cracked in me, so deep I couldn't stop it. For the first time since that night I gave it all away to Hope's father, I felt my heart open up just a slither. It was too much to bear. I had to go. Now.

With one last look at Hunter's broken and beautiful frame, I ran out of the room.

"Coryn!" Hunter called after me. I could hear his heavy footsteps trailing, but then there was a crash. Rhett cried out again with Rico yelling over him.

I took in many unsteady breaths and forced myself not to look back. This was probably it, the last time I'd see any of them ever again. And as much I understood him, I couldn't let Hunter stop me. Not this time.

Somehow, I made it to the newly rebuilt back door. I unlocked every safeguard and sprinted into the night. The darkness bore nearly as thick as the fog did two days ago when Hope was taken—as did the silence. My skin prickled. Though I couldn't see them, I knew someone saw me, watched me, studied me…

I curved toward the vast woods on my left. The second I stepped beneath the shade of the first tree, a deeper darkness swallowed me. The grass crunched softly beneath my feet. An owl hooted somewhere further in. Then another. Maybe this wasn't such a good idea. I was running blind into enemy-chosen territory. They could kill me in an instant with one jab of a knife or shot of a gun. Then what chance would Hope have at escaping? Who would come for her? Who would—

Someone appeared in my path. I dug my heels into the grass, but I still bumped into their hard chest. Two arms entangled me, the pressure awful.

"Coryn!" Hunter called from somewhere in the darkness maybe a hundred yards behind.

"See you on the other side," the man from the radio spoke. One of his hands released its clutch. A damp cloth with a putrid odor shoved against my face. I writhed beneath his binding grip, but I felt weaker with every fleeting moment. A new darkness overpowered my vision… and my mind. Hunter's cries were miles away now… My head lulled as my everything…shut…down.

Hunter

16. LEAVING IT BEHIND

"Coryn!" Though barely making out my surroundings, I could make her out, limp in her captor's grasp. I drew near, feet pummeling the ground beneath them. Just yards away, I stashed my gun, not able to take a shot in the dark. I raised my fists, closing in.

The man laughed, and a cut whipped through the air. Something dark and fast flew in between us, and the man vanished, taking Coryn with him.

"No!" I stumbled into the place they just stood. The weight of my loss toppled onto my back, and I dropped to my knees. "No!" I slammed my fists into the earth. Cuss words flew from my mouth. I trembled as an onslaught of images bombarded my mind.

Allison in her hospital bed. The heart monitor flatlined and rining. My last SWAT mission. The old couple held hostage. Their son-in-law's face before I pulled the trigger—over, and over, and over again. The look on my teams' faces as they watched their commander lose it for the final time. Krista getting her blood drained by the savages. The Blood Thief taking Hope... and now Coryn.

"God, why?" I yelled to the night around me. Why? Over and over and over again. So many taken, and I couldn't stop it. I couldn't save them no matter how hard I tried. How many times did I have to see evil prevail?

I hit the ground again and again. I used to love You. I used to trust You, but how could You let me see so much I couldn't change? What was the point of it all?

Surrender to Me, son.

Tears fell in the darkness.

Mine will be with Me. Judgement is coming to the others. Remember My return. A robe dipped with blood. No one will escape My wrath except the forgiven and all those who trust Me. Will you endure until the end?

My heaving breaths slowed. My fists stopped breaking the earth as I looked up. A break in the canopy revealed the moon, full and bright. Where had it gone before? I hadn't seen it.

But it was always there.

A new image filled my mind. Allison's blonde waves shimmered. Everything about her shined, from her wedding gown to her blue eyes. I did, too, in my white tux, face beaming as I beheld my new wife. It somehow seemed so long ago… some vivid dream I had in another world. It was four years ago, right around election time…

We got the news nine months into our marriage. Allison started having nausea. We thought it was a baby, but after three tests, we went into the ER. I hadn't let her hand go once, only when they took her for a CAT scan. She'd been so peaceful about everything, though she felt like garbage. She knew who she belonged to no matter what was going on inside.

The moonlight's glow surrounded me in a pool of light as the vision continued.

The doctor came in. Black glasses, black hair, black eyes. He'd been quick on his feet all night, but he came in slow with those papers in his hand. He looked down on us and spoke as slowly as he came in. "The CAT scan results reveal something more serious than we'd previously expected."

My grip on Allison's hand tightened.

"Allison… It appears you have stomach cancer."

My heart dropped like a stone. Allison didn't say a word. She just lay there, eyes locked as he explained just how far it had spread. The liver. Lymph nodes. He wanted to start aggressive treatments as quickly as possible. Much of what he said went over my head, but I could tell by his current demeanor versus his previous one that he didn't seem very hopeful.

But I had been—at first. I had everyone at our church praying. I took time off of work, and when I wasn't tending to Allison, I was praying. I prayed while I helped her, too. Not much was changing. In fact, she'd gotten worse. In a few months, she'd transformed from the seemingly healthy, vibrant girl I'd fallen in love with to thin and frail. She was quiet most of the time since she'd been too weak to hold conversations for long. Still, she had that peaceful look on her face. It was like she could see Jesus sitting in the rocking chair in our bedroom or out on our porch. She feared nothing because He was waiting for her…

That's how I knew she was going to die. Though I'd been believing, fighting… and praying for a miracle, Allison knew she'd be with Jesus soon, and she was okay with that. More than okay, really. She had peace about leaving it all behind… Leaving me.

The white rays exposed the dirt on my hands. How many times had they sinned against Him? How many times had I used them outside of the Spirit, losing control when I didn't have to take it that far? I didn't— and still don't—understand why He had to take Allison so soon. I also didn't know why He chose to forgive me over and over again. I exhaled a prayer through falling tears.

"Lord, I'm sorry. I've let my anger control me so many times. I wanted to take control, but I only kept losing it because I lost my trust in You. But not anymore. I'm taking back control of my trust. I will choose to trust You today, even when I don't have all the answers, because I've known You, and I've known Your Word. You've always kept it and always will." I turned my sights up at to the heavens again, the moon glowing brilliantly.

"Here I am in a world where Satan roams while my old lady's in paradise." My heart gave a hard thump. "Now there's gals living in this hell and getting preyed upon by minds so depraved I wouldn't be able to comprehend it had I not believed in the devil." The flickers of anger trembled within, but… Quietly, I breathed in the cool air then released my anger with the same breath. "I offer myself to You. I want to serve You. Let me be Your hands and feet in this mission to get these girls back, Lord. This time, let Your Spirit fill and lead me. I'm willing to die for them, and for You—send me."

An owl hooted in a tree while I sat and thought. We'd searched all over the woods with no signs of a hideout, and if the Blood Thieves could just come and go, did that mean they could come from somewhere farther out, like the city? I rubbed my temples. For we do not wrestle against flesh and blood, but against principalities, against powers, against the rulers of the darkness of this age… Therefore take up the whole armor of God, that you may be able to withstand in the evil day.

Black Hearts. A still, quiet voice whispered in my thoughts.

"Black Hearts?" I said aloud. "Black Hearts… Why does that sound familiar?" An image struck my head. There was a barricaded individual, a mob boss who owned a club in downtown. One of the clubs in the area was called Black Hearts Night Club.

And take no earthly weapons.

"No guns, Lord?" I sat and waited, the shadows growing larger again.

Not for this fight.

I exhaled, a shake in my breath. I'd never gone on a mission without firearms. But I couldn't let myself become Kyle and the others, especially when Coryn and Hope needed me. And God works in mysterious ways…

"Hunter! Coryn!" Voices called from behind. I rose to my feet and ran back toward the Barnes'.

17. COMING FOR YOU

The moonlight covered the Barnes as they approached the forest's edge, Gunner covered in dirt—And blood, too?

Dixie clasped her heart as I ran their way. "Oh, no. What happened to my sweet Coryn?"

"She's gone." Even though I knew where she was, the words still took the breath right out of me. "Did y'all find any of the others?"

Gunner wiped sweat from his grimy forehead. "We already buried three. A few of 'em made it and are helpin' buryin' the others." His tired blue eyes latched onto my gaze. A simmer boiled in my bones and on my tongue. I knew what Kyle had in mind wasn't going to end well, but Gunner didn't put up much of a fight. Now look at how many more souls met their Maker before their time. Indeed, this war we were all in was so much bigger than goons and guns. We were gonna need a lot more than bullets to end this.

Gunner perched a gray eyebrow. "You got something you wanna say?"

Dixie set a hand on his back.

"I want the keys to Sheriff's cruiser," I answered.

Gunner exhaled. "Well that ain't happenin'."

"I wasn't asking."

Dixie rubbed Gunner's back and spoke quickly. "Let's get in and get you boys a drink." She cusped her arm in Gunner's and bustled to their door, littered with Bullet holes. Some patched with wood while others still exposed... How many more battles would their home have to go through before all was said and done?

As Dixie fetched the water, Gunner set a fist on his hip. "You goin' to the city, huh?"

"Darn right, I am."

"All right, tone down the sass. I'm pissed at myself, too, okay? You think I wanted any of this to happen?" He sucked his teeth. "That girl became like a daughter to me, and her little girl like one o' my grandbabies."

"Then let me have the keys."

"Oh, I'll let you have the keys," Gunner said as Dixie approached with two glasses of water. "But I'm goin' with you."

Dixie handed over the glasses with big eyes.

Gunner turned to his bride. "Now sweetie, you and I both know how much this whole Coryn and Hope thing has been eatin' us up. We gotta try to get 'em back somehow."

Dixie sputtered. "We?"

"I mean me, in your stead. There's no way in hell I'm lettin' you go—"

Dixie raised her flowery dress to unveil a thigh holster with a glock. "All right, lemme get the rest of my girls." Dixie turned towards the staircase.

Gunner grasped her shoulders. "Now hold up, pretty woman. I said I ain't gonna let you tag along. You got folks here who could use your help and it's just too dangerous—"

She snapped her shoulders back and gave him a glare that made him gulp. "Dangerous? Oh, I'll give ya danger, Gunner Blaze Barnes! If your courage is finally gonna kill you, I wanna at least be there to say I told you so one last time and give your stubborn butt a kiss goodbye!"

A chuckle left my lips and dissolved the rising heat in my blood. Gunner chuckled, too, then Dixie. Tears quickly followed them both. When his laughter slowed, Gunner took Dixie's hands. "Darlin', we been married... what now, forty-somethin'-odd years—"

"Forty-four."

"Forty-four years, and you know I always try 'n' done what's best for you—"

"Lyin' is a sin, ya know."

"Mostly what's good for you."

She crossed her arms as he continued.

"Right now is one of them times, sugar. If you'll just let me go on my own with the boy, you can give me a nice see ya later, and we'll call it a night."

"I'm goin', Gunner." Dixie stared at the man like she could see his very soul. Not more than five seconds passed before Gunner dropped his hands from her shoulders.

"Well I know that look." Then he faced me. "Looks like we got ourselves a tag-along."

She uncrossed her arms. "Not a tag-along, backup. Now like I said, let me grab the rest of my girls—"

"I don't want to take weapons," I said.

They both opened their mouths, "'Scuze me?"

"We're all Christians here, aren't we?"

"And?" they answered again simultaneously.

"And we're supposed to walk by faith, not by sight, right?"

Gunner held his hands up. "Now listen, Kyle and them were heathens, God forgive me, but ain't we supposed to be balanced? Why can't we pray *and* take our guns?"

"I think for this particular battle, we need to rely fully on the Lord."

Dixie and Gunner traded looks.

"I hear what you're sayin', son," Gunner started.

"You do?" Dixie asked.

"But," he shot her a look before continuing, "My bride and I have been holding down the fort with both prayer and bullets, so—"

My blood kindled again. "And this last fight?"

"Like I said, Kyle and them were hell bent on doing things their way—"

"Isn't this the same thing?" I kept my tone even. "Listen, you don't have to come with me if you don't want to. But I know this is different. This is the kind of thing you just can't let your flesh lead in, and somehow, God's gonna win this battle one way or another, and I trust He doesn't need our guns to do it, which if I recall, Rico and the two of you witnessed firsthand back there in the barn. Now the clock is ticking so if you can decide already, that would be great."

With one last lengthy look at each other, they mumbled an agreement and compiled two bags of essentials. As Dixie finished packing, Rhett appeared at the top of the staircase with his arm in a makeshift sling and Rico behind him.

As our eyes met, an arrow pricked my heart. Though I knew the man was trying to take advantage of Coryn's vulnerability, perhaps a good clock in the face would've been sufficient to get the point across. And I imagine the Good Lord wanted me to humble myself—just a tad.

"You all going somewhere?" he asked as they descended.

"Yessir." Gunner slung the bags over his shoulder as Dixie posted beside him. "Might be a li'l while. Can we trust y'all to guard the place 'til we get back?"

Rhett frowned as he and Rico reached the bottom and neared. "How long you think exactly?"

"Could be a few days," Dixie responded. "Y'all can keep this place up 'til then, right fellas?"

"Yes ma'am," they replied.

Rhett gave a nod at me, his mouth twisted funny like he was almost… embarrassed for some reason. My suspicions now confirmed, I called him out in front of them all. "I'm sorry I broke your arm, but I expect much more from a pastor. You understand me?"

Another quiet nod.

"I also expect you to resign from your position, effective immediately, understood?"

"I understand," he said in a little voice.

Dixie and Rico looked at each other while Gunner cleared his throat. "All right then. Here's the keys." He handed me the keys to the cruiser and slapped Rhett's arm before quickly apologizing. "You boys keep us in prayer."

"Lots of it," Dixie added, tapping their cheeks.

I marched out into the night toward the cruiser. *Hang in there Hope and Coryn. We're coming for you.*

18. SHOWDOWN

I gripped the wheel with both hands as I drove the cruiser through near blackness. I kept the lights dim so at least whoever saw us coming wouldn't see us from too far ahead. We'd only been able to see about twenty feet in front of us, but left, right, and behind, darkness reigned. Gunner rode passenger with Dixie in the back. We'd hardly said a word, though Dixie had whispered a few prayers since we set out.

I took a glimpse at my right hand man. His jaw was tight, and he still had dirt smudged on his cheeks. Poor fella and his wife didn't even shower off the grime from having dug yet five more graves on their property. Lord knows I could only bare washing my face and hands ever since Hope went missing. I'd figured praying was more necessary than washing.

My chest knotted. That precious, bright-eyed little girl stole my heart the first time we met officially at First Baptist Bells Ferry. I'd seen her a few times with her momma. They always stood out to me, these two young ladies that I'd figured were sisters at first even though the only feature they shared was their full mouths. Other than that, they were night and day: Hope with white-blonde tresses and baby blues and Coryn with thick, dark curls and stunning browns.

My heart picked up just like it did when I saw her up close when I returned the little baby doll I noticed Hope carried around in a pew by its lonesome. I tried to keep it short and sweet so I wouldn't break out in a sweat in front of the woman, but as I turned to leave, that bold girl of hers – I'll never forget it – said, "Wait, aren't you going to kiss my mommy goodbye?"

Good Lord, it took everything in me not to burst out laughing. Coryn's olive skin had lost a few shades, though, so that helped me hold my tongue. Little Hope went on to say I must've been a prince since I returned her babydoll like Cinderella's prince found her slipper. I didn't really know what to say to lessen the awkwardness so I blurted out, "I don't think he was trying to kiss her just yet, ma'am. He waited until the end of the movie, after they were married, remember?"

That's when Coryn's color came back—red hot like a chili pepper and just as spicy. That beautiful face turned fierce real quick and she said something like,

"Yeah, because good ol' Christian boys like yourself wait until the girl they're chasing is their wife."

Before I could figure out how to respond to that one, she about-faced and marched off. My grip on the wheel tightened. *Please, Lord, keep them safe...*

Another thirty or so minutes went by before Gunner decided to break the silence stuffing up the cruiser. "So... What was all that about with Rhett?"

"I just don't want him near Coryn – or any young women for that matter."

Gunner shifted in his seat and peered over his shoulder at Dixie. "He and Rico can find their own lodgings when we get back just fine, don't ya think, hun?"

Dixie wagged her finger. "Two grown men like them'll be just fine."

Gunner clasped my shoulder. "I think us grown men can take care of the ladies, whadda ya say, son?"

I glanced at the rearview. Dixie had a funny curve to her lips. My gut twisted. So even they knew I had a thing for Coryn. Apparently I had more controlling of myself to do; but for now, she just needed me—needed us—to love her like Jesus. I couldn't bring myself to fall for a girl who didn't love my Savior like I did.

Heat entered my neck, and my grip on the wheel tightened. All I knew was I had to get her back— and I would, that precious Hope of hers, too, or all heaven would break loose.

Someone appeared in the road, and I slammed on the breaks. A man with scraggly white hair and a trench coat stood there as he gave us a toothless grin. I swiftly reversed, but several palms slammed the windows. A bang rattled the trunk. I threw the cruiser back into drive and gunned it. Something banged on the roof, then clanged over and over until a blade pierced through the ceiling right by my ear. I swerved as hard as I could.

Dixie yelled as the knife wiggled by my head. "We rebuke this in Jesus' name!" she screamed. Someone else appeared in the road, a black man. He jumped up several feet as we neared. A loud crash sounded atop the car.

"What in the heavens!" shouted Gunner as the man apparently landed on the roof. I floored it to 115. Several bangs clamored above until someone went rolling alongside my window. Heavy footsteps tramped above. The black man dove off on the passenger side and vanished into the darkness.

Dixie clasped her chest. "I think I'm too old for this."

Gunner whipped his head back. "I told you to stay at the house, woman!"

"Don't you woman me! You were just as scared!"

"Whatever happened, we thank God we still got our lives and the cruiser is in one piece," I said, wiping sweat from my brow. "Speaking of, we really gotta figure out the best place to hide it."

"There should be an old junk yard comin' up, right outside the city," Gunner replied. "We'll throw the tarp over it and some rubbish as best we can. I suggest you kill the lights once we spot it."

There it was on the right. I quickly shut off the headlights and slowed to a crawl off the road, praying we wouldn't catch a flat in the mess.

Gravel crunched beneath the tires. The car rose bumpily a few times like a saddle wagon on an old, beaten path. The cruiser's bumper hit something solid. I shifted to park. Dixie handed Gunner the tarp she packed, and we all crept out of the vehicle. Moving slowly, Gunner passed one end of the tarp to me. The moon cast just enough light to see we'd parked behind a school bus. We finished covering the cruiser and swiftly piled on some scrap metal. Best case scenario, we'd be getting Coryn and Hope before dawn, but Lord knew how long it'd take on foot to get to the Black Hearts nightclub or what trouble we'd run into along the way...

Something toppled over a few yards on the other side of the bus. Dixie stood behind Gunner as we crouched. Shuffling neared and another ding of something falling, much closer. Someone hawked up a nasty loogie just feet away now. I balled my fists. Silence. Then a stench...

"'Ey!" A man jumped to my left, wielding a pipe. "What're ya doin' in my yard?"

"We're not here to cause trouble." I stood and dropped my fists. "We just came to find a woman and a little girl."

The man coughed wetly before spitting again by his foot. "Well there ain't many of those 'round here. Unless you count my good 'ol Suzie." A massive Rottweiler emerged alongside him, growling as drool dripped off the corners of her mouth.

Gunner's hands flew up. "Sir, the man told you our business in these parts. Now if you do us a little favor, we'll do one for you."

The man rubbed the pipe. "Whatcha got for me?"

"That cough don't sound too good," Gunner continued. "If you and Suzie here keep an eye on our ride, we'll give you some echinacea tea and three vitamin C's."

"What else ya got?"

"Listen." Dixie opened her bag and lifted the tea bags and vitamin bottle.

The man's gaze glued onto them.

"We don't wanna fight, and I don't think you do, either, so if we aren't back by sunset tomorrow, how about you get the teas, vitamins, and this nice stick of jerky to share with your good girl?"

The dog panted with her stare glued to the stick of beef Dixie flaunted.

The man pat Suzie's head. "What's keepin' us from takin' your lives now, eh?"

I shrugged. "You wouldn't want the three of us hollering bloody murder for all your nice neighbors to come fight you and Suzie to the death for these goods and the cruiser, now would you?"

He puckered his cracked lips. After a moment, he chuckled. Wet coughs quickly overpowered the laughter.

Dixie opened the bottle and gave him a vitamin. "That should hold ya over 'til tomorrow. Now if you'll excuse us..."

Suzie growled as Dixie passed on through. Gunner joined at my side with a small flashlight.

"We gotta use that sparingly," I whispered as we stepped over debris.

"Just until we get outta this mess," he replied and addressed his bride. "You did great back there, hon'."

"Ya learn a thing or two when you've got some grays to show for it."

"Some?"

She gave him a look as we weaved through gutted cars. "Any idea where this nightclub is?"

"Somewhere in Downtown."

"Thank God we're on the right side of down, at least," Gunner said. "Bad news is downtown ain't a small place."

"We'll head straight to Adams Ave first," I said.

As we neared the end of the junkyard, Gunner clicked off his flashlight. We found a gash in the metal fence and carefully slipped through. The night obscured much in the distance, mostly outlining skyscrapers and storefronts. For some reason, the moon didn't shine like it had near the Barnes' place. The deadly silence felt like being swallowed by a grim reaper. Trash littered the streets and sidewalks. Every shop window lent its glass to the ground, the insides exposing looted clothing, jewelry, furniture, and the like.

What a sad wreck the world had become. After America's fall, other countries panicked. Citizens turned against their governments. For some, that meant freedom from tyranny and new beginnings; for others, it meant chaos and ruin. Lord knew when any sense of order would return, but it would eventually to make room for a bigger, badder ruler…

I focused on my uncertain surroundings. For now, one thing was sure: we had to find Coryn and Hope before this time tomorrow night.

Broken signs and shattered or graffitied doors made discerning names difficult. Only a few letters remained in tact, if any. I kept my eyes peeled for any signs of trouble and any indication of a nightclub as we made our way down the sidewalk. So far, we'd passed a lot of boutiques, which meant we strode Bakers Avenue. Adams Ave would be three roads West of here in the heart of Downtown. The police precinct and courthouse sat on the road behind, but most—if not all of them—got overtaken by thugs with guns, so many in their early twenties or younger. The images of them opening fire and burning down my old station burned my own mind. Before the grid went black, there was plenty to see on social media. I had to stop watching and start praying like I never had before— except for when Allison was dying.

"Y'all, I'm getting' an icky feelin' that we're bein' watched," Dixie whispered as she pressed close to Gunner.

"I feel it, too," he answered.

I scanned as far—and near—as I could. We hadn't much of a choice. Without lights, back alleys wouldn't offer any clues as to what places we passed. We needed the buildings' fronts to help reveal what lay within. I squinted at Gunner and Dixie. Their dirty garbs made them blend in a bit more, but me? I may not have smelled like a million bucks, but in comparison to what we'd encountered so far, it had to be plain I wasn't from these parts, like where I came from had it much better than here…

I quickly stepped off the sidewalk and over the broken doorway of a shop on our right. Dixie and Gunner trailed me inside what appeared to be a coffee shop. I ripped a sleeve off my shirt and rubbed my hands on the ground. I lathered grime on my cheeks, neck, and jeans. Footsteps drew close from outside— several pairs. We ventured deeper into the shop. Blackness swiftly consumed. We felt around until a hallway opening emerged. Crunches and murmuring came from the front of the building. As I rushed ahead, my hands hit a horizontal slab of metal, and I pushed the back door open into an alley.

I veered left and broke into a run, Dixie and Gunner close as whistles rounded the building. My shoulder swiped a dumpster, and I gritted my teeth at the searing pain now eating it up. "Lights, Gunner."

He obliged instantly, illuminating our surroundings. It appeared we had a quarter of the way left to go. Men's excited voices filled the air behind us. I picked up the pace, Gunner and Dixie miraculously keeping step. We turned right and continued booking it past more shops. Just two more roads until Adams Ave.

I stole a glance over my busted shoulder. Twenty men burst out of the alley.

Gunner panted. "I don't know... how much longer... I can keep this up."

"You ready to take on twenty men?"

"Might be... easier… than this." He and his wife slowed.

I took another glimpse behind us. There was no way we were outrunning these boys now. I tossed up a prayer and about-faced, fists ready. Gunner handed Dixie the flashlight and bent some as he heaved in a few quick breaths. Dixie stood back, flashlight raised like a police baton.

In seconds, the men charged. I ducked and dodged, then grabbed one goon and slammed him into two others. I countered and landed blows to another on my right. A lick brushed my brow, and I pivoted before I uppercut someone.

A yell tore into the madness from somewhere, and two men landed on the ground in front of me. Another, higher yell, and Dixie appeared on a man's back as she bashed him with the flashlight.

More punches crashed into my sides. I dropped my elbows and threw out a sidekick before lunging to my left and tackling someone. I pressed my forearm into the neck of a boy, who was maybe sixteen-years-old.

He gasped as terror filled in his light eyes. "P-Please, d-don't kill me."

Five other guys turned and jetted in the opposite direction. Dixie released the one she'd bear-hugged from behind, and he took off with them. Fourteen men lay unconscious around us. I stood up as I grabbed the boy by his collar.

I held him close to my face. "How old are you, boy?"

"Sixteen," he squeaked.

"How long did you think you could keep this up before trouble found you out?"

"I—I don't know, sir."

"What would your momma say, boy? Runnin' around with a brood of vipers and preying on innocent folks?"

"I-I don't know, sir. She died when I w-was three."

My heart stung like my injured shoulder as I set the boy loose. He staggered back and onto his butt. I held out a hand, and the boy's wide eyes locked onto it like it were a piece of ribeye. With a trembling arm, he took hold of it, and I pulled him up straight. Gunner wiped blood from his lip while Dixie came over and dusted off the boy's back.

"I know what it's like to lose your momma young. Mine passed giving birth to me."

Dixie glimpsed back at me, and a frown curved her lips.

"I grew up in rough parts, and these hands have hurt plenty, but I know one thing deep in my soul. I don't wanna be like those men, and if I were you, I wouldn't wanna be like them, either."

"Yes sir. I-I mean, no sir."

"For a boy with enough mind to use manners, you sure ain't using it running with these killers." I dusted my chest. "You know who took it and didn't even fight back though he could've destroyed every single soul spitting in his face?"

"Y-You, sir."

"Maybe, but no. I'm talking about Jesus, boy."

He nodded his head swiftly, desperate to run.

"He offered those sinners a second chance like I'm offering you." I reached into my back pocket and removed a small New Testament booklet. "And if I were you, I'd take it."

The boy reached for the book even more cautiously than he had my hand. When he grasped it, he spat out a thank you, but before he could race away, I grabbed his arm. "One more thing. You ever heard of the Black Hearts Club?"

A new kind of terror smattered his face.

I kept my tone even. "Where's it at?"

He pointed past us. "In the middle of Cunningham Drive."

Cunningham Drive… That was about four streets further than Adams Ave.

"Thanks, kid. What's your name."

"B-Beckett."

"You know anything else about the club that could help us out, Beckett?"

He slowly nodded. "Don't go."

Before I could answer, he ran the opposite direction his gang had gone.

Dixie removed a handkerchief from her pocket and dabbed Gunner's lip. "I think he knew more than he spilled."

"If he'd seen anything like we have recently, can you blame him?"

"Maybe he's got a li'l hope to hold onto now." Gunner smiled at me, revealing a missing front tooth. "Son-in-law of a preacher if I ever saw one."

I rubbed my shoulder. "Ex son-in-law." As I walked on, an old familiar ache that once plagued me didn't take its usual place. Something else did. A calm, knowing… hope. Whether it was that I'd witness yet another moment of God's goodness in the land of the living or simply for the next life to come, I couldn't say. But I knew this much: I'd make darn sure I saw Coryn again before I took my last breath.

Coryn

19. ENEMY'S HAND

A golden glow filtered through my eyelids. My limbs hung heavy, but stiff… bound. I opened my eyes. I stood on a platform in the midst of a large room… my hands and feet tied to a pole by black leather. Several candelabras mounted tables, casting various shadows. But oddly, the air in the room felt cold.

"Finally." A silver-haired man sat at a table nearby. His face shown free of wrinkles, almost as if he were in his late twenties and had only dyed in the gray. His voice, deep and rich, revealed he was much older than his looks paraded. He traced the collar of his black robe as his equally dark eyes scanned me from head to toe. "You are one intriguing piece of flesh." His stare halted at my wrist. "Tell me, Coryn, how did you get that… very special jewelry?"

Heat seared within. "Where's my daughter?"

"Of course you wouldn't cooperate without seeing her."

A door opened from an entrance at the end of the room behind him. That white-haired woman in the catsuit who'd attacked Krista that night at Gunner's glided in, wheeling a steel cot— Hope laying atop it. My heart slammed in my chest as the vile woman drew closer until she stopped at the man's side. He leaned over, and his pale finger brushed Hope's forehead.

"Don't touch her," I growled.

The man snickered. "Oh, we're beyond that already, don't you think?"

More heat like the fire burning all around us raged inside. I trembled. "What did you do to her?"

"She's in a deep sleep. Certain drugs will do that to you." He crossed his hands. "Would you like to see what other things can do?" The man vanished, then reappeared inches from me. A coldness emanated from him. My skin prickled as he peered into me with completely black eyes…void of whites and light. He squeezed my chin and pressed his lips hard to mine.

I shook at the cold, painful grip and squeezed my jaw shut. My stomach grumbled and rolled. The man released, still so close his icy breath touched my face. "You're beautiful and bizarre… like me. You've tapped into something greater than your typical witch. This light power… I want to see it." He scratched beneath my chin. "If you don't show me, I'll put on a show for you with Hope as my lovely co-star."

I pushed against the leather bonds. Not an inch. They bore into my wrists and legs and made them throb. I'd tried before to show Pastor Mitchel and Rhett, but I couldn't make anything happen. This light power wasn't something I could turn on and off like a switch... Almost like it had a mind of its own, and I merely carried it as an unwilling vessel. But if I told this beast that, he'd hurt Hope in an effort to break me…

"I'm too weak… I need to eat something."

He blinked his black eyes and snapped his finger. The woman vanished. The man grasped my wrist and rubbed the stem-bracelet. "While we wait on that, answer my question."

My throat itched for water. Should I tell him the truth? If I mentioned Dixie and Gunner's farm, he'd probably want to go back there and search for the plant.

"Someone gave it to me."

His eyes narrowed. "Who?"

"My mom."

"Your mom?"

"The same day she died." The half-truths flowed freely.

"Before the car accident?"

"How did you…?"

He curled his mouth. "I thought I told you that I have sources."

I observed his hollow, unnatural eyes. Did he mean demons? And if so, why couldn't they just tell him where I got the bracelet? Wouldn't they know?

"So your mother was a witch?"

"In more ways than one." My answer flowed easily again, but my heart stung.

"Did she teach you how to wield the light magic before she left you forever?"

"No."

"Who taught you then?"

The truth sat on my tongue, but would he even believe me if I confessed it? Clearly, he believed in the devil, but did he also believe in the God who made him?

"What are you hiding, Coryn?"

I clenched my jaw again. Oh, God, what do I do?

The white-haired woman reappeared beside us with a silver canister. The man took it from her and unscrewed the top. Steam emitted from it, carrying a gentle aroma of chicken broth. He put it to my lips. I opened my mouth and drank. The warm liquid tasted amazing. The salt, garlic, and vegetables that had shed their juices to create this life-giving food…

The man patiently waited until I guzzled the entire thing, which foolishly wasn't long. I dug my nails into my fists. Hope and I needed time, but I let my stupid appetite take over.

He returned the canister to the woman and when she disappeared again, he stepped back. "Showtime."

I closed my eyes. I know I can't summon this thing awake. I can't make this bracelet obey me; but please, just let something happen. I need a distraction. Just a flicker or a flash... anything to satisfy his sick craving for power.

Warmth pulsed three times around my wrist.

A thick drop of blood spilled down his left nostril. He wiped it with the back of his hand. Every candle in the room flickered as his ebony eyes glinted, and darkness covered his countenance. "A brief intermission. I'll be back soon." He vanished, and the room vibrated in response. Several chairs shifted, the flickering stopped, and an eerie stillness returned as if I'd still been watched... like in the dream I had before I woke up to the living nightmare of Hope missing.

I set my sights on her little frame on the cot. She lay there like a mini Sleeping Beauty. Her golden hair neatly rested on her shoulders, one hand over the other as if... she'd been posed that way on purpose. A chill inched up my spine. These twisted souls arranged her like if she lay in a casket. What if he played a game? What if she was...

"Hope!" I half-whispered, half-called. "Hope, please. It's Mommy." Tears hazed my vision as nausea gagged me. Please. Please don't let her be... No, not here... Not this way, God.

White fog crept into my peripherals. I shut out her beautiful image. My head throbbed as the pain came sharp and fast. I can't do this. I can't. Me dying is one thing, but seeing Hope die? I know I'm a sinner, I know I messed up and maybe this is my rightful punishment, but I can't bear the weight of this...

I already bore it for you.

The warmth on my bracelet flowed around my skin in a circle.

What… What does that mean?

Who did I give for you?

My hazy brain wracked deep beneath all the madness of recent memories to when I was Hope's age. Seven-year-old me stood in a room with about fifty other children. Upbeat music blasted and a handful of kids danced on a stage at the front of the room with older, teen and twenty-something volunteers. One of the twenty-somethings in neon with braided hair sang into a microphone. "Who am I? I'll never know why, the Father sent His Son to die, to die for me. All He asks is for my heart to believe. So here I am, with nothing to bring, but a yes and amen, a yes and amen."

The words pushed themselves into my little heart and I began crying, hard. My shoulders shuddered. I stopped dancing and wept into my hands for the rest of the worship.

Oxygen found itself in my nostrils. I took it in, slowly. I used to believe, but middle school brought new emotions and new ideas, things I'd never contemplated before. All the little girls talking about boyfriends and kissing, and much more…

I just wanted to fit in at first, do what the cool girls did: date the cute boys, show off a little more of my body. Slowly, more wasn't enough, and I had to keep going. I didn't know what I was doing then, but the years flew by, and I found myself in high school, a big one, with plenty of new cool girls and cute boys from other neighborhoods. With them came marijuana and drinking, pills and injections, but I wasn't brave enough for those. It only takes a few drinks for a petite, newly sixteen-year-old to start feeling risky in other ways, though. The right words and the right timing for the wrong guy is a jackpot; but, like lotto winners, the high of the win only lasts for so long. What's the point of playing the same number over and over when you've already won? There were other lottery games to play; and play he did, "winning" many other girls who – like me – fell for the charm then got thrown away for the next one.

All the value I'd worked so hard for, the approval of the cool clique and the arm of the hottest "Christian" guy I could ask for, all crumbled with the breakup. It only worsened after the shame my parents rendered afterward. I forgot all about that seven-year-old crying in a children's service because she truly believed she was loved enough to die for, and not just by anyone, but by the King of Kings and creator of the universe Himself. Yes, I didn't know why, but He loved me... and I foolishly got distracted from that love. Little by little, that Adventure Bible got read less and less, those prayers got shorter and shorter, I got busier and busier until I just stopped going to the Wednesday night service entirely. I habitually missed the Sunday one, too, until my parents gave up fighting me on it. Perhaps they felt they'd push me away, but the opposite happened.

Then they were too ashamed to take me back to the same church. Starting over wasn't easy, not after everything I'd lost, so I figured it was better to not even try. I should just keep quiet and go to shut them up, though it never really did. Not until after I gave birth, but at that point, I was done. So a little over a year later, when I turned eighteen, I wrote them a goodbye letter with the name of my new town: Bells Ferry. It didn't take Mom long to find my exact address being as small as it was.

My heart stung again. When my parents showed up at my door asking how I was and if they could see Hope, I said she was at daycare, and I was busy working on a wedding edit. Then I shut the door on them for good.

I half-lied. I was working, but Hope wasn't at a daycare. She was napping in our room. She'd been moments away from meeting her grandparents at an age she'd actually remember them. Maybe if I knew that'd be the last opportunity she'd ever have to do so, I would've let them in.

A sob trapped itself in my throat. I held it in as best I could, sucking in breaths. I could die at any moment just like them, like Hank, Bill, and Krista... and so many others. What do I gain by continuing to shove my parents from my heart, to hold back the love I felt they failed to show me, at least in a gentler way.

They made me feel like I had to hide my sin from others, which made me hide from God. But here I stood, supernaturally pricked by a power I didn't seek out. He found me there, alone in the strawberry patch, and gave me a gift that had only helped keep myself and others alive.

Why I was chosen will probably never make sense to me, but I'm still here. It's not much, but I'll give You whatever little trust my battered heart can offer. No matter where that leads me.

Hope groaned, and I opened my eyes. "Hope!" I whispered louder than I had before.

Her glossy eyes opened sluggishly. Another soft groan. "Mommy?"

"Yes! Yes, sweetie, it's me. I'm right here, baby."

"Mommy…" A weak smile lifted part of her mouth.

The warmth on my wrist grew, and a purple glow reflected off of the pole. I peered over my shoulder. Lavender light radiated from the bracelet as it enveloped the leather bonds. They loosened and slipped from my wrists. I rapidly shimmied out of the rest of the bondage on my waist and legs, then jumped off of the platform and raced to Hope. The moment I reached her, every candle in the room extinguished. Darkness encroached, and the chill in the room increased. I felt around for the straps on Hope and fumbled to pull them loose. Whispers sounded in various parts of the room as if someone—or something—rapidly teleported all around us.

I pulled off Hope's binding and scooped her into my arms. She felt so light and yet so heavy at the same time. The whispers grew louder. A wind touched my right cheek. "Coryn. We see you."

"Mommy, make it stop. Make it stop." Hope burrowed her face into my chest. My heart banged as sweat moistened my clammy hands.

I willed my body to move, to head toward the door at the other end of the room, but my legs locked me in place.

"Here is where you will die... Both of you."

Every hair on my body rose, and a painful vibrating pushed against my skin. A chair toppled over on my left, then behind. In front of me. I squeezed Hope tighter. Her muffled voice filtered through. "Make them go away, Mommy, please." She cried into my shirt.

I opened my mouth. "Je—"

Something hissed.

"Je-Je—"

A chair scraped the floor, then crashed against a wall. Hope screamed.

My heart pounded harder, and I parted my lips again. "Jes—"

Every candle relit. Something huge and black stood right next to us, and the other ones glided closer from every corner of the room. I clasped Hope's head tightly so she couldn't turn it, every inch of me shaking. The demon closest to us bent its black face toward mine. Two gleams where its eyes must have been latched onto me. The hatred… Even though black engulfed this beast, loathing shed so plainly from its hollow irises. It vibrated against my skin, more painfully now than ever before.

I forced my tongue loose. "Jesus, help us!"

Shrieks everywhere. The demons flew back as if being blown by a fierce squall. My legs unlocked, and I sprinted to the door. I grabbed the knob and opened it. A long corridor stretched ahead. Torches dotted either wall as I bustled through it, passing door after door.

The fire here seemed petrified as if holding its breath, and that out of place coldness filled the hall. Each door I passed seemed to whisper its own taunt…

Hope's head turned as she watched each room go by. My clamoring heart suddenly slowed. A gnawing, buried somewhere in my heart, called from the depths. It rose within, summoning me… to the rooms.

I forced my face forward. No. It had to be a trap… A distraction. This whole place was one big abomination. Nothing good lay behind these doors, nothing that was worth scarring my baby's mind with any more than it already had been.

But… What if…?

As I passed another door, the draw in my heart intensified. The twig bracelet glowed purple. It pulsed gently, slowly, almost as if to confirm what I had to do even though most of me didn't want to. And Hope… Could she brave what lay beyond them?

I am with you in the darkness.

"Mommy, why aren't we leaving?" Hope's tired eyes concentrated weakly upon mine. "I want to go…"

"I know, honey. Trust me, I do, too. There's just one more thing I need to do."

"No," she whimpered, crushing my soul. But I couldn't…could I? Just take my girl and leave the shadows behind for good? Never know what horrors hid in this place that needed exposing by the light?

The light on my wrist brightened, and the purple shined off of Hope's eyes. She looked down at it, then up at me. I gave her a gentle nod and faced a door on my right. Shaking, I reached my hand to the cold, ornate handle – gothic in design like everything else in this club.

Heavily, the door slid open. A black diamond chandelier glimmered in the room, exposing six open coffins.

My insides twisted. Hope's fingers dug into my flimsy biceps that ached terribly.

"I'm gonna set you down for just a little bit, okay?"

Hope nodded. I stood her on the floor and took her hand. "Keep your eyes closed."

She quickly obeyed. I inched closer to the coffins, knowing I should be much faster, but I couldn't bear to see too soon what – or who – was in them. My heartbeat pounded in my ears, making them ring; but the warmth and lavender light on my wrist remained, giving me just enough strength to carry onward.

I held my breath, then reached the first coffin. My stomach dropped. A little girl, blonde like Hope and likely her age or even a little younger. Her eyes were open, but glossy and distant. Deep gashes marred her arms, and it appeared every fingernail had been removed. I covered my mouth and swallowed a cry. No. No, no, no. I coerced my head to look at the other coffins. They all carried the same thing: little girls, four to around eight-years-old, hazy-eyed and tortured unspeakably.

Oh God, how could this happen? How can people be this sick?

The chest of the first little girl who looked like Hope rose barely. She was alive? I slowly walked down the line as I squeezed Hope's hand. Every chest hardly lifted. There was no denying they were somehow still alive... But how could I help them? How could I get them out of here if they couldn't move?

I softy pressed my hand on the chest of the last girl, a curly brunette that looked like a younger me... She flinched and blinked, then her eyes widened. Fear and utter terror. My heart screamed within me. I gradually raised my glowing wrist, and her eyes trailed the light.

"I'm Coryn. I'm not here to hurt you, I promise. This is Hope."

Hope opened her eyes. Her jaw dropped, eyes as wide as the little girl's. She stepped close to my side. "Nice t-to meet you. What's your n-name?"

The girl's lips barely moved. "Emma."

"This is my mommy. She wants to help you."

Emma's eyes gradually returned to a more normal size, though the fear remained.

"Can you try moving, Emma?" I asked.

She nodded. I placed my hand behind her back, Hope doing the same, and together, we helped push her upright. She winced with every inch. Her wounds still appeared new…

"Can you try walking, sweetie?"

She nodded again, and Hope and I took her arms as we carefully aided her out of the coffin. She wobbled weakly. Then the other girls began to stir.

Hope, face scrunched with growing concern, marched over to them. "I'm Hope. Me and my mommy are going to help you get out of here."

Though my stomach still wrenched within me, my heart swelled. I managed a smile as we quickly helped the other little girls out. Holding Emma's hand, Hope and I started for the door.

The chandelier flickered.

The white-haired woman appeared a few feet away in the door's path. "Taking off with our supply now?" She glowered at me though a smirk curved her black, painted lips. "I don't think so."

"Supply?" I spat. "These are children—They're not products to be sold!"

She chuckled. "Who said we sell them?" She strutted closer, and the girls shrunk toward me. "How old do you think I am, Coryn?"

The churning in my stomach bubbled worse as I answered. "Twenty-one?"

She clapped her hands. "Guess again, sweetheart."

"Thirty-two?"

A laugh, high and eerie flowed from her. The girls huddled behind me as White Hair drew inches away. "I'm celebrating my eighty-third birthday next week."

Bile stung my throat as she continued to revel in her disgusting form of consumerism.

"See, these girls are products, Coryn. Their precious youth, fear, blood… fuels us. So you see…" She stopped eye-to-eye before me. "You're not taking them anywhere."

She slammed her head into mine. I staggered back, accidently knocking a few girls onto the floor. As Hope scrambled to help them up, the woman vanished and reappeared beside me. Her boot rammed into my ribs, and sent me across the floor until my back crashed against a coffin. Old White Hair slunk near, heels echoing sharply in the room. She lifted a palm toward me, and painful vibration tingled beneath my body. I lifted from the floor and floated into an upright position. Only the tips of my toes touched the ground. The vibration pressed in from every side, binding my arms and legs inward.

"What's wrong, Coryn? Your little purple light magic not up for this fight?"

I peered above past the ceiling. God, a little… assistance. Please…

The light on my wrist flashed.

The woman stopped. The light vanished. She puckered her lips. "Aww. I suppose not." She disappeared, then materialized a foot in front of me. Her cold hand squeezed my neck. Her metallic, cat-like nails punctured my skin. Trickles of blood dripped down.

"Stop it now!" Hope yelled.

White Hair's eyes narrowed. "You know what, Hope? I will." She released me and turned toward my daughter. "Your mommy needs to learn a few things about members of the Black Hearts. The first of which is—" Her upper body convulsed in one jarring motion, and her voice deepened. "We are not alone."

Hope cowered back, arms outstretched protectively over the six little girls that surrounded her. Though her blue eyes shone fear, they showed something else, too. "Neither are we."

A slow chuckle, still deep and masculine, emitted from the woman. "Seven little girls against us?"

Hope and the girls bumped into a wall. White Hair drew closer and closer.

It is my power in you, so trust in Me, Coryn. That still small voice whispered in my thoughts. I exhaled, and a soft wind stirred in my hands. I trust You.

The wind strengthened, rising up my forearms and stirred in my feet now. The air traveled up every limb in my body faster and faster toward my chest. Like a stream from all sides, the wind washed over my heart and consumed it. My tongue unraveled and began to move on its own. Rapidly it moved, up and down, making a certain sound… like a language I'd never heard. Joy enveloped every fiber in my being, a joy I'd never before experienced, not even the first time I heard Hope call me Mama.

White Hair spun around. For the first time ever, her black eyes expressed what she'd so freely imposed on innocents for God only knew how long. Something not even the deepest darkness could hide: fear.

The vibrating ceased, and my feet dropped firmly to the floor. I stepped forward as my tongue still spoke whatever language this was. Warmth engulfed my right hand where the bracelet clung, and I raised it. Violet light illuminated my palm and burst at the woman. The girls dove aside as she slammed into the wall and collapsed onto the floor. They hurried to me, eyes now wide with awe and wonder, and I approached the woman again.

Her black eyes stared widely into mine. I suddenly remembered that story about the man Jesus met in the tombs.

"What is your name?" I asked, halting the indiscernible language that had overtaken my mouth.

Her jaw jerked from left to right uncontrollably. "Zarah." She spoke in her natural voice.

If I had the power to do what I had done back at the Barnes', and now here, it was worth a shot. "Come out of Zarah right now – in Jesus' name."

She convulsed, writhing and groaning like a dying snake. Her mouth stretched open wide, and a shriek like nothing I'd ever heard in my life roared out of her petite frame. A violent vibration raced passed me and upwards. The chandelier swung. The sensation vanished, and Zarah lay still, eyes no longer black but hazel.

A bitter scowl covered her mouth. "Go ahead and finish the win."

I looked down at her. Though part of me wanted her to die right there for her vile crimes, something greater told me her vengeance would come in a far less merciful way, worse than anything I could ever dream of doing.

"No, Zarah. I'll let God deal with you as He pleases. But know this: You will never – ever – harm another child in your life. In fact, for whatever time you have left, you'll do the opposite." I looked at the door. "How many others are there?"

"Fifty."

Breath left my mouth. Fifty children in the rooms. "And how many Black Hearts are there?"

"You took out one, so that leaves three." She spat blood from her mouth. "Make that two." She turned on her side, gripped her stomach, and coughed out more blood. I grabbed Hope's hand and rushed out of the door, every girl lined up single file behind us.

I hurried to the left and started at the first door after the hall's entrance. More coffins, more little girls. My heart ached for each battered one. I thought the end of the world would come sooner than this... After America fell, that's exactly what it felt like. You'd see and hear the horror stories on social media before the grid collapsed. Hope and I lived through more than one. Our whole town did.

So many said Jesus was coming back any day now, and yet we all were still here, and lawlessness was everywhere. Evil seemed so triumphant like it had taken dominion and reigned over God... But maybe that's just what the devil wanted us to believe because it wasn't the end yet. There was still work to do.

I thought my life was over when my ex abandoned me with our child; but I had Hope, and raising her gave me a sense of purpose. Then the war tore everyone apart. Politicians disappeared, abandoned their homeland, and settled on islands or fled to other countries while Americans fought sleeper cells – and each other.

I had nothing left to give my daughter but suffering and starvation. Then the Los Daggers gang attacked us, and Dixie and Gunner took us in. Doing whatever house and field work I could to thank them for keeping us alive also gave me some sense of purpose... like I wasn't living in vain, but for a reason. Even if it seemed so simple for Hope and I, it was so much more...

I looked around me at the growing number of precious little girls following Hope and I. Much, much more.

"Miss Coryn," Emma said as we finished helping the last girl from a coffin. Emma's little brown eyes darted before whispering, "There's one more girl."

My toes turned cold. "Do you know where she is?"

Emma slowly nodded. "Wolf keeps her down there."

"Wolf?" I asked.

"The gray-haired man."

"Down… where?"

Emma pointed beneath her feet. The chill in the air added to my own decreasing temperature. Underground…

Hunter

20. HELL IS COMING

As we neared Cunningham Drive, two things shifted: the moonlight over the shops and towers grew even darker, and the air became crisp and colder. Gunner walking on my right with Dixie, wrapped his arm around her. "I got that feelin' again," she said, "Like we're bein' watched."

I squinted through the darkness. The last three street signs had been blacked out, and this one was no different, but we had to be close. We'd gone five roads over and seen a handful of homeless on the sidewalks, most asleep, others mumbling to themselves; but the last two streets had been vacant, minus wandering cats and scavenging raccoons.

As we neared a cut in the sidewalk leading to an alley, I stopped, holding my arm out over Gunner and Dixie. My heart rate climbed. I took a few quiet steps forward and planted myself behind a shop-front wall. I peered around the corner.

Posts with black velvet ropes stretched alongside a wall that led to double doors toward the end of the alley. The fading moonlight just illuminated a metallic heart on either door. My heart rate spiked more. I was finally close to seeing Coryn again and that precious Hope of hers. God, please let them be okay…

I motioned Gunner and Dixie over. They followed my stare.

"What's the plan?" Gunner asked. "March up in there and hope for the best?"

"Let's pray for backup." I faced my companions, fellow soldiers on this dangerous mission, and clasped each of their shoulders. I bowed my head and closed my eyes, then I started to speak. "Father in Heaven, we come to You with nothing but our faith and hope. We know this battle isn't ours to win, but Yours, Lord. We have enemies we can see and those we can't. We ask You to send us help. You said You make Your angels spirits and ministers of fire on our behalf. We know Michael isn't your only warrior angel. We need part of his team now as we enter a war zone that's run by the enemy.

"The wicked have their supernatural forces, and now, we're asking for ours. Holy Spirit surround us, fill us… give us everything we need to get Coryn and Hope out of here alive. For Your glory, in Christ's name, amen." I stepped into the alley. Another few degrees lower. Our steps echoed along the stone enclosures. A hard vibration pressed against the skin on my arms and chest. A gust and a tearing wailed from above.

Something dark slammed down six feet in front of us. A black-hooded figure bent, wide-shouldered, then straightened. A man around 6'5 lowered his hood. Pale-skinned with upside down crosses tatted on his forehead, nose rings, and snake bite piercings. He snarled at us like a dog. "Lost?"

"Nah," I replied, my breath visible in the cold. "We're exactly where God wants us to be."

The man hissed. Black covered the whites in his eyes like mud in the snow. "God doesn't belong here and neither do you." He charged like a lineman ready to tackle the quarterback. I side-stepped, but his long arm and shoulder crashed into my abdomen and brought me to the ground. My upper back smashed into the asphalt. Gunner swooped in, but the man vanished, then reappeared from behind. He lifted Gunner off the ground and chucked him halfway down the alley.

Dixie backtracked, rummaging through her bag. She removed her Bible and held it up. "In the mighty name of Jesus, we rebuke whatever the hell is in you!"

The man cocked his head and a grin broke out. "I told you," he spat as he stepped toward her, "God doesn't belong here."

I pushed myself off the pavement. Adrenaline coarsed through me as I rammed into the man, but he only staggered. Dixie yelped as she hopped aside and raced to Gunner. The man grabbed me in a headlock. His arm cut off all the air in my throat. I punched his side, and he tightened his grip. I stomped his foot. Nothing. My head throbbed. My punches waned, and the alley spun. My arm grew numb. I stopped punching. My eyes began shutting out the night. My heartbeat grew heavy. Jesus... I have to...see...Coryn. Help me...help her...and Hope...

A flash like lightning erupted in front of us. A warm wind rushed past. The man's grip unlocked, and I collapsed on my knees and coughed in breaths. Shining calves and sandaled feet stood before me. I lifted my aching head, still panting for air. A man larger than the possessed watchdog towered over me. His skin and the white tunic he wore glowed. I winced at the brightness, almost painful after all the dark my eyes had adjusted to.

"Rise." He spoke in a vibrating baritone that echoed through my skin. Nothing and everything in me wanted to heed so I did, albeit slowly. His heavy hand grasped my shoulder. A wild warmth filled my neck and back. I straightened, blood flowing like a river breaking through a dam. The searing in my throat was gone.

Something shrieked above as a shadow flew by, then another. Two large shadows rapidly encircled the angel. He reached for his belt and unholstered a glinting dagger. As he swiped it around, I turned back. The possessed man stumbled around squeezing the sides of his head. He barked, growled, and cussed over and over. Dixie knelt beside Gunner as she wrapped gauze around his bloodied head. I gradually approached the madman. Spit followed every sound that came from his mouth. He clawed at his cheeks and neck now. "Don't send us to the pit!"

I curled my fists. "I've heard that one before; unfortunately for y'all, there ain't no pigs around here this time."

The man's head jerked violently in my direction. Another grin, but hopelessness reigned in his eyes. "Hunter, Hunter, the one who's lover died."

My gut tightened. I ignored the demon's taunt. "What's your name?"

"Hunter, Hunter, where is she now? In a grave alone, in a grave, in a gr—"

"Come out of him in the name of Jesus."

The man took three strides forward and closed the gap. He stood in my face, spitting. "She's dead and you're next! Your life is over!" His hands reached for my throat.

"Stop it," I said, the anger inside a settled simmer like a burner on a stovetop.

The man's hands halted at my command. He hissed and clacked his tongue all kinds of obnoxious ways. I rolled my eyes. "Get out of him now and go to the pits of hell where you belong."

The man wailed, and his shoulders convulsed. He collapsed on the ground, still writhing like a snake. I knelt beside him and rested a hand on his chest. "I rebuke you in Jesus' name!"

He groaned, and his veins protruded violently from his forehead and neck. With another harsh convulsion, he opened his mouth and darkness surged from it. The shadow shot into the sky like a geyser. Misty clouds parted from over the moon, and moonlight flooded the alley.

I looked behind where the angel had battled the demons. All three beings were gone. I returned my focus to the man who was still as stone. I nudged him with my hand. The whites had returned to his eyes, and they landed on me, full of fear.

I snatched his shirt by the neck and jerked him inches from my face. "What's your name?"

"R-Rage."

"Okay, 'Rage,' you're taking me to Coryn and Hope or I'm sending you to hell early."

Rage nodded a lot, whole face tight. I yoked him to his feet and marched over to Dixie and Gunner, who had finally found his footing. Gunner rubbed the back of his head, his face pale.

"You don't gotta go in, Gunner."

He smiled, then winced. "I know I don't, kid. But I'll—"

"Probably slow them down," Dixie interrupted. She cupped her arm in his and addressed me. "We'll start headin' back to the junkyard and try and get the cruiser."

"All right. Just be on standby."

"I'll be prayin' the whole time," Dixie answered.

"And I'll be mumblin' agreement," Gunner said.

Dixie took a radio out of her bag. "For when you need backup." She glimpsed up. "Though, if my eyes are still workin' right, you got somethin' else watchin' your back."

"Thank you, ma'am." As she and Gunner made their way out of the alley, I clipped the radio on my hip. My other palm grasped Rage's shoulder tightly. "Lead the way."

Rage strode to the double doors down the alley. He removed a necklace from under his cloak with three keys on it, unlatched one, then unlocked a door. Cold wintery air stung my face like small needles as he led us inside.

Red victorian couches filled a space leading into a large room with tables and throne-like armchairs. Candlelit chandeliers hung over checkered marble. Several poles on platforms stood in the center, and two curved staircases lined either side of the place. Rage led me to the one on the right while I looked around.

I trailed him up the steps. Despite all the candles and torches, the chill remained, but I knew it wasn't AC.

We slipped past more couches and tables into a hallway. We passed some bathrooms and landed at a door at the end that read *Employees only.*

Rage opened it. Torches lined the walls of a lengthy corridor. Face forward, Rage swept past door after door. Something gnawed in my gut. It grew with each room we passed. "What're all the rooms for?"

Tension emanated from him. He stopped and slowly turned to me. More fear filled his eyes. Sweat mounted on his forehead. He tapped his shaking hands together and cussed under his breath. "He's gonna kill me. I know it."

Gut now a rigid wad, I turned to the nearest door and opened it. I didn't peel my palm from Rage. He spit another swear word and muttered his demise as I entered the place. Six open coffins stretched in the middle of the room. My heartbeat quickened. I strode to the caskets, taking Rage's arm and pulling him with me. I sucked in a breath. Empty.

Rage's face dipped to white. "No. This… This isn't possible."

"What?"

"They're not here. Where are they?" He rubbed the back of his head.

"Where's who?"

"The girls."

"You mean Coryn and Hope?"

"Zarah," he said more to himself than to me.

"'Ey."

He scratched the back of his head like a dog getting at fleas.

I shook him hard, and shoved my face in his. "Remember what I told you."

He stopped scratching. "C-Come on." He peeked out into the corridor before stepping inside. He hurried to the end of the hall and opened the last door on the left. Another room with candelabras on tables, but this one had a platform with a pole in the midst. Leather bonds lay in a heap at the foot of the pole, and a surgical table on wheels lay nearby. Rage cussed again. Eyes still large he whispered, "Well, it looks like Coryn and Hope aren't here." He rubbed his hands together.

"Where else could they be?"

He stopped rubbing his hands and grasped the keys around his neck, knuckles white. "The Burial Grounds."

The knotting in my gut strengthened. "What did you just say?"

"Underground, where he keeps Little Red Riding Hood."

"Who's that?"

"His main energy source."

"The guy who runs this abomination?"

Rage exhaled. "Something like that." He rubbed his hands again. "I just don't know why he'd move all fifty-two of them down there."

My heart jumped. "Fifty...two?"

"Well, including Coryn and Hope, yes. Fifty-two girls."

"Lord have mercy." Now I clasped my head and closed my eyes, that simmering heat starting to rise quick. Fifty-two girls need saving, Lord? How am I gonna get them all out of this place? The cruiser's literally big enough to fit Coryn and Hope, and that's it. My heart jumped again. The bus in the junkyard. If it even works...

I unclipped the radio from my waist and turned it on. "Dixie," I whispered, "Dixie, do you read me?"

After a moment and some crackling, her faint voice came through. "I read you."

"See if that bus in the junkyard works."

"Umm… Okay, then what?"

"Bargain for it, and bring it over. Forget the cruiser."

"Sounds like a lot to give up for a banged-up bus, but I'll try. Let's hope we can make it before sun-up with this slowpoke."

Gunner grumbled something in the background.

"Prayin' for you!"

"Roger that. Thanks, Dixie. I'll check back in two hours. Over." I turned off the radio.

Rage shot his trembling hands up. "Wait-wait-wait. You're gonna try to get them all out?"

The simmering spilled into my hands, and I grabbed Rage by the neck. "It's taking everything in me not to rip your head from its mount right now, so if I were you, I wouldn't question me."

He swallowed with chapped lips and whispered, "Wolf's gonna commission all of hell before he lets that happen."

"And I'm commissioning all of heaven so it does."

Rage gripped the key on his necklace again as sweat dripped into his darting eyes. With a slow rock and a gulp, he looked at the ground beneath him and mumbled, "Hell, here we come."

Coryn

21. KILL ME FIRST

Forty-nine girls trailed Hope and I through the dimly lit tunnels. Wickedly cold, the fog of our breath shown visible in the torches' lights. Our steps echoed and we'd heard other things. Whispers… Moans… Inhuman things. I shuddered, but continued. Every girl mattered. And this particular girl meant more to that demented 'Wolf' than any of the others.

I glanced back at Emma, right behind Hope, and asked, "Have you ever spoken to the girl Wolf keeps down here?"

"A few times…" Despite the warm light, her thin cheeks appeared pale. "Her name's Maya. Her mommy and daddy took too much medicine one day. She found them on the couch, and they wouldn't wake up."

Another shudder wracked through me. Drugs. How many were on them? Especially now with no regulation, and no law enforcement... How easy it was to trade in the streets, no longer having to hide in the shadows with consumable death. And what better time to peddle it?

Despair reigned over the once great land of the free. Though, really, I don't know how free we really were before everything hit the fan. The government had grown with so few willing to keep it in check, and it seemed every month new restrictions rose on everything from homeschooling to travel. There were so many protests I couldn't even go to the store once a week without driving past one. Inflation had crippled so many. Hope and I miraculously got by with just enough every month, but we had government assistance; and a very low rent to pay, too, thanks to the Barnes' kindness.

My heart sank. Good old Aunt Dixie and Uncle Gunner. How were they holding up? Would we ever see them again?

And Hunter... My heart hung heavier. How he shouted my name echoed in my ears. It broke me in more ways than one, but I couldn't look back at him. I had to leave. I didn't have a choice. I needed to get my baby, and there was no other way. I hope he knew that... that if things were different, if Hope was safe with us, maybe I wouldn't have run away... Maybe I would've stayed.

I focused on the winding path ahead. Thinking of those we left behind wouldn't help any of us down here. We had nothing to hope for except one more moment, another second of life. This living nightmare would end eventually, and I couldn't predict when or how, or if any of these precious girls and I would even make it through the night…

The torches crackled and flickered. An icy gust swept past. The girls huddled all the closer, and Hope squeezed my hand hard.

A scream reverberated in the tunnel from somewhere in the distance. A little girl's scream: Maya. I halted. My mind raced. This battle—if there even was one—did these girls really need to be caught in the crosshairs of it? Perhaps, if I distracted Wolf, the girls could at least find a place to hide and figure a way to get out.

Heart still heavy, I faced Emma again. "How many others are there besides Wolf and Zarah?"

"Just Rage, but he watches the outside."

My temples throbbed. Nowhere was safe for these girls, but they could try… And if I died, at least they'd be spared from witnessing it.

I knelt before Hope and took both of her little hands in mine, trying my best to keep it together. "Sweetie, you remember how Rapunzel had to escape the witch?"

My sweet Hope nodded.

"She was brave and escaped." I held tighter, my voice thin. "These girls need us to be brave. Can you be a brave princess, Hope?"

She nodded fast, sapphire eyes burning like the fire around us. A million needles stung my chest. So many thoughts threatened to overtake my fragile calm. I spoke quicker. "Take them back to the club and find places for them to hide until Mommy comes back for you all. And if I don't, you get them out of here, understand?"

Tears fell from Hope's eyes. "But Mommy—"

"Remember Prince Hunter's God?"

A little crinkle lined her brow, and she whispered as if she uttered a secret. "Jesus?"

"Yes. He's Mommy's God too now; and no matter what happens, He is able to help you girls. Just ask Him."

Hope gave another nod through tears, and I pulled her into my arms. I kissed both of her cheeks as I squeezed her little body tightly. The needles in my chest were unbearable. Oh God, please give these girls the strength to carry on no matter what…

I rose. "Hope's going to take you girls back to the club until I come to get y'all, okay?"

Some nodded, and others just stared with fear. That wretched fear. If only I could somehow crush it for them... For all of us. The ball and chain I wanted to throw out of a skyscraper and never experience again. I breathed out a shaky breath. "Go on now."

Hope wiped her eyes, then turned. They all began their trek back the way we came. I waited until their patters quieted to a rustle, then I turned to the darkness ahead and the other demons waiting for me. I stepped forward. Faster. My heart kept pace with my steps. The torches flames flickered wilder and wilder as if warning someone of my presence... Or warning me.

Another cry echoed through the tunnel. My heart screamed back, and I ran through the passage. My shoes slammed against the hard pavement until the tunnel broke open into a wide space with two other passageways: one going left, the other right. The domed top reached high, maybe a hundred feet up. Torches quaked.

"Wolf!" I shouted. The torches stilled unnaturally. My ears rang with rushing blood. I drew in slow breaths. Every part of me ached worse. My weak legs begged me to take a seat, but I forced them to stand.

The wall torches doused. Dense darkness pressed in on me. I stood as still as the flames had. Not a whisper. Not an echo. Emptiness. But this place wasn't empty. It was filled... with evil.

"I see you want a tour." The torches reignited to reveal Wolf standing in the center, several yards away, in the midst of the fork. "And I've been wanting a show, so why not?" A twisted smile eased onto his lips and he called in a high, playful voice, "Little Red Riding Hood, come out to play."

The torches' flames grew and shifted to a vivid blue. A deafening shriek raged behind me, and a rippling blue wave crashed into my frame. I flew forward and rolled until my back slammed into Wolf's calves. He stood unflinching, like a Greek statue. Wind knocked out of me. I blinked rapidly, everything whirling. A little figure in a crimson hood glided closer from where I'd stood. Her pallid, bare feet pointed like a ballerina, barely touched the ground beneath her. I struggled to push my arms against the floor as they trembled with the effort. The little girl stopped five feet away. She lowered her hood, and her eyes glowed like a sky on fire.

"What kind of ringmaster am I?" Wolf stepped over and kicked me down on the way. He stood at the little girl's side. "Little Red, this is Coryn. She dreams of rescuing captive children like you." He laughed while the girl stared at me. Her face looked dead, minus the blaze in her eyes. Full of rage, of hatred...

"She also has a special power that I've been dying to see." He clapped his hands. "Come on, Coryn. Up, up. Let's see it."

I squinted in a feeble effort to quench the spinning. I took another deep breath and quivered slowly to my feet.

"You're wearying me, Coryn." Wolf's corrupt grin disintegrated. "Don't make me have to go fetch Hope and wake the little sleeping beauty to a nightmare unlike anything she's ever experienced before."

My heart thrummed. So he had yet to learn his Zarah was gone and the girls were roaming... But how long could I keep him down here? I moved my fingers as if playing a piano, body still shaking like how the torches flickered. Put on a show, Coryn. For however long it takes. At least until the girls can escape…

Wolf crossed his arms, gaze rapt on my hands. I rolled my wrists, then focused my attention on them. I raised my heavy, shaky limbs, and I swayed my arms in front and above myself. I mimicked the wind as best I could, trying to get lost in my own guise. If I believed it, maybe he would, too…

A minute passed, then another. And another. Wolf's gaze never left, but his toe tapped the floor.

I kept my focus on my wrist, the bracelet that remained unlit… How much longer before—

"You're stalling," Wolf hissed. "Little Red."

Maya watched me too closely. So young, yet her stare looked like it'd seen ages. Her jaw slowly opened like an alligator's. That deafening shriek erupted from her little body, and another wave three times her size emerged and pummeled me.

I tumbled backwards until I hit a wall. More breath shoved out of my lungs, and I coughed blood. Pain spread like water over my ribs. The girl floated toward me rapidly now. She stopped at my side and peered down at me. Her face spun in circles. That dead face. Pain knifed at my back and ribcage. I coughed up more blood. I blinked hard against the spinning, holding onto her eyes with mine. *You're just a child. A child… who doesn't… know… what's happening. You need… help. Je—Jesus… can help you.*

Her head tilted to the side, matching the angle of mine. She bent down. A chilling, distant voice slithered from her lips. "Don't look at her."

I held my gaze all the harder. "Get out. Get out of her... in Jesus' name."

Her eyes glowed brighter, and the flames jostled. She grasped my wrist with the bracelet, and her little hand crushed it despite her size. She choked the blood flow, instantly making my hand numb.

"Her parents were ours, and now she belongs to us." The girl growled. "She will always belong to us."

"Jesus. Loves. You," I panted through the rising agony in my body. "He wants... to save... you."

She pulled me onto my knees with my hand still restricted. I forced my thighs to hold my weight. Those eyes seared into mine. So much hatred for such a tiny person, but none of it was from her… was it?

Tears rolled down my cheeks for this precious little girl in front of me whose life had been ruined by these monsters and all the other girls, too; and for my own babygirl whose innocent life had been cracking from the time she began to ask why she didn't have a daddy, to now, being shattered by monster after monster who came for our blood. The government, the gangs, the looters, these Blood Thieves, and the child they tried to turn into something just as terrible... But she was just a child, not much older than my own. Did she really understand what she was doing?

We battle not against flesh and blood, but against principalities, against powers, against the rulers of the darkness of this world, against spiritual wickedness in high places.

The words seeped into my spirit. No, this wasn't all her. She had been held captive by not just wicked human beings, but wicked spirits who invaded her little body and sought to wreak havoc through her. She was just their puppet, but not anymore.

"Maya." Every syllable wrought agony. "Jesus. Can set. You. Free."

Her head tilted slightly – or had I imagined it? The pain that coursed through me shouted so loudly I couldn't trust what I saw. Her eyes squinted, didn't they? Yes. Just a—Maya released her grip on my wrist and turned around.

Wolf's eyes also narrowed. His shoulders squared, and lowering his chin, he peered up at her challengingly.

Feet planted firmly, Maya unleashed more screams. An array of blue waves burst from her and pummeled into Wolf, then proceeded into three of the four walls.

Wolf staggered back a few feet, but held his footing. "That's enough, Red!"

She continued to holler out the sapphire energy. The ground trembled. Everything did.

Something cracked beneath my palms. The floor… Cracks grew underneath and beside me.

"I said enough!" Wolf trudged ahead, forcing himself gradually through the waves closer to Little Red.

Cracks now lined the walls. The whole place was going to cave in; and the girls above, would they get out in time? This had to stop. I pushed myself up. My flesh wasn't willing, but my spirit knew what it had to do now. The pain deepened.

Wolf stood a few paces from Little Red, his eyes enraged and just as hate-filled. He swung a fist at her head. She snatched it and sank her teeth into his forearm. The blue waves ceased and Wolf growled as he grabbed her hair with his other hand and yanked her head back. She roared. A stream of blue light blasted from her mouth and into Wolf's face. He lurched onto his back and slid yards from her.

I inched upwards. My legs burned. My chest. My head. The ground quaked. Dust and tiny rocks fell. She's going to kill everyone. But how do I stop this?

Bigger rocks dropped from above. The cracks enlarged. Flooring split between my feet. I prayed through burning tears. God, I have nothing. I am nothing. And I can do nothing without Your help. It's not for my sake. But the girls. Please don't let them die here. Please give them hope. Give Maya hope.

Warmth ignited on my wrist, and the purple stem glowed. I raised a trembling fist at her. Please don't let this kill her. Heat radiated up and down my arm like electric pulses. For a moment, a burst of energy filled me from head to toe. I swallowed a breath, closed my eyes, and opened my palm. A pulsating stream emerged. Violet pierced my eyelids, and I opened them.

Purple light flowed from my hand and engulfed Little Red in an orb. She hung in midair with toes floating a few inches from the broken ground. Her eyes stared straight ahead, and her mouth was slightly agape as if frozen in time. I inched near. The purple orb hummed gently in melodic buzzes. I stepped inside. A warm wind slowly stirred, in sync with the rhythmic vibrations that emanated from the orb. The light shined off of Little Red's blue eyes... turning them indigo.

"Maya," I spoke.

The little girl's irises glimmered and she blinked.

"I know you can hear me, Maya. I know what it's like to lose your mommy and daddy. I lost mine when I was younger. I felt like I was alone and on my own for years, but I found out God has been watching all along... waiting for me to look at Him."

The floor beneath us cracked more. A wall torch dropped to the ground in a burst.

"Anger gives the devil a foothold in our lives, but Jesus said He came to set us free. Let Him free you from this."

A tear fell from her eyes. Then another. And another. Her lips moved slow. She whispered, "Free me... Jesus."

The purple light engulfing us pulsed toward her, then seeped into her little frame. She exhaled. Black shadows raced from her mouth. One... Two... Three... Four... Five... Six... Seven. Her body lowered onto the concrete, and a jolt ripped it open. Maya stumbled forward, and I caught her. As soon as she was in my arms, we rushed toward the tunnel I'd come in from.

Fire lashed around. Smoke swelled. Someone snatched my wrist. I turned – Wolf.

Blood seeped from his forearm, and his ebony eyes raged. He raised a dagger with his other hand and brought it down. It crashed into my bracelet and ricocheted back... into his neck. As he staggered backwards and clutched his bleeding wound, coughing, I clasped tighter to Maya and ran ahead. The smoke burned my eyes and throat. Maya coughed now. My head pounded. Darkness crept into my peripherals. Lightheadedness. I breathed as deeply as I could, but it only worsened the coughing. My legs slowed. My grip on Maya loosened. Her coughs sounded further and further away. The darkness grew as another tremor hit. My arm slipped from Maya. I collapsed into something hard... then nothing.

Hunter

22. IN MY ARMS

Coryn dropped into my arms. I held her against my chest and reached for the little girl coughing up a storm beside her. I quickly hoisted them over either shoulder as the dungeon's ground screamed and smoke enveloped the area. I raced back through the tunnel. Tremors stalked us through the winding passage. I fumbled my steps, but I couldn't give in. I pushed harder. My body could hate me all it wanted later, but my heart had found what it came searching for, and I had no plans to lose her now. The entire club shook five minutes ago so the place would cave in any second now... Stones pelted from above, trailing us like devilish rain.

Lord, cover us! Rocks dropped on each side. I side-stepped and jumped over the ever-growing debris. The smoke strangled my lungs as the ground inclined.

More jolts barked at my feet. I prayed some more, my chest on fire. Stairs appeared ahead of me. I climbed up, the girls heavier with each step. The door to the lengthy corridor of coffins greeted me. I kicked it open and barged through, sucking in the fresher air though the fire followed close behind. Walls cracked, the ground quaked, torches fell.

Dodging new flames, I reached the end and again kicked open the last door that led into the second floor hallway. I raced past the bathrooms and falling tables and chairs. I turned toward the spiral staircase on my left and descended. The girls weighed more with each step. It had been so long since I had trained for anything like this...

Black chandeliers swung wildly overhead, then crashed to the ground. More flames descended. I hit the bottom and climbed over red couches and burning carpets.

I winced through smoke. The double-doored entry came into sight. And so did something else: Rage.

Blackness consumed his eyes again. Flicks of red bounced off the bottomless orbs. They bore into me as a grin like the devil himself spread across his mouth. "Hunter!" he roared, and somehow, I knew exactly who was speaking—and it wasn't the demon I'd cast out earlier.

Embers rained around him. Unfazed, he strode toward me and the girls I held as his heavy steps crushed the faulty floors beneath them.

Fire lapped at my sides. The heat threatened to incinerate my legs. No way I could set the girls down or I'd lose them to the flames, but I couldn't charge through this guy. Unless I—

In a blink, Rage disappeared. Another and he stood a couple yards from me. Energy pulsed against my skin so strong it slowly pushed me back, closer to the chaos burning behind. Above the racket, a baritone like thunder in the night taunted. "Like a star I fell, but now here I stride, roaming to and fro on the earth—" He vanished and reappeared inches from my face. "—Seeking someone to devour."

Grip tight on the girls, I front-kicked him in the gut. He doubled over and slid back as if on ice. Peering up with those soulless eyes, he grinned again. "Pathetic." A flap of wind, and he was gone like lightning. Something crashed into my back, and I staggered forward, clutching the girls as I fumbled to catch my footing. A puddle of fire waited to consume us all. Miraculously, my feet caught the ground. Applause rang out from behind, then steps beside.

"He shall give His angels charge over you, to keep you,' and, 'in their hands they shall bear you up, lest you dash your foot against a stone.'" A swipe to my leg that brought me to both knees. The fire grew closer.

Smoked burned, blurring my vision. Satan paced in front of me, the flames blending with his black visage. "You know who killed Allison, right?" His deep voice pounced over the falling debris once more and vibrated its brutal pulses into my skin. "I did."

My head pounded against the smoke, adrenaline, vibrations, and his words… The vibrations rammed against my aching chest like a snake striking its prey. I coughed deeply, the pain unreal.

The devil comes to steal, kill, and destroy… I forced my muscles to move, but they remained frozen.

"I approached God about his servant Hunter. 'God, he serves You because You've put a hedge of protection around him. Everything he does flourishes. His soul and health prospers, but what if I touched his beautiful wife…?"

The devil, still controlling Rage, appeared right in my face. His icy breath defied the flames' heat. "He said yes."

Now the vicious vibrating eased in more, slowly, like a knife being driven in with care… precision…

I coughed again. My hands trembled as they clasped Coryn and the little girl. *God…let him? But—No. I can't do this, Lord.* I drew in a slither of air and opened my mouth. Hardly a whisper came out. "For the weapons of our warfare are not carnal, but mighty in God for pulling down strongholds—"

The vibrations viciously drove themselves deeper into my heart, and my breath caught, trapping even a cough within.

"I touched her that night of the storm," Satan jeered, "When you lost power and she fell asleep in your arms."

I winced at the memory. Every part of my flesh wanted to shut down, to let go and give up. *Jesus, help. Me.*

A tiny breath entered in and I muttered, "…casting down arguments and every high thing that exalts itself against the knowledge of God—"

"And I watched every moment she suffered. In the hospital, during worship service—" He hissed so hard his cold breath stung my lips.

"…bringing every thought into captivity to the obedience of Christ—"

"Pathetically praising the God who abandoned her to me!" he yelled in my face. Chunks of ceiling collapsed somewhere close. The heat intensified.

Sweat poured like water from every weakening limb. I couldn't… hold on… much… longer. "And being ready… to punish… all… disobedience." Every word became harder to utter. The smell of smoke overpowering. "When… your… obedience… is… f-fulfilled." I coughed out the last word. Suddenly, a surge of strength rushed through me. I slammed my head against his and rose to my feet. As his deep, endless ebonies eyed me, the hate-filled vibrations eased—No, they had weakened.

A rushing wind doused my sweat-soaked legs and I opened my mouth, this time loud and clear. "The Lord gave and the Lord has taken away. Blessed be the name of the Lord!" I kicked him in the chest, and he flew back into roaring flames. Screams ripped from Rage as his mouth opened. A massive black figure burst from his lips and shot upwards through the ceiling. The vibrations fled with them.

Another chunk fell to my left. I readjusted my hold on the girls and searched for a path to the double doors. Smoke covered most of the room. I found myself in a tailspin as I tried to find any direction safer than the other. The fire engulfed left, right, behind, and forward. The only path to the door was straight through the flames. I closed my eyes and ran ahead.

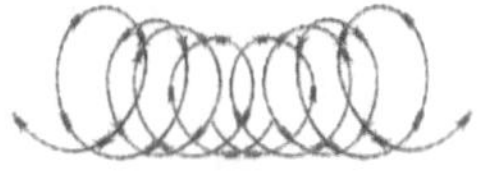

A white light shone all around and hummed peacefully. A new vibration pressed on my skin, warm and soft. It flowed over me like a breeze gently moving water. Slowly, I opened my eyes.

A figure stood before me in the midst of the flames. He glowed like the lightest and brightest part of the fire. Long, white hair draped either side of his cheeks. As my eyes adjusted to the light, a robe appeared, long and white like his hair. His eyes, amber and flickering as fiercely as the inferno, peered – not at me – through me.

My heart forgot to beat for a few moments. I opened my mouth, but nothing came out. A smile graced the man's lips. A pop of air entered my lungs. I inhaled, and somehow, rather than a swell of nasty smoke, clean air – sweet even – eased in. Yes, a sweet fragrance, myrrh… I took another fresh inhale. And frankincense… The only reason I could identify them was because Allison loved essential oils, and every Christmas Eve and Christmas Day she'd burn them in her diffuser.

"Follow Me," the man said. He beckoned me with His hand and led me onward through the flames. Though the fire consumed everything: the floors, walls, and imploding ceiling, it no longer held heat, but shined and boasted only breathable air like some sort of mirage. I held fast to the man walking before me like I held fast to the girls in my arms. I realized their weight was no longer a burden. They were as light as mere feathers.

He stopped, then put his hands forward. Holes bore through each wrist. As my heart skipped again, He pushed against the double doors. They burst open, smoke pouring forth like a flood, and He vanished in their wake.

I ran through the opening. Purple skies surrounded the fading moon. All the little girls I'd found on the way to the dungeon huddled together at a storefront across the street.

I raced toward them, never letting go of Coryn or the child. "Where's Hope?" I called.

"Right here, Prince Hunter!" The little angel squeezed through the horde as I set her momma and the girl, who was finally stirring, down on the sidewalk.

Hope's worried little face peered at Coryn, limp on the pavement, as the child's eyes opened. Glassy and pink, she looked around as she slowly sat up. "Where... Where am I?"

I let out a sigh I didn't know I had been holding. "You're outside of the Black Hearts," I answered, "And it looks like you're gonna be okay."

"Mommy!" Hope dropped beside Coryn as I removed my focus from the child and quickly did the same.

I dipped my head face-level with her chest. I couldn't discern any rising. My heart jostled. *No, God, please don't take her from me, too.* I placed both hands on her chest and pressed down. *One, two, three.* I counted and prayed in my mind. *Please, Jesus, just this one thing and I'll never ask You for anything again. Let her stay.*

I pinched her nose and pressed my mouth against hers. Her cold lips sent a shockwave through my bones. I prayed and pumped harder. I gave her my breath. If only I could trade my renewed lungs, I'd do it in a heartbeat.

Lord, take me instead. Please. Let Hope have her Momma back. I'm begging You. More pumps, more prayers. Hope prayed, too now. Her little lips moved so fast. Then more whispers as more little mouths opened. Even the child who'd just woken from the nightmare's mouth moved.

I kept going, and the sweat returned like I'd been dumped into a wildfire. It dripped onto Coryn's still chest. A minute passed. Then two... three.

My own words pricked my heart like thorns on a rose. It was a selfish prayer. She was in a better place. She was at peace, and she was safe – like Allison – and I'd dare ask God to send her back to this?

The fire roared behind. The building continued to fall apart as the noise threatened to drown out the praying whispers of the little girls; but their whispers grew louder… Hope's voice broke through.

"Send her back, Jesus! Like You did with Lazarus! Please!"

"Yes, Jesus!" the little voices echoed in agreement.

Though I'd secretly let Coryn go into the arms of her Heavenly Father, I kept pumping for the girls' sake. If they hadn't given up, I couldn't show them that I'd let go of the one woman who had stolen my heart and made me blush again.

My forearms and lungs seared at the effort. As I rested to catch my breath, I gazed down at the woman I'd hunted down at church two years back. The woman I'd selfishly wanted to see again, although I did want her baby girl to have her doll returned; the woman I thought about from time to time, though I'd fought to forget; the woman who made my heart skip when I saw her again at church after the Blood Thieves first struck; Coryn, the woman I never wanted to lose sight of again after I thought I lost her to them forever.

Now my tears fell on her lifeless chest, and I couldn't bring myself to keep trying. I closed my eyes and whispered, "I'm sorry. I'm so sorry."

The girls' voices grew quieter and quieter until the only sound that remained was the blazing edifice behind us. The silence felt like I, too, had entered eternity. A dark one where the fire consumed earthly hopes and dreams and only left ashes that would someday be turned into beauty.

A gasp pierced the silence—Hope.

I opened my eyes. Coryn's browns had shot open, and she coughed out a torrent. My heart rate instantly slowed at the sight of her irises: bright, alive, and… new.

"Mommy!" Hope squealed again and threw her arms around Coryn. "You did it! You saved Maya!" Hope beamed at me as she pulled away. "Well, with the help of your prince, of course."

Coryn's eyes lowered a moment before she focused on me. "I wouldn't say he's my prince—"

"It's fine with me if it's fine with you," I said all too easily.

A small smile lifted her pretty lips, and Good Lord, it took everything in me not to grab her face and kiss her as if no one were watching. Instead, I slipped my palm beneath her back and gently sat her upright. As she looked into me, I couldn't stop my other hand from grazing her cheek, nor could I stop my heart from practically jumping out of my chest. I breathed in slow and deep, then exhaled even slower. I had to calm it down before I started sinning. "Hi, princess," I said with a purposeful smirk.

She chuckled and coughed, but managed a weak back-handed slap to my chest.

A crash resounded behind us. I turned just quick enough to see the roof of the Black Hearts Club topple inward, and the rest of the edifice followed suit. I rose and grabbed Coryn's hand to help lift her up.

Hope tossed her arms around her momma again. "Jesus did it, Mommy. He answered all our prayers and brought you back."

My heart blazed like the crackling building. Jesus brought us both out of certain death on the same night, and I'd never, ever forget it.

Coryn smiled down at her daughter, though a hint of sadness dimmed it. She stared up at the moon. Her eyes were glossy and distant... longing. This time, I kept in my sigh. I couldn't blame her. She'd tasted Heaven just as I did, and we stole her back from it.

As if knowing what I'd thought, she turned her eyes to her daughter. "And I'm glad He did, baby. I'm glad He did." Then those browns settled themselves onto me.

My dang face warmed, and I gave her a smile in return as I beckoned her and the girls to follow me through the alley toward the street. Another crash. The demonic nightclub crumbled in a burning heap. Good riddance.

A few homeless stragglers ran into the rundown shops as I unclipped my radio and brought it to my mouth. "Dixie, do you read?"

As I waited, I forced my eyes on the smoke rising beneath the moon. Though darkness continued to reign all over this broken land, light still prevailed in what seemed like pockets. A streak here, a streak there, but even that was an illusion. The dark attempts to skew reality, and often, its deception succeeds in that scheme... but not tonight. A portion of hell lost to the power of Almighty God, who still sat enthroned upon this wasteland and would return to it someday. I knew my Bible so I understood more needed to happen, and until then, we all have to just endure…

"Hunter," Dixie's voice sounded low over rackety static. "Got the... Gunner... Killed him."

I gripped the radio as Hope gasped, and Coryn held her.

"Don't…there…you…out." Static consumed.

I sucked my teeth as I clipped the radio back onto my hip. Tears slipped from Hope's eyes.

I wiped them with my thumb and conjured a distraction. "You and your momma are heroes. Look around you."

All the precious little girls encircled and drew in to Coryn and Hope. They embraced, thanking them.

"You said you always wanted a sister," I continued. "Now you've got fifty."

Hope managed a cute little smile as the girls released and agreed in unison.

I braced myself to look at Coryn again. The moonlight illuminated her messy curls and war-torn appearance. Her eyes met mine. They shined in the darkness, so different than when they first peered at me in the parking lot of First Baptist Bells Ferry. She'd looked like a stray puppy then. Hurt, guarded—and sassy. But concern muddied the new peace they held.

I tried to hide mine well. "We have to make our way back to the Barnes'…" I looked over the group of gals. I gave them a short brief on their – hopefully – new home, though Lord knew what had become of Gunner, if we'd make it back, and where all the girls would go; but that would be worked out later. Now we just had to—

Our heads shot up as a rumble came from down the road. A ragged bus bumped its way toward us, one headlight flickering. I laughed nearly as loud as the thing and clapped my hands. "Girls, your chariot has arrived."

The bus jolted to a stop with a pop of smoke from its exhaust.

Coryn grasped my bicep. "Did you orchestrate this?"

I smiled at her. "I didn't, God did."

She smiled back, that new gleam in her eye making her all the prettier. "I couldn't trust that before, but I do now."

I shook my head and had to catch myself before tears fell. So that was it. Jesus didn't just bring her back from physical death, but He'd brought her to life spiritually. She'd been reborn tonight, no longer the woman I met way back when. She loved the One who died for her now... And that meant I could unleash what I'd been holding back like a dam all this time.

She released my arm, and I forced my attention on the bus as the door opened, praying it would reveal Gunner.

Dixie sat at the wheel with dried blood on her forehead. "Well don't just stand there. Y'all get in!"

Coryn and I helped the girls onto the bus before we filed in after them. The moonlight darkened with the smoke climbing from the club. Not a soul showed itself, though it felt as though several eyes watched.

Coryn staggered up the last step. I grabbed her waist and steadied her. She felt as frail as Allison had the last few months before the cancer took her home to the Lord. A sharp pang struck my heart. I held on tighter as I walked Coryn to a seat at the front. Please, Lord, if you'd let me, I'd steady this woman for as long as we have left…

"Thank you, Hunter." She sank into the chair while Hope sat in the one behind with one of the little girls.

As Dixie veered the sputtering bus around, I stood alongside her. I barely got the words out. "Where's Gunner?"

"Gunner? Ha!" She nudged her head toward the back of the bus. "He nearly got eaten by that junkyard mutt, but he managed to escape with all his limbs intact."

I let out a sigh as big as Gunner's courage before marching to the back of the bus to check on him. He snored on a seat with both of his forearms wrapped with bloody cloths. I winced at the old man. He'd need a lot of tending when we got back. The bus grumbled and jerked. I clasped the top of a seat.

"Yeah, I forgot to mention – no standin' in the bus, kids!" Dixie called out.

"Roger that, ma'am." I made my way back to the front. Coryn faced the window watching the storefronts go by as we were jarred by the bumps in the road. "May I, your highness?"

She looked back at me, wearing a darn cute smile. "I'm took weak to say no, so... sure."

"I'll take it." I sat down beside the beautiful battle-worn momma. Her mocha eyes shone glassy and tired as I wrapped my arm around her. She felt dang good after being away for what felt like ages. Shyly, she let her head rest on my bicep, and I whispered what I'd told God when I thought I lost her. "I'd die for you and your little girl, Miss."

She breathed in slow and steady as that cute smile returned to bless me. "I pray you never have to."

"And I'm gonna need you to stick around for longer, understand?"

She laughed softly, then exhaled as she set a hand on her stomach.

My own stomach twisted. "We can chat later. Just rest."

"Hunter…" Her eyelids grew heavy. "I just wanted to say… I never thought I could…"

Though I had to know what she desired to confess, she needed to get some sleep. Who knew what we'd—

The bus lurched. I held my arm out to prevent Coryn from falling from her seat.

"Thank you again, Prince Hunter," she whispered as her eyes slowly closed.. I rested my cheek on her head. A simmering took over my heart. Stuff I hadn't felt in a long time deepened. As I held her and we drove onward into the night, I didn't know what lay ahead, but I knew one thing: I had three words to tell her when she woke up.

Coryn

23. CAN'T RUN

*W*hiteness everywhere. Blinding, yet it didn't burn my eyes. Chords played somewhere gentle and soft... like a harp? Its sweet sounds tingled against my skin somehow, the kind of sensation I'd get when I visited the club with my ex a few times. The blasting music vibrated through my body in an almost violent way; but this, it wasn't violent, it was... healing.

"Coryn."

I froze. Dad's deep voice, tinged with a Cuban accent, echoed in my brain. I turned around. He stood across from me in the midst of the unending brightness. His deep brown eyes shined, as did everything else about him. He wore a white robe, even whiter against his tan skin. A warm smile stretched his lips. "How are you?"

"Dead again?"

He chuckled that hearty chuckle I used to say sounded like a latin Santa Claus. "Not yet."

My heart sunk in my chest. Though Dad hurt me so much, this place we stood in... I couldn't feel it here. All I could feel was… love. That same love I felt when I had died and seen Jesus…

Dad took slow steps toward me. "Mija, if I could tell you I was sorry, I would a million times over. I was so hard on you." He stood just paces away. "I knew that boy was trouble, and I wanted so badly to spare you, to protect you. But in the process, I stopped trusting God, and I held on too tightly…"

His eyes gleamed as he stopped, and he lifted his hand. His fingers, vibrating like the harp's waves, brushed away a tear on my cheek that I hadn't felt. "I forgot you weren't just my little girl, you were His." He lowered his hand as tears rolled down his face. "Just like I couldn't force you to obey me, I couldn't force you to obey Him... I could only show you His love in an imperfect way, and pray you'd discover His perfect love in time." The vibration wrapped around my hands as he held them. "Have you?"

I peered at the light all around me. I breathed in the harp's sweet song and suddenly realized the melody… *"Who am I? I'll never know why, the Father sent His Son to die, to die for me. All He asks is for my heart to believe. So here I am, with nothing to bring, but a yes and amen, a yes and amen."* The song I'd heard in Sunday school when I was seven. The song that melted into my little heart and opened it up to the truth that I was loved... perfectly and completely, by a Perfect Father...

I clasped Dad's hands tighter. "I have, Dad. I have."

My eyes opened. Something firm yet cozy pressed against my cheek. I moved my face back. Hunter held me like I'd never been held before. I felt so small in his encompassing embrace like I swam in an ocean; and suddenly, my heart quickened despite the wreckage that was presently my body. Terrified of drowning if I looked up and happened to find his eyes on me, I kept them down on his lap.

I busied my fingers with the rips in my jeans, half-hoping he slept. How he could make me feel so safe yet so scared at the same time just worsened the possibility I didn't want... The one I couldn't let myself accept...

"Good morning, Sleeping Beauty." Hunter's voice made me jump.

"Hey, hey," he said softly, his hand now rubbing my shoulder. "It's okay." His voice was so close... I pulled away some.

Then I stupidly stole a glance. Hunter sat there beautiful and frowning. Hot pink painted the skies behind him, kissing his skin in a warm glow. Dawn had finally come, but instead of embracing the light, I shuddered at it.

Hunter frowned again. "We're almost out of the city, then we can get you back to the Barnes', and I'll take care of you—"

"Please stop," I blurted before I could stop myself. "Just stop."

"Stop what?" He managed to keep his arm on me, unflinching.

"I don't know, I just don't want to think about being at the Barnes'."

He adjusted himself forward some, concern still etched on his magnificent frame. "You don't have to worry about Rico or Rhett. The Barnes and I already discussed that they're gonna leave."

"That's great, but that's not what I meant."

"Then… what did you mean?"

My tongue sat heavy in my mouth.

Hunter's concern colored his voice now, but he spoke softly, resolutely. "Tell me."

My tongue snapped into action. "I don't want to be around you, Hunter. Okay?"

His arm eased from its mount on my shoulder. "Is it something I did, ma'am?"

I sharpened my tone. "You've done more than enough, and I'm good now. The Blood Thieves are gone, me and Hope will be all right. I don't need you worrying about us."

"Coryn." His tone, serious and brewing with… something, demanded my attention. "I don't just worry about you and Hope." Those eyes set on me as firm as his tone. The brightening sun highlighted every detail; the specks of gold, the lines of grey, even flickers of blue blazing like sapphire in the light.

Warmth overtook my aching body, but it wasn't the sun's rays. It was him – Hunter – and what was behind his eyes…

"I told you I'd never let you out of my sight again. And it wasn't just because I worry about you." He grasped one of my hands, then the other. Weakness crept into them as his thumbs traced my skin.

I tried to look away again, but couldn't.

"Coryn, I—"

My upper body jolted forward. Hunter released my hands and shot his arm out, which kept me from slamming against the divider. The bus squealed onward. Loud dings clanged the outside. Something smashed into the window on my right, and it cracked.

Hunter reached over to Hope in the next seat and hauled her under his left arm. "Everyone stay down," he shouted, as he drove Hope and I in.

I ducked. Sticks, bats, pipes pummeled the windows. Dixie hunched over the wheel as more clanging barraged the bus.

"Run 'em over!" Gunner hollered from the back as he crawled out of his seat into the walkway.

"The bus is a tad too slow for that, dear," Dixie hollered.

A pop sounded from the back of the bus. Was that the exhaust? Gray smoke rose from the outside rear, and the bus crawled slower.

"I don't think this thing's gonna make it!" Dixie shouted.

Hunter carefully drew me out of the seat onto the floor with him and Hope. "Lord, we need You right about now." He set his hand on my back and murmured quietly, his words a mystery other than some pleases and Jesus's.

Something entered my back suddenly. A warmth like the one that often radiated from the bracelet on my wrist. I looked down at it. It was still there, faithfully clinging to my skin. The warmth saturated and soothed my body, and my aches melted away.

Hunter sighed a thank you and set his stare on me. "Ready to fight some more?"

Stomach a bit fluttery, I gave a nod and let out my own thanks to God, then looked past him to Hope, who pressed her head tightly into his side. "It's okay, sweetie. Remember who got us out of that other bad place?"

Hope's wide eyes found me, and she nodded.

"He can do it again. Just believe."

"Amen." Hunter rubbed her back, eyes scouring as I checked on my bracelet and whispered, "Please, help me help them in Jesus' name."

The bus rocked to the left. I slid, falling onto Hunter as he held out his arm and barely stopped himself from crushing Hope. Another rock, this time toward the right. Everyone slid again. I slammed into the side of the bus, Hunter stopping himself from mashing me in further. "Grab hold of something!" He yelled, just as the bus rocked once more. I clung to a pole on the bottom of the seat, my legs swinging.

"Everyone over here!" a man ordered from outside. People yelled ravenously as the hammering on the left stopped, but then the banging continued on the right—worse.

The bus leaned with a deafening screech. It tilted farther than before. My fingers squeezed the pole, but sweat loosened my grip. Another screech rattled as the shouting continued. The bus leaned further, then toppled onto its side. I lost my hold and fell atop Hunter still holding Hope. I rolled aside and placed my arm around them. The noise outside turned into scratching and thuds as our assailants scaled the bus. Windows broke above us, raining down glass.

Hunter's strong arms closed us in tighter. "You girls are mighty, you hear me?" he called out, "Because He who is in you is greater than he who is in them."

A head peered down at us from the shattered glass. A woman with several bald spots like if someone tore the hair from her scalp sniffed our way with a drooling mouth, her lips white and chaffy. "Foooooooood," she crooned before bashing her head against the other intact parts of glass, spilling more shards. Hunter flipped himself onto his knees and shielded us from the onslaught. He winced as the sharp pieces rained on him.

Anger—and something else—smoldered inside of me as the now bloody woman clawed at him. He grunted as Hope screamed for the madwoman to stop.

"Y'all get to the back!" Hunter cried.

As Dixie and the rest of us scrambled in that direction, something smashed the windshield. A brick fell on the ground close by. A horde pounced onto the hood and pulled apart what remained of the broken glass.

As the girls screamed, the psychotic woman fell atop of Hunter and clung to his back, trying to bite his neck.

I grabbed Hope's hand, pulled her in between Gunner and Dixie, then approached Hunter and the psychopath. I raised my hand. The bracelet slowly brightened, and a familiar purple, translucent light filled my palm. I grabbed a handful of the woman's remaining hair and yanked her back. Light traveled up the thin strands and covered the top of her head. Smoke rose from it as she screamed and convulsed, crashing into a bench then onto the floor.

Hunter looked down at her, then up at me. "Thank you, ma'am."

Two men barged in from the now-demolished windshield like wolves ready to consume. They charged at me—and Hunter. I jumped in front of him and raised my hand. The first man's head rammed into it. Purple light crawled on his face in electric spurts. He staggered back as he clawed at his cheeks, wailing and eyes aglow. He stumbled into the second man and they both fell back.

I walked forward with my palm still lifted. The bracelet's violet glow shined off the bus walls. While the first man continued howling, the second backtracked on his bottom. My hand shone, and a thin beam shot from it and pierced his chest like a bullet. He fell backwards and stayed still as a statue. The clamoring outside ceased. Through the windows, wild-looking women and men gawked at me. I narrowed my eyes and waved my shining hand like I was Dixie wielding a *chancla* at Gunner and wasn't afraid to use it.

They dropped their weapons and fled in every direction like roaches when the lights come on. Hunter appeared at my side as the light slowly faded and quiet sun rays stretched through the battered bus. Sweat and dirt smudged his face, and though tired, his green eyes brightened the morning all the more. I hid a swallow as he stepped close. Very close.

"Coryn…" It seemed almost to pain him to say my name.

My hammering heart filled my head. I dug my heels down to keep from swaying. He's too close. Why is he this close?

His warm, strong hands all too easily found mine again. His thumbs remembered their previous path on the lines in my palms before he gently turned them over and brought each to his lips. As he exhaled onto the skin his grip tightened. "It's taking everything—and I mean everything—in me to not kiss you right now."

His words pounced on my heart, and my knees bent at the pressure. Hunter's hand caught my back and steadied me. I quickly firmed my footing again—mostly. "Hunter… I…"

Hunter held my gaze and took a step closer. "You what?"

I couldn't breathe. I opened my mouth, my next words hesitant to come out… "I…"

His hands, his touch, his nearness. The warmth in my heart wanting so badly to burst forth.

I stepped back, my words a whisper. "I can't." I slipped my hands out of his. Something new entered his eyes, the now fully risen sun making it all too clear, and I had to look away. No, I had to get away. I turned

—

Hunter grabbed my arm, firm but gentle. "Ma'am, I can't let you go again."

"Pardon me?" I squeaked.

"I said," he stood in front of me like a rock, "I'm not letting you run away this time." He cradled the back of my head and pressed his mouth against mine. Strong, soft, and intoxicating. Every ounce of fight left in me fell at his feet. Heart full of fear yet erupting with warmth. He released me from my wonderful torment and said, "I love you, Coryn, but I can't let you make me sin again."

"Pardon me?" I squeaked again more pathetically than the first time.

"I'm gonna need you to marry me."

The warmness all over my body turned cold like forgotten coffee in a microwave. I blinked at him. Maybe I didn't hear what I thought I just did. I'd gone through so much in the last forty-eight hours I very well could have been hallucinating at this point.

"Mommy, you are going to say yes, right?" Hope approached, not exactly asking but demanding. All the girls – Hunter and Gunner included – watched with eyes like flipping owls. Heat found its way back into my cheeks. So that's a no on the whole hallucination thing then. I mustered the courage to face Hunter.

His mouth lifted into a right-side up curve. "I ain't got all day, ma'am." He gestured his head toward the girls though his eyes remained on me. "We've got some princesses to tend to."

My heart cut at the reality of what we had to do when got back to the Barnes', and yet it made my answer easier. Hunter almost died for all of us. If it weren't for him, I wouldn't be here with my babygirl or any of these little ones – and the Barnes, my new family.

I rested my hand on his cheek. He closed his eyes briefly before he slowly opened them again, and his weakness for me strengthened my own weakened heart. "Hunter, I don't think I can ever escape you."

The smirk – that killer smile of his that should have been forbidden during the apocalypse that I now found myself thanking God for – widened. "Is that a yes?"

I tapped his cheek and gave him a nod.

"Woo!" He bear-hugged the small of my back and lifted me off my feet in a spin.

Hope clapped wildly, leading all the others into applause and cheers. Her little arms wrapped around my waist as I turned into her and pressed her close.

"Does this mean I'm going to have a daddy?" she whispered in my ear.

My heart tugged on its chambers, wanting to break into a million little pieces like the windows' glass; but the feeling dissipated at Hunter's smile as he knelt beside her. Now he took both of her little hands in his. "Princess—"

"Queen," she huffed.

"Queen Hope. Would you allow me to not only be your momma's prince, but—" His voice broke. He cleared it as I clasped my brimming heart, then continued, "To be your daddy?"

"A million yes's!" She crashed her little frame against his, squeezing his neck like she did her favorite baby doll when he returned it all those years ago as a five-year-old without even the slightest concept of what a father was.

Hunter smiled as he took her into his arms and carried her like a princess. He turned to me he said, "It's time to get these girls home."

"And this old man, too." Dixie trudged our way, Gunner hanging on her arm, a little pale and hunched.

"You're just—" His voice cut off in a cough, "As old as me, darlin'."

She offered a forced smile as her concerned eyes darted to Hunter. Also seeming to take much effort, he let his gaze break from mine. "I'll check how far we are." Hope still in tow, Hunter strode to the front of the bus and peered out of the broken windshield. He rejoined us after a few moments. "I'd say we've got a full day's walk, but might make it before nightfall if we leave now."

Gunner began coughing again, worse. Much worse. Hunter set Hope down and hurried to Gunner's side and quickly helped Dixie sit him on the floor as Hope walked over and squeezed me.

Gunner shook his head and spoke between coughs. "I think I'll just... hang out a bit... 'n' catch up with y'all later."

Tears dropped from Dixie's blue eyes and misted mine. I squeezed Hope back.

"Don't make me give you a piggy back ride, Gunner," Dixie said through more tears.

After a few coughs, he managed a smile. A shaky thumb met her cheek and wiped the drops. "I love you more than baked beans and hummingbird cake."

"Okay," Dixie sniffed, "Enough games, Gunner Barnes. We gotta get these girlies home."

Gunner held her gaze, a weak smile on his chapped lips. As she shook her head no, he slowly turned his toward me and Hope. He beckoned with a trembling hand. My stomach knotted as I obeyed, Hope's hand in mine. I kneeled beside him.

He spoke quieter and slower. "You take good care of my bride... and my grandbaby." He offered another weak smile at Hope.

Dixie let out a single sob before she covered her mouth and shook her head back and forth. Tears fell from Gunner's eyes as he studied her. "Y'know where I'm headin' to, Dix'. You don't got a... fork in that bag by chance, do ya?"

A laugh mingled with her weeping. My heart began to crack, and I shuddered at the pain. I lost my mom and dad. Dixie and Gunner were the closest people I had to that... Hope never had grandparents... He couldn't leave us, not now. And Dixie...

I braved another look at her. Face red and puffy, she cried harder. Her breaking broke me more, and I let the tears fall. Now Hope started. The little girls watched quietly around us, still as deer when caught in the headlights of a vehicle. Hunter wrapped his arm over Dixie.

"And you, son," Gunner coughed very weakly. "You keep all these girls in line, a-and give Dixie lots'a other grandbabies." Then he winked at me.

Through the tearing in my soul, a faint flutter entered in.

Hunter chuckled, his own eyes shedding tears before he closed them and rested his free palm on Gunner's head. As Hunter whispered a prayer, Dixie pressed her cheek against his chest.

The color fled from Gunner's sunburned face. He peered above as his vision seemed to go farther and farther away, and that light all living things held slowly drained out of them. I shut my eyelids as tight as I could. Hope squeezed my arm, wetting it with her tears. I couldn't help but think of Dad again and what I'd give to say goodbye... To tell him I forgive him and say "I love you" just one more time.

As if hearing my thoughts, Dixie spoke. "I love you. I love you so much." Then her sobs became muffled.

Eyes still closed, I found Gunner's cold hand and whispered my own I love yous. The warmth of the new morning contradicted the coldness of Gunner's skin beneath my fingertips. Somewhere in the distance, birds chirped a bright song. Their rhythmic tweets mingled with Hunter's soft whispers. As I listened to their voices, the warmth under my palm strengthened.

I opened my eyes. My hand glowed purple along with the bracelet still adorning my wrist…

Dixie wept on Hunter, still silently praying. His green, wet eyes concentrated on my palm before he lifted them up to mine. He breathed a barely audible "Amen." His intense stare seemed to ask what my heart was asking, but too scared to believe.

Gunner remained still, but… Tinges of reddish brown seeped in, revealing once more all those sun-kissed years on his skin. Something rose under my hand, and I jumped.

Gunner's eyes opened. He blinked at the sunlight. "Who left the curtains wide open?" He spoke steadily like he had before getting battered.

As Hope and the little girls gasped in unison, Dixie tore her head from Hunter's chest.

"'Ey, why are you snugglin' my bride, boy?'" Gunner sat upright with a twitch to his lips.

Dixie's mouth fell open before she slapped her palms against his cheeks and kissed every inch of his face.

Gunner laughed. "Whoa, whoa, li'l lady. Not in front of all the kids now."

She laughed as she fell into his embrace. "Don't make me send you back."

"Send me back?"

Hunter chuckled. "I guess Heaven wasn't ready for your stomach."

Gunner's eyes widened "So it wasn't a dream..." he said in a hushed voice.

I shook my head. "Glad you're back... Poppa Barnes."

Hope threw her arms around him. "Poppa Bear!"

He kissed her forehead as the rest of the girls drew close. My heart overflowed like a fancy fountain with gratitude to God for not only sending me back to fight alongside these precious souls for a little longer, but also Gunner. We had almost lost it all to the Blood Thieves, the fire, the devil and his army... Some of us gave it all.

I thought of Krista, Bill, Sheriff Hank, and all the others who fought these battles with us from the start. Though bodies perished, we never gave up; and if hell would continue fighting until Jesus dealt with them a final time, we'd also wage war on the enemy on behalf of the King until He returned— or until He took us to our eternal abode.

Hunter rose. His gaze brushed over them before it fell on me. "I think it's time we all go home."

24. BELONGING

Sunlight reigned in the room from the large open window over the bed. Butterflies tumbled in my stomach. I caught myself staring at the queen-sized bed with a simple, taupe quilt and two pillows…

I refocused on the mirrored closet door in front of me. How different I looked from before everything fell apart…The lacy white dress sagged in a few places, whereas it would've hugged my hips had I worn it six months ago. My dark curls were fluffier, more wild without access to cream or moose; but they were decent and obeying the crown braid they flowed from.

Dixie insisted on not only letting me wear her wedding dress from fifty years ago, but that I'd let her do my hair and makeup – which consisted of mascara and lip gloss – and the real diamond earrings she wore on her big day as well. It was the only other jewelry I'd accept besides my stem bracelet which hadn't lighted since after that last fight on the bus when we'd almost lost Gunner…

My eyes welled with tears, blurring my reflection. Dixie put her pink, fluffy slipper down when I told her those diamonds should be traded not worn by me. *Now I thought you done learned by now not to tell me what to do with my things. Besides, it's just for today, then I'm takin' 'em back.*

Today. What am I even doing…

Taking in a shaky breath, I shunned the mirror and made my way to the dresser. That neat stack of Mom's letters rested atop it. I couldn't decide when the right time was to read them. I suppose there never would be a good time since those days seemed far away or maybe even gone forever.

I fought hard to keep the tears at bay even though Dixie swore the mascara was waterproof. The way my hands shook made my fingers twitch as I carefully ripped open the first letter. Mom's clean cursive flowed down the page. Already, a teardrop fell on her words.

My dearest Coryn,

How I miss you, baby girl. I'm not sure where to start anymore, but I figured I have to begin somewhere. I'm sorry is a broken record by now so instead I'll say a prayer. I pray one day Joy Himself will find you. I pray you will grow old with Jesus, with lots of wrinkles more from laughter and less from concern. I pray one day you'll realize how beautiful you are to Him, and that you don't need to ever be afraid again because He already loves you and always will.

I pray precious Hope sees her momma strong and brave, unwavering in faith no matter what comes her way. I pray no weapon formed against you both prospers, and that Satan is crushed beneath your feet at the end of every battle.

And lastly, I pray God sends you a man who loves Him more than He loves you, who will go to hell and back to fight for you and Hope, and be the very best Daddy you've ever seen.

I love you forever, and can't wait to hug you again someday.

More tears poured out. I quickly closed the letter and shakily put it back in the envelope as I sucked in breaths. Oh Mom, He did it. He answered every single one of your prayers, and one day, I will get to tell you I'm sorry, too, and hold you for as long as I can since time will be of no consequence up there.

As I cried, I imagined Mom's beautiful face in all white like I'd seen Dad's in the dream. I pictured them both now in heavenly robes glowing with love and light, arms wide open, waiting for Hope and I to go be with them forever.

I had no idea when that would be, but I knew that day would come eventually. Until then, I had people here in the land of the living to love and cherish, care for, fight alongside, and create new memories with…

A gentle knock rapped the bedroom door. I flinched before wiping the tears from my cheeks and set the letters back on the dresser. "Come in."

The door softly opened, revealing my sweet Hope. She wore the prettiest, puffiest tu-tu dress she had. I'll never forget how she squealed in the thrift store and caused so many heads to turn. "Mommy, Mommy!"

she'd continued quite loudly, "It's a Cinderella dress! I need it for the ball tonight!"

It was seven dollars outside of budget, but I couldn't bear to say no, especially since her last birthday I was only able to get her a dress for Ariel; and I'm so thankful I didn't have to be the one to go back to our old home to get it…

I breathed in, slow and steady. I didn't have to get it because *he* did…

Hope waltzed toward me and spun before landing in my lap. Her little arms draped my shoulders. "You look lovelier than Cinderella did at the ball."

I chuckled. "I'm glad you think so, princess."

"Well today, I'm actually a butler."

"A butler?"

"Well, I guess you can say a butler-ess since I get to carry the special pillow."

I chuckled again, though a flutter of fear climbed down the walls of my stomach.

"You were wrong, Mommy…"

I set my hand on her warm cheek. "Wrong about what, baby?"

"About never finding a man who would love us."

My brain fumbled. "I—what do you—"

"I heard you crying once." She pressed her palm to my belly and fiddled with the beads. "It was pretty late. I was supposed to be asleep, but I was thirsty. I didn't want to wake you so I made sure I tip-toed real quiet. I heard you through the door as I passed by… It was a little cracked so I could peek in."

I pushed my lips together as she continued to reveal her secret discovery.

"You were on your knees by your bed. Your head was down, and you were sniffling a lot like if you were sick... I knew you weren't sick, though. Just really, really sad." Her own lips turned downward. "You were talking to someone, and you said, 'I know I'll never find a man who will love me and Hope. He doesn't exist and never will.'"

Her hand moved from my stomach to a gold necklace around her neck of a cross that looked a bit big for her small frame. "I know now who you were talking to because He gave you what you wanted."

More tears rose in my eyes and threatened to spill all over my face, but I spoke quickly. "Who gave you that?"

"Your pastor prince."

I laughed at her word choice. Maybe Duke Deacon would have been more accurate, but all those titles were a bit difficult to explain. Another knock rapped the door. Dixie's head peered in from behind it. "You done stallin' already? It's getting' chilly out there, and Gunner's about ready to park his ol' butt inside by the fireplace... Or in it if he gets any colder in his words."

Hope hopped off my lap and pulled me to my feet. She darted behind me and pushed me out of the bedroom. "The princess won't be hitting a midnight game over on my watch!"

Graciously saving me, Dixie grasped Hope's hand and steered her downstairs then out into the backyard where everyone waited… Where he waited…

I descended the steps slowly, squeezing the railing like a lifeline. Each step grew heavier. Could I really do this… Should I do this? The end of the world was here—or it sure felt like it, at least. Was it even okay with God?

But as the days of Noah were, so shall also the coming of the Son of man be. For as in the days that were before the flood they were eating and drinking, marrying and giving in marriage, until the day that Noah entered into the ark…

I'd just read that verse earlier in the morning. I couldn't sleep. I tossed and turned on Dixie's guest bed wondering if what I was doing was foolish or not. The answer never really came, though I'd thought maybe that verse was it. Basically, to keep on living until the end came, to focus on God and receive whatever gifts He has for you, since He isn't going to stop giving until you're safe at home in His arms. So here I was… stepping slowly, uncertainly.. to death do us part.

I managed to make it to the sliding glass door, already open where Gunner was waiting outside for me. A chill instantly bit past my gown and into my skin—worsening my shakes. I braced myself and stepped onto the deck. Gunner lifted his arm, and I cupped mine in his as I held on for dear life. I could sure use some of his legendary courage right about now…

Gunner smirked. "Try not 'n' break it now."

I bit back a response, petrified to look up, but I knew I had to. A crowd of maybe 350, nearly the whole town, including the sweet girls we'd rescued and managed to find homes for each, stood crammed on either side of a simple stone walkway that led to a white oak tree still containing some of its orange autumn leaves… and a man in a fitted black tux standing beneath its shade.

My heart breathed in the sight of Hunter. Pastor Mitchel was on his right, Bible in hand, and Hope on his left with the special pillow in tow. The most gorgeous smile etched the mouth of the man waiting for me at the end of aisle. The sun sparkled down on him as he lifted his chest and gave his tux jacket a tug, those green eyes of his glimmering like waterlilies.

"You can do this, Coryn," Gunner side-mouthed. "Love is waitin' for you at that altar."

I took another step. Fear fled, replaced by a heart hammering with excitement. I'd only known Hunter for three months, but it felt like a boy I'd grown up with. He helped… restore me. Me and Hope both.

It's true I never believed a man would love her and I, let alone nearly die for us; but a man that could claim to be God's and actually keep his word and hold back from his desires—minus stealing a single kiss?

I hastened my gait—but not too much. I didn't need to trip on my way to my soon-to-be-husband and father-of-my-child…

Every inch closer to that smile grew lighter, and then I landed right before him. His smile widened before he said, "Lord have mercy." Me and a few others laughed. Gunner pecked my forehead before he joined Dixie in the front row with Mitchel's wife, both dabbing at tears with their handkerchiefs.

"Coryn." Mitchel stepped aside and gestured for me to stand before Hunter. Hope beamed at his side with the pillow that carried our gold bands – donated by the Barnes' who nearly spanked us for putting up a fight. They both were positively certain they'd never fit in 'those old skinny things' ever again, and they'd just been catching dust on their dresser for two decades. We finally caved when Hope said it won't be real unless we wore the symbols of forever on our fingers and got to carry them for us to the altar.

I blew a kiss to our little butler ring bearer, and she tapped her feet together like Dorothy from Wizard of Oz, threatening to bust out in a *salsa* at any given moment; but I couldn't blame her, really. This day was as much hers as it is mine. Then I returned my focus to my soon-to-be... husband.

My heart swirled at the word, almost in unbelief. Though I stood in a daze, I'd learned what sleep-walking was, surviving, and now... I was learning how to live. Really, fully live.

"It's to my understanding that the two of you have prepared some words for one another," Mitchel announced.

Hunter gave a nod, eyes still locked firmly on me, then smirked. "Ladies first."

Some of our friends—Dixie and Gunner loudly included—let out a chuckle and some whistling. I shook my head at him as I slipped my fingers beneath my sleeve where I'd tucked a small paper.

I unfolded the note, forcing myself to take my eyes off of this man whose side I never wanted to leave. I cleared my throat and began. "Hunter Freeman: From the moment I saw you standing in church two years ago, I knew you were trouble."

A few gasps and playful boos made their way through our rowdy audience as I continued. "Not because you were evil, but because you were good... Too good." I glimpsed at my angel beside him. "Ain't that right, honey?"

She gave several enthusiastic nods.

"I was so scared of you... Scared of letting myself even think of you, but circumstances—" I glanced at Hope again, "—And a little pestering princess ensured our paths kept crossing." I looked up at Hunter. I read the note so many times I had practically memorized the words. So I let the paper hang at my side.

"Then the world turned upside down. Earthly angels took us in, and soon, we were embraced by not only the Barnes... but you."

His eyes shined like his soul. Glowing, just glowing. He never looked more handsome – though every day he grew more beautiful to me, anyway.

"I didn't want to fall in love, God knows. Love was never safe for me before. But since the moment you walked into the Barnes', you've only protected me—

protected me and my daughter both. You're just one man, but you've become our family, and now, you've ruined me in the best way possible because I am so dangerously in love with you."

Hunter took a bold step forward that garnered more whistles, but Hope lifted the pillow between us. "Uh, uh, uh, Mister. The ceremony isn't over yet."

He held up both hands like a cop had just cornered him, and he took a step back.

Dixie clapped. "You tell 'em, baby!"

She gave a little bow, then Hunter raised his voice over the noise. "All right, little lady. Now it's my turn." His eyes were blazing into me, peeling back every hidden layer.

Hunter finally spoke. "Coryn Diaz, the moment I saw you, I knew I was in trouble. Something I hadn't felt in a long long time tugged me closer to you, but I wasn't ready – or prepared – for all I'd find. You made your mark as someone I couldn't easily forget, though trust me, I tried." He smiled down at Hope. "This little girl haunted me, too—"

Hope gasped.

"In a good way. I'd never met a little girl who looked at her momma the way she did... And it made me want to look at you more."

My stomach did another dance, and I grasped at it with my hand as if that'd make it settle, but no such luck. Hunter's piercing gaze was just too much. There was no settling until he freed me from his focus, which apparently wasn't any time soon.

"I prayed for you every night after that day in the parking lot... Prayed that God would keep you and Hope safe in His arms, and His hands would heal every hurt. I wanted Him to make sure you'd know how much you were loved, and someday, find a man who'd love you like He does. I didn't realize I'd been praying for myself or that He'd heal my hurt in the process; and that someday, I'd find a woman who'd love me like He does, too..."

He paused for a moment. "I thought I was healed before I met you, and in some ways, I was; but truth be told, I was afraid of falling in love again." He cleared his throat and exhaled hard before continuing. "Afraid I'd lose you." He grasped my hands firmly, but his thumbs grazed my hands gently. "But when I saw you fight for all of us time and time again, you made me brave. When I watched you come out of that fire a new woman, like beauty from the ashes, I knew I'd risk losing it all again just to have you for however long He'd give me."

A tear traced my cheek and met the bottom of my chin. Hunter smiled as his thumb left my hand and wiped it away. It melted into his touch and joy began to bubble within. Every moment I grew closer to for the rest of our lives...

"Ring bearer," Mitchel beckoned Hope.

She inched forward with her head high like a knight on his way to being knighted. The gold bands gleamed in the cool sunlight as she lifted the pillow. Hunter took mine and raised my hand.

"Repeat after me," Mitchel spoke. "In the name of God, I, Hunter Freeman, take you, Coryn Diaz, to be my wife…"

"In the name of God, I, Hunter Freeman, take you, Coryn Diaz, to be my wife."

"To have and to hold from this day forward."

"To have and to hold from this day forward." Hunter's tone grew more serious with each declaration. "For better, for worse. For richer, for poorer. In sickness and in health. To love and to cherish 'til death do us part." Hunter slowly slid the band over my finger. Perfect fit. You'd think we had it sized... Only God.

Mitchel turned to me. "Coryn, repeat after me." As I stared into the eyes of the man who gave himself for me and my daughter over and over again, I could barely get out the vows. I stumbled over a few, which only garnered tender smiles from Hunter until I finally let out the last one, firm and clear. "To love and to cherish 'til death do us part."

Hope bounced – and even shimmied – as I slid Hunter's ring into place.

Mitchel drew close and raised his voice over the strengthening wind. The chills threatened to have me bust out in shivers all over again, but I kept my focus on Hunter.

"By the power vested in me by God Almighty, for such a time as this, it is with great reverence and honor that I, Mitchel Sligh, now pronounce you husband and wife. Hunter, you may kiss your bride."

In a single stride, Hunter closed the distance and clasped my waist. He drew me in, strong but slow, like leading a new boat rushing into shore; and I held my breath as I closed my eyes to go under his waves, then his lips met mine.

My head reeled as I tasted true love's kiss for the second time in my twenty-three years of living. Every part of me eased into his gentle sway, drowning out the burst of cheers from our crowd of onlookers and Hope's ecstatic squealing. I don't know how many moments he trapped me in his kiss, but I know it had to be long enough to have me gasp for air after his release.

Hand still on my waist, Hunter chuckled as he steadied me. "Come here." He scooped me up like a princess, and Hope applauded. "You too, little queen." He bent down, and Hope hopped onto his back. He walked forward, chest high, as my − our − daughter beamed on his back and laughed as our friends hooted and hollered us down the aisle back to Hunter's home —our home, just a half mile from Nana Dixie and Poppa Gunner's.

As we reentered our living room against Hunter's chest, my heart exploded with a happiness I never thought I'd experience again. Fun? In this new era? Unimaginable; but as Hunter spun us around, mine and Hope's giggles were very real. We'd been through the valley of the shadow of death together over the last several months, and here we were in green pastures carried by Light Himself all along.

Hunter set us down and took each of our hands, giving us twirls as he waltzed us around the brown leather couches and dipped us before the brick fireplace. As time danced on, we laughed some more, sang a few hymns—and some princess classics, our guests outside patient to celebrate with us as they prepared a backyard potluck.

The generators had all run dry, but so many farmers had shared their crops and quite literally saved Bells Ferry from starvation. No one had exploited, demanded, or turned on the other in our town of six hundred. We'd prayed together, cried together; heck, we even fought together, but we never turned a blind eye to each of our plights. The three of us rejoicing in this living room were part of a bigger family, and though so much of this was incomprehensible at times and took much adjustment, I can't help but wonder where I'd be right now had it not all fallen apart.

Would I still be alone in our little home, just Hope and I? Would I have found my way back into the arms of my Perfect Father or ever stepped another foot into First Baptist Bells Ferry and allowed myself to fall in love again?

I don't know, but I do know this: I was dead, and now, I'm alive. I was lost, but now I'm found; and no matter what comes, I know who I belong to and where I'm going after this life. Until then, I have a husband and daughter to love and to fight alongside.

Hunter took a break from the spins and dips, and stole another sweet kiss, making me lose oxygen again.

Hope curtsied and saw her way back outside for a drink.

"Coryn Freeman," Hunter purred.

"Yes, my king?"

His eyes widened some as he rested his hands on the small of my back like a snug belt. "King? Ooh, I like that." He lifted my chin and pierced my soul with his stare. "Thank you for letting me in. I know that wasn't easy, and I'll do my best every day to make it all worth it... And love you and Hope like Jesus does."

"I wouldn't have said yes if I believed otherwise."

"Good." He dipped me for another kiss.

I pushed him away as I tried to play down my panting.

He chuckled. "You do know I've even watched you in your sleep, Coryn. You're not gonna be able to hide much from me, and I don't want you to ever think you have to."

Cheeks warm, I sighed into his truth. "Yeah, yeah, I know there's no hiding from Hunter."

"Nope." He scooped me up again like a princess. "No running away, either."

Face warming all the more, I opened my mouth to give a pitiful response, but then my wrist warmed.

The bracelet glowed lavender and pulsed slowly, pausing a few seconds between each. Hunter followed my gaze. The pulsing continued as the warmth spread up my arms and eased toward my heart. As it enveloped, my heart blazed with a joy that surpassed understanding. I breathed it in, then the bracelet's light dimmed until it faded completely. The bracelet's grip on my wrist loosened, and it unraveled, then fell to the ground.

Hunter set me down, and I carefully picked up the strange jewelry I'd worn nonstop since the moment it wrapped itself around me at the Barnes' strawberry patch three months back. A wave of relief washed over me like warm waters after winter.

The previous threat had been quenched so perhaps I didn't need this… mysterious power anymore.

My power is with you always, because I am with you always. I will never leave you nor forsake you, even unto the end of the age. I am yours and you are Mine. And I will come to you again soon…

Spiritual Warfare Prayer

Father, in the name of Jesus first I give you the glory, the honor, and the praise that is due your majestic and mighty name. I thank You that You set captives free and died to deliver me from every device of the wicked one. Father, please forgive me for all of my sins, known and unknown, deliver me from every stronghold, from every sin I am clinging to.

I confess I need You to break off these chains and empower me to live the new life You died and rose again to give me. Father, I rebuke all demonic activity that has risen against me because of doors I have opened. I close them now by the power and authority of Jesus Christ of Nazareth. I take every thought captive right now that comes against the knowledge of Jesus Christ and I tear it down in Jesus' name.

Lord, fill me with Your Holy Spirit. Help me not to quench You, but to build myself up in my most holy faith. Lead me not into temptation and help me to be brave and bold enough to cut off all bad company in my life and to trust you to deliver me from every circumstance that would cause me to stumble. Lord, I thank you now for the victory that is mine in Christ Jesus. Wash me with the water of Your Word and prepare me for every battle I'm facing and for those which lie ahead.

In Jesus' name, amen.

Stay in Touch

Thank you so much for believing in my work. I truly love writing these stories that not only entertain, but edify. To continue staying up to date on new releases or to sign up for a low-cost monthly subscription where you get all of my romance books, four chapters a week, visit:

https://natashasapienzabooks.substack.com/

Until next time, happy reading!

-Natasha